I0783885

Blame It On Nantucket

Titles by Doreen Burliss

Blame It On Nantucket
Fogged In
That Nantucket Summer
We'll Always Have Nantucket

Blame it on Nantucket

Doreen Burliss

Copyright © 2025 Doreen Burliss

All rights reserved. No part of this book may be reproduced in any form or by any electronic or mechanical means, including information storage and retrieval systems, without permission in writing from the publisher, except by reviewers, who may quote brief passages in a review.

Paperback: 979-8-9861095-6-5
Ebook: 979-8-9861095-7-2

Library of Congress Control Number: 2025909084
Printed in Boston, MA

Blame It On Nantucket is a work of fiction. The names, characters, businesses, places, events, locales, and incidents are either products of my imagination or used in a fictitious manner. Any resemblance to actual persons, living or dead, or actual events are coincidental.

*For my dear Billy, my husband and the father of our three
children. You slipped away so suddenly and unexpectedly as I was
finishing this book — we pictured you here forever. I will miss,
among so many other things, watching you read this one....
the way you always laughed and cried in just the right places.*

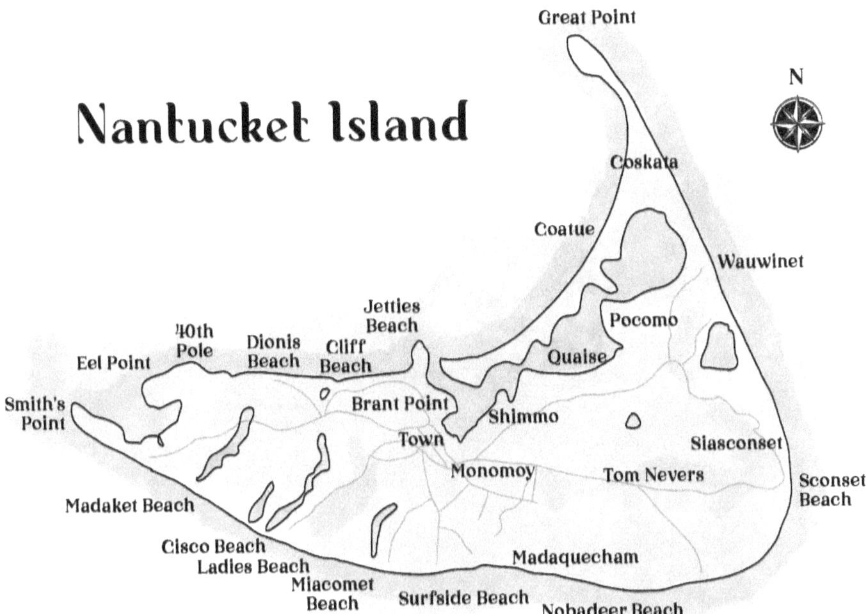

Nantucket Island
N
Great Point
Coskata
Coatue
Wauwinet
Pocomo
Quaise
Jetties Beach
40th Pole
Dionis Beach
Cliff Beach
Eel Point
Brant Point
Shimmo
Smith's Point
Town
Monomoy
Siasconset
Tom Nevers
Sconset Beach
Madaket Beach
Cisco Beach
Ladies Beach
Miacomet Beach
Madaquecham
Surfside Beach
Nobadeer Beach

Chapter One

SHE FROZE IN HER sleeping bag, hearing the distinctive huff and low grunt of a large animal outside her tent. Carly's heart beat in double-time and her blood thumped in her ears. Had she strung her backpack up high enough in the tree? Did she get all the trail snacks out of her pockets?

She was afraid to peek out the top slice of the mesh window. Her bowels shifted and she swallowed a scream as she looked out at a black bear not ten feet from her tent, swiping up at her pack like a pinata. She ducked back out of view, burrowing deeper in her cocoon to wait out the bear. It was barely morning.

Was this how it would end? Dumb girl alone in the White Mountains mauled by bear?

A barrage of thoughts pushed in from the corners of her brain. Her life passing before her in a movie reel, just like people said. Why had she made this solo trek? What was she trying to prove? That she didn't need some guy there to protect her, to do the heavy lifting, to read the maps, build the fire? She wanted to be able to do all those things for herself. But how fine was the line between being strong and independent versus careless and irresponsible?

Almost thirty years old and without a permanent address. Not exactly where she thought she'd be. Her Boston lease was up and her roommate was already en route to the Great Barrier Reef for her year in Australia. Temporarily moving back home to her parents' house in Andover, Massachusetts hadn't even been on Carly's radar but she'd lost a couple of clients and money was tight. *Happy last year of my twenties* she thought, reaching to scratch a mosquito bite on her ankle.

Had it been ten minutes or an hour that she laid still waiting for silence? Her heart had restored its regular rhythm and the last of the rain pelted the ceiling of her two-man tent as dawn broke over the Whites. Tuned keenly to every sound, Carly noticed the raindrops growing further apart, and the wind kicking up as the trees shook water down in a new rush. Like the tears she smudged from her face. Her deep sigh filled the small space.

Faint voices of early hikers along the Appalachian Trail echoed and Carly let go of the breath she'd been holding. The bear had moved on. It would take several hours to finish the Franconia Ridge Loop down the west face of Mount Lafayette, wrapping up her final New Hampshire White Mountains adventure before Nantucket. She listed in her mind all that needed to get done before then, as one bird at a time started the morning chorus. A watery shard of sunlight splintered through the trees and the piney air wafted in through the unzipped windows. She breathed it in deeply to slow the tumble of thoughts. But they came in anyway, like the snowmelt rush of the stream babbling over the stones beside her campsite.

Carly exchanged sleeping layers for hiking gear and ate a protein bar for breakfast instead of firing up her pocket-rocket stove. She shook the rain from her tent as best she could before loading everything into her pack and lacing her boots tight for the trek down.

The descent always seemed like it would be a breeze after the climb. But it never was. Her quads were spent and shaky and her feet were hamburger, smashing into the toe box of the boots she'd had since college. Her pack was heavy with gear along with the fears and insecurities she'd stuffed in on top. How she missed car camping and day hikes with her brothers and cousins back in the day, cracking themselves up the whole way — doing SpongeBob and Grinch voices with nothing on their backs but water and a windbreaker.

Surrounded by dense woods along the narrow rocky trail while roots crisscrossed the steep terrain, Carly had to remind herself to look up every now and then, away from the ground and her feet. In the distance were glimpses of the Presidential Range through breaks in the trees, with peaks that stretched toward the sky. The air was fresh and earthy and the light filtering through the canopy of trees cast the trail in dappled shadows. Carly found her pace making her way down the trail, focused and mindful of each step. She let serenity land as she celebrated the challenge.

The trail wound singularly down the mountain for about a mile and a half before it appeared to fork. She stopped and reached for the straps of her pack to ease the burden away from her body as she pulled a long sip of water from her CamelBak. She looked down at the split — both paths appearing equally worn with one steeper, cutting sharply to the right. She paused, waiting for recognition to dawn, for her instincts to kick in on which way would lead her to the lot where she'd parked her Jeep.

The air grew still and the trees seemed to close in around her. She felt a tug of uncertainty but decided that her sense of direction was leading her down the path on the right. Invigorated by the water, the small break, and having made a decision, she continued down. But the ground underfoot became more uneven, loose rocks and fallen branches obstructing the way.

As she continued, the trail began to descend more sharply than before and the forest grew denser and the light dimmer. She pulled out her phone to access her All Trails app but there was no signal. She'd forgotten to take a photo of the trail map that she'd have easily accessed now, she berated herself for this rare lapse in attention to detail and the possibility of a major misstep.

The happy sounds of the wilderness were replaced by the crunch of her boots on the rough ground. She pushed forward, but with each step a nagging feeling took over that she'd chosen the wrong way. The trail became less defined the further she went, disappearing into the wild, and she knew she'd screwed up.

She felt clammy with cold sweat as she backtracked to the right trail at the fork — feeling stupid and like she couldn't do anything right. Her quads burned with every steep step, the pack's heft soaking her back. Fatigue kept fear at bay — no time to go down the rabbit hole of the worst case scenario. *You got this*, she said aloud, replacing images of being stranded alone on the mountain with photos she'd seen of the gorgeous island of Nantucket. Miles of pristine beach, rose-covered cottages, rolling heathered moors, shell lanes and cobblestoned streets.

Before she knew it she was back on the right track and making good time. Her feet had gone numb, which was an improvement over the pain of smashing into the front of her boots. Relief flowed when she heard the distant rush of traffic on the highway opposite the trailhead where she'd parked.

Carly's black Jeep was right where she'd left it, she'd never been so happy to see it. Her parents had bought it for her right before college and it was about the only thing she owned in the world. Shrugging out of her backpack and kicking off the boots was all she wanted to do. She poured herself into the driver's seat then pulled down the mirror to assess the state of her appearance. She scraped her soaked honey-blonde hair into a fresh ponytail, noticing how sweat had darkened it, and how her blue eyes were like sparks against her flushed face.

Checking to see that no one was around, Carly peeled off her wet t-shirt and sports bra in exchange for clean, dry ones from the back seat. Then she put the Jeep in drive, and headed south. Andover was just a little over two hours away, where her childhood bed awaited her. Before that too would disappear out from under her.

Her parents' had just put the family home on the market — heading to Asheville, North Carolina for their second act. Hello Blue Ridge Mountains and boho art scene. It seemed everyone was living large, moving on to bigger and better things — did everyone have a direction but her? At least a chance opportunity had forced her hand, a new experience had fallen in her lap. Or, more accurately, her inbox.

Her boss, Keith, at the travel group for which she was a social media content creator, had an enticing offer — to manage the weekly summer renters of his grandmother's Nantucket house, and immerse herself in the summer season there while creating content that could change the perception that the island is just for the ultra-wealthy.

But it wasn't as simple as it sounded. Keith had explained that his grandmother had believed in supporting young artists and writers back in the day by offering the individual rooms to rent in the big island house rather than renting out the whole property to one person or family. A boarding house, he'd described, filling each room rather than entire floors and wings going unused. It wasn't necessarily just artists and writers anymore, but couples vetted by Keith looking to defray the enormous price tag of a waterfront vacation home in exchange for shared spaces and less privacy. It sounded like the perfect gig to her.

But wasn't "gig" by definition temporary? More fly-by-the-seat-of-your-pants living for Carly? Every time she'd tried to pause and reflect on her path, another exciting side-hustle presented itself, further preventing her from digging in and putting down roots. She'd always blamed Jake for being the one afraid of commitment, but what if it was her all along? The realization had her foot involuntarily easing off the gas in her Jeep.

Miles sped by under her wheels. What was she afraid of? Since the traumatic loss of her little brother years ago, she was obliquely aware of not feeling worthy of her own happily-ever-after. But it was her fear of failure that loomed larger. She needed time to switch gears. God, she hoped her parents' home hadn't sold already, she need a day or three to get her shit together.

Chapter Two

CARLY MADE IT TO Andover before dark. Daylight seemed to stretch forever this early in June. The *For Sale* sign pounded into the front lawn dimmed her mood but it all still looked the same. She was relieved that her parents hadn't started packing yet — boxing everything up left a place so chaotic and depressing.

"Well hello dear," her mother said, as Carly hauled in her cooler and gear, "I hope you don't mind my saying so but you look a little worse for the wear — how were the mountains?"

Carly's mother, Cynthia, was more spa than wilderness, standing there in linen trousers and a crisp white shirt, with perfectly styled, highlighted hair and freshly lacquered nails. Carly felt both protective and wary of her mother's reactions and was never sure how much to confide to her — nearly being eaten by a bear for breakfast and losing her way down a mountain would hardly inspire confidence. Carly wasn't in the mood.

"Just tired, Mom, but thanks." Carly put the small cooler in the kitchen on her way back to the laundry room to sort through her backpack. Cynthia followed.

"You can't leave all this here and there you know, we'll be showing the house."

Though Carly understood her mother's need to control the things she could, sometimes she was exasperated by her obsessive need to keep everything on a rigid schedule. "*Tonight*, Mom? Yeah, no, I didn't think so. Don't worry, I'm dealing with it, see?" Carly said, depositing items straight from her pack into the washer. Then, regretting her snark, nudged her mom with her shoulder and smiled. "I'm almost thirty years old you know, not twelve. I got this." But who was she trying to convince more?

Cynthia nudged her back, "I know, honey, I'm sorry, I'm just a little wound up about everything — trying to keep things clean and perfect so we sell this place as soon as possible."

Carly considered the meaning of that statement — disposing of her childhood as quickly as possible so her parents could get on with their glam retirement era. They absolutely deserved it, but she wished her big brother Grayson were here to commiserate. But he was long gone. Thirty-five years old, UNH Biodiversity Conservation professor *and* head coach for the men's division one alpine ski team. He was badass and not looking back. She sighed, grabbing her camp dishes to bring to the kitchen sink where her mother was already poking around in her cooler.

"I got it, Ma, don't wreck your manicure. I promise, it'll look like I was never here."

"Oh you know your father and I love having you here, don't be silly, I'm just—"

"I get it, moving is a nightmare, believe me I get it. And I can't imagine having to pack up a house you've lived in for thirty-six years," Carly said, suddenly wondering if she really got it at all. Having to literally box up your whole adult life; your tender newlywed years, those brand-new baby years, and the two babies who came along after him to grow your family even more. Every milestone and birthday cake, thirty-six Christmas trees, all the firsts and the lasts. It would split her wide open if she let it.

"You got that right, Cricket," came the booming voice of Carly's dad, Jack, from around the corner, "did I hear that you and Grayson are going in on a storage unit?"

Carly studied the playful look in her dad's eyes under his waggling eyebrows. If the storage unit was anyone's idea, it was Jack's. "I'd be down for that," she said, turning into his hug and staying there a few beats. North Carolina was going to feel far.

"You all set for your next adventure?" he said, releasing her but holding her ice-blue gaze with his identical one, "Nantucket Island... hobnobbing with the rich and famous... Hey, tell Bill Belichick I say hello!" Carly could hardly picture her father any other way than with the wide smile he wore now, the way it rode all the way up into his eyes.

"Hobnobbing? Sure, Dad. You're a kook, you know that? But I love you anyway."

"I love you too, Cricket. Am I still driving you to the ferry? And remind me, why aren't you taking your Jeep to the island? It's the perfect dune buggy!"

"Agreed, but the $700 price tag for a ride on the steamship — not so perfect, you know? That place may be loaded with billionaires, Dad, but my banking app will confirm that I'm a solid fifty-dollaraire. Plus the owner says the house comes with a car. Well, it's not so much a *car* as some vintage Toyota Land Cruiser. No idea what that is — I'll google later. And Auntie Donna said I could park my Jeep at their place for the summer."

"Sounds like you got it all figured out. Land Cruiser, huh? How old? That's actually a pretty cool machine. " His eyes were hopeful but with a shadow of concern, "As long as it runs and is safe."

There was something about her father's love — steady, undemanding, always there — that made her feel safe in a way nothing else did. Like if she stumbled, he'd catch her, no matter how far she'd wandered or how old she got. It felt good, comforting in a way she didn't always admit to needing. Which made it all the more disorienting to think of him moving so far away. She was nearly thirty, a grown woman by every measure. So why did it shake her, this thought of losing the nearness of someone who'd always been there to catch her? It felt almost childish to admit how much that comfort still meant to her. Shouldn't she have outgrown the need for a safety net by now?

"I'm told it's in great condition, Dad, I don't want you worrying about me, okay? And Keith said it would be up and running by the time I get there. The lawn mowed, the house cleaned and ready to go." She met his blue gaze with a soft smile — something to ease the crease in his brow, soften the concern clouding his eyes.

Her mom had materialized by her dad's side, and in that moment she felt it all at once —the gratitude, the ache. How lucky she was to have them. How much she'd miss them.

Carly trudged up the stairs to her room, stopping in the doorway of Grayson's old room, beside the closed door of Dillon's. Neither brother had lived there in years — the rooms were time capsules, a museum of who they'd been, of a life they'd never get back.

Grayson's dusty trophies sat crowded on a shelf their dad had made, a quiet echo of achievements long past, a reminder of days that felt both distant and simpler. A Nirvana poster above the bed beside another of Megan Fox, edges curling from age, a snapshot of a time when music and teen dreams filled every empty space.

Carly hesitated in front of Dillon's door. She wouldn't open it, couldn't bear the thought of seeing his stuffed animals still perched on the bed, or the toys scattered just as he'd left them. She could almost hear the whisper of his laugh and the little voices he did when he played vet.

It was all too much — each relic of their past pulling her into a moment that she could never return to. She stood there, weighted by nostalgia so thick it felt like gravity itself, holding her in a past that wasn't hers to keep.

Chapter Three

S ITTING ON THE UPPER deck of the island-bound steamship Carly thought how she probably either packed way too much or all the wrong things. She'd never been to Nantucket but she'd read things. Was it a quaint little island with charming cottages draped in roses, cobblestone streets and a Quaker history? Or was it a billionaire's playground with multi-building estates on sweeping lawns with themed bougie galas that had replaced family barbeques? Was it gin and tonics with glass swivel sticks and cheddar-garlic breadsticks that looked like branches in an enchanted forest? Or was it burgers, dogs, beers and s'mores? Somehow it was all of it.

As a social media content creator for Custom Escapes Travel Group, Carly was getting better at distinguishing fact from fiction, cutting through the hype to get to the reality, but still. Glossy photos and pretty words were seductive. And she'd be kidding herself if she didn't admit to feeling a little intimidated by this new assignment — what stellar content could she, Carly Hill, create about the famed Nantucket Island that hadn't already been done?

She was excited to see for herself if the house on Baxter Road on the eastern edge of Nantucket would be as she imagined. *Driftwood Dream* it was called. When Carly had been approached by Keith Thatcher with this unique summer rental situation, in conjunction with crafting a campaign to entice more mainstream, regular-budget people to visit the island for more than just the day, she'd jumped at the opportunity.

She'd be paid a decent amount of money to organize and loosely supervise the vacationing couples and singles who'd been selected from a deep applicant pool to stay in each of the three bedrooms of the house, and to create social media content that showcased not just Nantucket's upscale charm but also its rich, storied history that was accessible to everyone.

The vetting process was based on several grounds to encourage compatibility and create the right atmosphere for guests. They not only had to agree to participate in the social media campaign — they also had to be open to mingling with each other, sharing space, and leaning into the communal energy. They'd be chill about each other's playlists, be into sunset drinks on the deck, and have an unspoken understanding that shoes were optional and the outdoors was part of the living room.

It wasn't a place for people who wanted turndown service or took themselves too seriously, white-knuckling their schedules and routines like a designer handbag. This house was built on a vibe, not formality. It all looked great on paper, she hoped it gelled as well in reality.

For the two-hour chug thirty miles off the coast of Cape Cod she reviewed the files of each of the renters to acquaint herself with names and personal histories. She hoped everyone was as chill as they sounded on paper and that this summer would be more fun than stressful. As well as a caretaker and landscaper prepping the property, there'd be a housekeeping crew to clean in between guests. All Carly would be responsible for were the initial pickups from the airport or ferry, light housekeeping, making certain no one snuck in a pet, smoked anything on the property, or threw raucous parties. She felt like the room mother of a boarding house — except she didn't have to cook and would only be laundering their towels. Piece of cake. And she'd have plenty of time to maintain the more basic content creation for her other two existing accounts, get to the beach, the bars, and restaurants — all the while expanding her photography portfolio and being given the reigns to dive deep into the island's history. Excitement rose up inside her like prosecco bubbles.

She was glad she'd taken the slow boat — it only seemed right for the journey to take time. She liked the idea of being thirty miles off the coast of the mainland with the next nearest thing east of Nantucket being Portugal. She needed the time to slough off her old life and to embrace this new one — even if it was just for the summer. She took a seat outside at the back of the boat and soaked up the rays bouncing off the water.

What she didn't want to think about was her housing situation come September, her shitty breakup with Jake, or the fact that she'd be the only one in her family still living in Massachusetts. She was happy for her parents' new life but she already felt lonely.

Why was she limiting herself to her home state? She could live *anywhere* — she worked for a travel enterprise for crissakes, spinning dreams into reality with every image and reel. Maybe she was ready to customize her own quest, one with more permanency. She'd traveled after college — to Verona, the famous Italian city of Romeo and Juliet, hiking in the Dolomites, and onto Innsbruck in the Austrian alps. But home was home. Except now that the family home was *poof,* gone, existing only in the pages of photo albums and in a corner of her heart, she needed to redefine *home.*

It was one thing to traipse all over the place with everything you needed on your back when you had somewhere to return to. Things felt different now — she was too old to be a drifter. Carly leaned back in her seat and closed her eyes against the sun. There was a perfect breeze blowing, the air salty and soft. She could invite her friend Paige to come for a weekend, she'd been toying with the idea of that, but she needed to get her footing first, get to know the island so she had some clue of how to share it with someone else.

It was a comedy show when Carly and Paige hung out, a never-ending standup routine with one laugh-out-loud moment after another — but was it weird that they were still friends? They'd met a few years ago when they were both dating the Miller brothers....it hadn't ended well for Carly and Jake, but Paige and Travis were getting married. They would all be at the wedding together next fall. Carly's stomach clenched just thinking about it. But she loved Paige and wasn't willing to let her be collateral damage. She'd text her in a few days, get something on the calendar. They'd share Carly's bed like they did that weekend in Vermont — it would be like old times.

When Carly opened her eyes she could see land, the historic island of Nantucket rising up out of the sea. It was just like she'd read about... big old summer homes lining the cliff beyond the jetties, the iconic Brant Point Lighthouse on a curl of sand framing the postcard harbor dotted with sailboats. She saw two church steeples; one a white spire, one a clocktower with a gold dome, both set among the cedar-shingled buildings weathered to a silver-gray. She had a sense of going back in time at first glance, until she spotted the rows of giant power yachts in the boat basin, like nothing she'd ever seen.

How did it all exist on an island fourteen miles long by three and a half miles wide?

The contrast must be part of what made Nantucket so unique—a place where the past met the present, and where the island's simple traditional values merged with modern luxury. It would take getting used to, finding where she belonged amongst it all.

Chapter Four

CARLY NEEDED TO COLLECT her luggage and secure a ride out to the house. The village of Sconset was at the eastern edge of the island which was about eight miles from town. She had just pulled out her phone to find a taxi when one materialized beside her. She felt lucky and relieved to get out of the crush of people.

"Where to, darlin?" the driver asked. Vicki, according to her badge.

"Hi, yes, 33A Baxter Road please, Sconset."

"Beautiful old house," Vicki said, her green eyes lighting up her face, lined by the years and the island sun. "You have a fair amount of stuff, here for the summer? You got family out in Sconset?"

"Yes and no," Carly said, settling herself in the back seat and smoothing a chunk of hair behind her ear, "No family here, just a summer job." The cobblestoned street had the minivan bucking like a bronco and Carly wondered if all the roads were like that.

"Working *and* staying out in Sconset? Pretty ritzy address, how'd you swing that?"

Carly wondered if on such a small island, everyone knew each other's stuff. And instead of feeling off-putting, it gave her a more welcoming vibe. "Actually I'll be staying at the house and sort of overseeing the guests who come to stay."

"Oh, right, right, the old Thatcher place. I heard she'd passed away. Hadn't been out here in a while — glad to hear the family will carry on the tradition.

"Did you know Mrs. Thatcher?"

"Knew of her. Quiet — you know those artist types — a painter, right?" As Vicki expertly navigated cobblestones and tourists, Carly feasted her eyes on the storybook aura of downtown Nantucket, her senses on overload while she considered what she knew about Keith's grandmother.

"Yes, a watercolorist I believe," Carly said, trying to remember what she knew. "I just know that it had been Mrs. Thatcher's tradition for the rooms of *Driftwood Dream* to be rented to other aspiring artists who couldn't afford and didn't need a whole house. I guess it's been empty for a while, neglected a bit until now."

"Yup. I could tell you stories...," Vicki said as they left the crush of Main Street behind and headed for Milestone Road. "Back in the day I drove more than a few folks out that way over the years, interesting characters, a few crazies too. You could tell the ones that wouldn't be back." It all sounded so mysterious to Carly, like the island had some secret past that belonged only to a select group.

"I bet you've crossed paths with some interesting people for sure — anyone famous? Didn't I read somewhere that the author of *Jaws* had a house out in Sconset?" Carly found herself leaning forward in her seat to be able to hear Vicki over the wind rushing in through the windows of the old Honda Odyssey.

"You'd be referring to Peter Benchley, yep, he had a house out on Baxter Road, down the way from where you're headed. And it was the early 50's, I believe, when John Steinbeck and his family actually stayed at the Benchley's place — worked on *East of Eden* while he was here if I'm not mistaken."

Carly couldn't wait to put her camera to the task of capturing this magical place through her eyes. She'd read about its storied past and enchanted light, now she would be part of it. She gave into a big yawn as Vicki looked back at her from the rearview mirror.

"Am I putting you to sleep?" Vicki said, with her kind eyes crinkling in a smile, bright green against her tan, ruddy skin, her silvery-white hair flying every which way. "It'll be nice and quiet for you out in Sconset, not the same bustle of downtown."

Carly leaned forward in her seat again as the long expanse of Milestone road tapered into the entrance of the picturesque village of Sconset, it was like entering a postcard dream with rose-covered, cedar-shingled cottages flanking the narrow road, the blossoms bright pink against a powder-blue sky.

"Here we are," Vicki said as they pulled into the semi-circle shell-strewn driveway. Looking out the window at the house Carly had a moment's thought that they were at the wrong place. The images Keith had sent hadn't captured its essence. Carly just stared as Vicki put the Odyssey in park.

There the house stood in all its glory, cedar shingles faded to silver, bright white trim, and pink roses climbing up a trellis on one whole side. Pale blue hydrangeas hugged the entire perimeter with wide stone steps leading to the front door painted forest green with a brass scallop-shell knocker.

What looked like an addition on the right had a wide picture window that framed the sparkling Atlantic beyond. Her focus was drawn to a model of a three-masted ship on a wooden pedestal in the center of the giant window. A clipper ship, Carly was sure of it. Her Grandpa built model ships, she knew more about them than anyone should. She could make out its red hull and fully rigged masts with its square sails, carefully shaped to simulate the look of sails billowing in the wind. Her heart knocked in her chest.

Carly was snapped from her musings by Vicki unloading the bags and coming to stand beside her. She was compact with a sturdy frame compared to Carly's willowy five feet, eight inches. Vicki had a shoulder-length mane of silvery hair that she wore free and Carly could picture her as a young woman, platinum blond with an hourglass figure. "Thank you, Vicki, so much, I enjoyed those peaks of the past." Carly fished out her debit card before wondering if Vicki even took cards.

"Sorry, hon, I'm cash only."

"Oh, no worries at all, hang on," Carly said digging out the bills that her dad slipped into her hand dropping her off.

"Do you have a bike, dear? How do you plan on getting around all summer?" Vicki said.

"Ah," Carly hesitated and then looked toward the garage, "I'm told there's an old Toyota Land Cruiser in this garage at my disposal," She walked to the garage door and pulled it up.

"You drive a stick?" Vicki stood whistling as the beautifully restored, two-toned green and white old vehicle was revealed. "She's a beauty, isn't she? That Brett did some job fixing her up."

Brett? It really was a small island. "I do actually drive a stick — who's Brett?"

"He's my cousin's husband's brother's son — does beautiful work — I'd heard about this project, well good for you. Enjoy, I gotta be heading back," Vicki said, reaching into the back pocket of her jeans for a business card. "Here, take this. Not that you'll need it — I'm sure that rig runs just fine. But in case you need anything — you don't hesitate to call, alright?"

Carly took the card and felt like she wanted to hug Vicki, she hadn't expected such kindness. So many people didn't talk to you at all anymore — it felt like things had become transactions more than anything else.

"Now, I know you young people *google* everything nowadays so you know everything," Vicki said, settling herself behind the wheel, "but if you're in the market for a good ghost tour or restaurant or tow truck recommendation, you give me a call, alright?"

So much to digest. Carly waved Vicki off as her minivan crunched over the shells out of the driveway onto Baxter Road.

Chapter Five

THE KEY TO THE house was under the fifth flagstone as Keith said it would be. It took a couple of tries to wiggle it just right in the old lock for the front door to open. Stepping inside, Carly felt the woosh of a hundred summers. Trapped salty air swirled to greet her, blending with the smell of sun-bleached linens, Coppertone, lemony citronella, and towels drying on sunbaked cedar railings. The briny tang of the sea had seeped into every board and beam. Dust motes drifted in the strips of golden light filtering through the windows, and the worn wooden floors smoothed by bare feet and sandy heels creaked underfoot.

Carly sighed at the perfection of the stone fireplace that anchored the room with its weathered driftwood for a mantel, a satiny silver from the years. Overstuffed linen sofas and chairs surrounded the low coffee table piled with well-loved books, and Carly could picture the warm golden light of the vintage brass sconces once night fell.

Had there been extravagant dinner parties once upon a time? Candles flickering from every surface, women in flapper dresses with fringe, beads, bobbed hair and cloche hats? The men would have worn sharp suits or summer blazers. Carly could hear the music — maybe a live jazz band or gramophone playing Louis Armstrong or Duke Ellington. There would have been dancing, the Charleston or the foxtrot.

Carly was frozen in place envisioning it all. A table overflowing with oysters, clams, finger sandwiches and lobster. It would have been prohibition 100 years ago, but the gin rickeys, martinis, and whiskey sours would have flowed freely behind closed doors, disguised in teacups and mason jars. When it got too hot inside, the party would have moved outside to the wide back deck and the lawn. She pictured it as a sepia-tone image. Carly walked through the French doors that opened to the deck that spilled out onto the generous lawn that opened up to the big blue Atlantic. She wished she could be back in those roaring 1920's.

A hundred years ago F. Scott Fitzgerald and Ernest Hemingway were exploring themes of disillusionment and the search for new identities. Did anyone in these current times even know who they were anymore, what they stood for? There seemed to be more questions than answers. We have the social upheaval down pat, Carly thought, the divisiveness, but was that the lasting impact they wanted to have? Her generation was in trouble.

Carly walked to the edge of the lawn, to where the narrow path of the Sconset Bluff Walk ran parallel to the ocean. She looked out across the moors and low dunes that rolled into the sea. Then she turned to view the house from the top of the long wooden staircase that lead down to the beach. *Driftwood Dream* was apt. Perched on the eastern edge of the island, keeping company with other stately homes. The gray shingles shimmered like fish scales in the light, catching the sun and keeping it. The generous deck ran the length of the house then curved to a gazebo on one end. Carly could picture guests across the years sinking into the blue-stripe cushions of the wicker furniture watching the dawn of a new day as the sun climbed up out of the ocean.

She could hear the tinkling of glasses and silverware at the weathered table where twilight dinners had been, candlelight dancing in wine glasses. Would there have been croquet on the lawn? Could there still be? Would these new guests actually connect and enjoy the place, or would they keep to themselves, treating the house as nothing more than a pit stop?

She wanted to believe that people who'd signed on for this kind of vacation would be down to collaborate in their experiences — enjoy each other's company. She was glad she had a few days before anyone arrived — so much she didn't know. This was shaping up to be the most fun research she'd ever done — benefiting both the guests and the Custom Escapes campaign she was creating. What are the must-see sights on Nantucket? Where can we learn more about the whaling history? Best place for local seafood? Easiest place to rent a bike or scooter? What hidden gems off the beaten path should we check out? Coolest spot to watch a sunset or sunrise?

Her thoughts spun with possibilities. She was itching to get her camera and get out there. She wanted to capture it all — the slant of afternoon sun on the deck, dew drops on the clematis vine, a delphinium spike bluer than the sea, the lip of the sun still clinging to the horizon, melting like spilled paint into the ocean. Capturing the nightlife might be a challenge, but she felt excited, hoping to experience it not just through her lens, but also through the perspectives of her guests.

Sometimes Carly wondered if the images she saw in her head — moody, artful, layered — were meant for something more permanent than a fleeting scroll. A book, maybe. Prints on a gallery wall. The way they would tell a story. But then she'd second-guess herself. Maybe that kind of ambition belonged to someone more certain, more legitimate. She hadn't figured out what she wanted from all this — only that the pull toward creating something real, something lasting, still hummed in the background.

She needed to settle into her room first, the primary bedroom on the first floor. While it was larger than the others and its bathroom had a clawfoot tub, it would not have as grand a view as the upstairs bedrooms would. She lugged her two huge Patagonia duffel bags into the room hoping the space was as cute as it looked in the photos.

The honey-gold floor throughout the house continued into the bedroom. She loved the knots and swirls of pine, its softness underfoot, and the way it aged — it would always remind her of her grandparents' summer cottage in Maine where the floors, walls, and ceiling were all the same rustic knotty pine. Her eyes were drawn to the queen-sized bed and the quilt, its carefully stitched patterns and softened colors told a story of the seasons well-loved.

There were two night tables and a bureau, all crafted from the same pale, buttery wood. Carly was relieved it wasn't dark cherry or a heavy walnut, nor buried under layers of paint — just natural and warm. The windows were tall with gauzy sheer curtains and accordion shades that she hoped did their job blocking out the light. She'd read that morning came earlier on this island thirty miles out to sea than anywhere else in the country.

She couldn't let herself lie down. She had to keep the momentum — unpack her clothes and get food in the house. How was sharing the fridge going to work out? She hadn't even taken a hard look at the kitchen. She left her clothes half hung to check it out.

HUGE fridge! Some modern, mega-capacity thing that stood in contrast to the vintage look of the place. But like the island itself, *Driftwood Dream* was a unique menagerie of old and new. Beside the new refrigerator was an old farmhouse sink, long and deep, with a vintage brass gooseneck faucet. The countertops and center island were soapstone set against rustic whitewashed oak cabinetry — Carly loved the cozy coastal/farmhouse vibe.

Chapter Six

ONCE SHE'D UNPACKED EVERY item of clothing and organized her toiletries in the bathroom, fatigue lassoed her. It was already late afternoon and she was definitely not in the headspace to deal with the Land Cruiser yet — her stick shift experience was feeling more distant than she was comfortable with. She would walk the bluff path in the direction of the village of Sconset and see what the little market had to offer.

The air had its own perfume. Some sweet mix of the beach roses blooming everywhere and the salt of the ocean. The sea and sky were a solid sheet of sparkling blue. Sunlight skipped along the surface of the water.

As she walked along the bluff, her eyes were drawn to the homes that lined the path — deep porches, lawn furniture both pristine and artfully weathered, gardens tumbling with color. It felt like spying, stealing glimpses of people sipping drinks on the lawns facing the sea. There was an aura of intrigue to the grand homes with their grand people and Carly couldn't decide if she wanted to be one of them or just know everything about them.

She considered her challenge of capturing the island's essence, and its hugely varied cross-section of society struck her. Nantucket was a mix of hard-working locals, tourists, and summer residents — an enormous spread of incomes, lifestyles, personalities and attitudes. It was no single one of these things, but all of them. And at the end of the day, they were all people, wanting the same things. Love, happiness, health, security, and purpose.

Carly would use this summer to want those things too, give herself permission to deserve them, to stay on a path to get them.

The Sconset Market was just around the corner, no bigger than a cottage itself with antique floors creaking underfoot. On one side were tidy aisles of provisions, souvenirs, and at the counter fresh-baked blueberry muffins scones and croissants. On the other side were neat rows of island-garden vegetables, postcards, and a small ice cream bar. A village frozen in time.

There was just about everything a summer visitor would need but Carly had a feeling it would come at a cost. She vowed to take the Land Cruiser to the mid-island grocery story the next day. The shrimp made her mouth water — she decided she'd sauté it with garlic, butter, wine and peas then toss it with penne. Damn, she needed wine too — would she find that in this little village?

She must have said it out loud because a lady next to her in tennis whites and a visor said, "Right next door you can get yourself some wine. The sign over the door says Bookstore, but there isn't a book in the place — you should check it out," she laughed.

Carly laughed with her and thanked her, wishing she had more to say. There was something about the woman — her posture, maybe, or the tilt of her smile — that reminded Carly of her mother. A rush of loneliness caught her off guard. Her phone buzzed in her back pocket, "Mom" lighting up the screen as if she'd conjured her.

"Darling! How are you?" It made Carly happy to hear the smile in her mother's voice.

"I'm good, Mom, how are *you* guys? Settling in?"

"Oh, honey, you would just love the Blue Ridge mountains, your father has already hit the hiking trails."

"You should go with him sometime, Mom, I bet it's so beautiful and it would be good for you."

"Well, you know that was never really my thing, honey, but I'm thinking about it! Kayaking too if you can believe it. Everyone here is so active."

"Good for you guys, that makes me so happy! Will you have a garden?"

"Oh, you better believe it. Farm-to-table is a whole lifestyle here. The food culture's amazing — and the weather makes growing things almost too easy."

Standing outside the little market, Carly pressed the phone to her ear, not wanting to miss a word. It had been a long time since her mom had sounded this light, carefree. It was like a weight lifting — one she hadn't realized she'd been carrying. Had Carly's sense of self really been so tethered to her mother's happiness? Or maybe more to the absence of it? A swell of joy and possibility rose up.

Back across the street she went to Bookstore Wines, in another totally unassuming gray-shingled cottage with forest-green trim and a pale yellow door. Carly quickly googled the best wine to pair with shrimp and garlic. Sauvignon blanc it was. And a six-pack of the island's own Cisco brews was an absolute requirement.

The walk back felt longer, balancing bags and zig-zagging thoughts. Everything and everyone was so beautiful — she wished she had someone to share it all with. Her friends these days were busy doing their own things — boyfriend things, fiancé things. Would Paige flake out on her? Come up with ten reasons why she couldn't visit after all? Her mom told her that she'd make new friends, that she'd always been good at that. And Carly thought how people visiting Nantucket were from all over the world — all she had to do was put herself out there.

She'd send her ideas and photos to Keith within the week, hoping to get a clearer sense of the campaign's scope — and to make sure they were aligned. She'd adapt to whatever direction he chose, all while figuring out what resonated most with her, what might point toward something lasting.

Because what she really needed at the end of summer was a place to live. She couldn't blame her bouncing around on a breakup anymore or losing a roommate to a new direction. She was past the point of living on a whim, beyond the desire for some rando roommate. It was time to settle into a steady career and find a place to call home. She really had to figure her shit out — she had the summer to do it.

The cavernous fridge was empty but for her few items. It would be a different place in a few days. Before she whipped up her dinner she wanted a shower — she remembered Keith saying something about an outside shower — that it was one of the best parts of summer on Nantucket.

As she walked the perimeter of the house with her towel, bodywash, shampoo and conditioner, she spotted the cedar-plank stall on the side of the house near the garage, tucked behind a tall stand of pink and white hollyhocks. The walls were full height, the top open to the sky with smooth wide stones underfoot. The smell of the cedar baking in the sun mingling with the salt breeze was ambrosial. Inside, the simple showerhead was attached to the house and there were cedar pegs and small shelves. The grass all around the stones was the lushest green.

She stepped in and found her way around the hot and cold until the perfect temperature rained down on her. It felt like the most luxurious thing in the world. The evening air was cooling off, swirling perfectly with the steam rising off her body, she didn't want to get out. Drying off she realized she didn't bring out a clean change of clothes — could she dash inside with just the towel wrapped around her? She figured she'd have a better chance of slipping by unnoticed if she went in the front instead of the back, where evening walkers might be passing.

She was almost to the front door when she noticed someone standing on the steps about to lift the brass knocker. *Great.* Finger combing her wet hair she had no choice but to own the moment. "Can I help you?" she said, standing there more naked than not in her medium sized white bath towel.

Chapter Seven

"OH SHIT, SORRY, BAD time?" the dude said, stepping aside to let Carly open the front door.

Carly just wanted to get inside the house. "Give me a minute," she said, closing the heavy door behind her. *Jesus*, he was not ugly. She rushed back to her room to throw on a t-shirt and shorts and run a brush through her hair. Though her brain was scrambling to figure out who he was and what he was doing there, she arranged her expression into one of calm and collected and opened the door. "Sorry, come in — who are you again?"

"Brett Kinsman," he said, extending his hands to shake hers, "my buddy and I did some work on your Land Cruiser and I was in the area so I thought I'd see how she's running."

Carly was trying to focus on the words coming out of his mouth but she was distracted by his formidable height — he had to be at least six foot, four — and by the way his eyes looked beyond her seeming to take in the whole space. His hair was the color of peanut butter, damp and kind of all over the place, and his eyes were chocolate brown. He was a peanut butter cup. He shifted his weight self-consciously shoving both hands deep in his jeans pockets.

"Is this a bad time?" he said.

"Not really. I'm sorry — my brain is a little fried, I kind of just got here and to be honest I haven't even checked out the car yet." Carly found herself fiddling with her own wet hair and shoving one hand into the pocket of her shorts.

"*Car*, huh?" Brett said, "That is a 1972 Toyota FJ55 Land Cruiser, a cult classic. We're talking F-series six-cylinder engine. Come on, let me show you," he said, leading her outside to the garage and hoisting the door. If only Carly could find a guy who would look at her the way this dude was looking at that old vehicle. "It's got steel wheels with these dog-dish hubcaps and just look at these meaty off-road tires. The interior isn't what you'd call *luxurious* but comfortable enough and she'll get you there. The thing is beautiful."

"Should I leave you two alone?" Carly said, biting back a smile.

It was like he didn't even hear her as he opened the driver's side door imploring her to check it out. Her fatigue and hunger took a backseat and she found herself drawn in by his excitement. "Alright, alright," she said, sliding herself in behind the wheel. "Whoa, bench seats — you don't see those anymore, nice." In that moment she was back in her grandfather's old Caddy going for ice cream with her thighs sticking to the seat on a summer day.

Before she knew it, Brett was letting himself in on the passenger side, folding his long self onto the seat beside her. "Let's take her for a spin," he said, eyes alight like a little boy on a tractor. He dropped the keys into the palm of her hand and she suddenly panicked trying to remember clutch, break, neutral, shift, and in what order. God, she was one hundred percent going to embarrass herself.

"You *do* know how to drive a stick, right?" he said, not condescendingly as much as suddenly concerned. She noticed his eyebrows shoot up under his floppy hair and she wasn't sure if she was going to laugh or cry.

"Yes, I know how to drive a stick," she said, with sarcasm lacing her voice and more confidence than she felt, "but it's been a minute so cut me some slack."

"Okay, now make sure the gear shift is in the neutral position like this," he said with his hand covering hers, wiggling the stick freely from side to side.

Not even a zing of sexual energy between them, Carly registered, he was all business. Which was probably a good thing. Carly needed to focus on who she was and what she wanted in this life before she lost herself to someone else.

"Now press the clutch with your left foot — all the way," he continued with laser focus, "This disengages the engine from the transmission, stopping the vehicle from lurching forward when you start it. Your parking break is on so we're not moving until you're ready. Go ahead, start her up." He was way too excited for this.

The engine roared to life and Carly shot a glance his way and let his excitement roll over her.

"Okay, good," he said, "now with the clutch still fully depressed, move the gear stick from neutral to first gear and release the handbrake. Slowly release the clutch while gently pressing the accelerator with your right foot. Good. Now remember, if you release the clutch too fast without enough gas, we'll stall."

She was grateful for the step-by-step, and for the way he said *we'll* stall instead of *you'll* stall. It wasn't like Baxter Road was the Autobahn — it was just a winding little road out to the lighthouse. Would she even get into third gear? She hoped pedestrians and cyclists were all home eating dinner.

As she released the clutch she could feel the engine engage and they started to move forward. It felt like a tank. "You may notice the low-end torque, right? Feel that?"

"Um, yeah, it's kinda rough, isn't it?" she said.

"That's what makes Land Cruisers great for off-roading. And they tend to pull confidently from a stop also, even on inclines, so be mindful of that."

"Great. I'm not used to having to think so much about driving," she said as they crunched slowly over the driveway. *Clutch, break, neutral, look both ways, and again, pull out onto Baxter slowly shifting into first.*

"Nice job," Brett said, as she shifted seamlessly into second gear, "you're a pro."

His praise washed over her making her sit taller in her seat. They cruised along the narrow road slowly while Brett talked about the erosion of the bluff as they got closer to the Sankaty Head Light, pointing out the homes that were destined to fall into the sea sooner than later. "See that one right there? It's called *Slip-Sliding Away*. It's like they always knew..."

"That's so sad!" Carly said, as the red striped lighthouse rose up into view. They sat idling looking out at the lighthouse while Brett gave Carly a brief history.

"Looks safe enough there doesn't it?" Brett said.

"What do you mean?"

"In 2007 the Sconset Trust took ownership of the lighthouse — it was sitting just 68 feet from the bluff — it was definitely in danger. And so they moved it 400 feet back. It was pretty cool — you can watch it on YouTube."

Carly got a kick out of the way his eyes lit up talking about it — a*dork*able — some kind of engineer? He couldn't just be a car guy. Not that there was anything wrong with that. "So where'd the name Sankaty come from?" She felt proud of herself for coming up with a decent question.

"Well, you've heard of the first settlers on Nantucket, right? The Wampanoags? In their language *sankoty* means highland. It was built in 1849 and by 1850 it had a state-of-the-art Fresnel lens that reflected the light of a single-wick whale-oil lamp that could be seen more than twenty miles out at sea. Crazy, right? Nantucket shoals are super dangerous — something like 23 miles of shallows east of here. Problem is the shoals lie just off a major transatlantic shipping lane — ships can and have run aground."

"Wow — you really know your history, Brett, impressive."

"Not that impressive really — when you grow up here I guess most of this stuff is second nature."

"Well, it's pretty cool to me — I might use it for work. I should be recording you!"

"You lost me," Brett said, with a self-conscious laugh.

On the drive back to the house, Carly explained her Nantucket tourism assignment for the travel group, the spin she had in mind to put on her content. "But, hey, what might also be cool is a sort of day in the life of a real rear-round resident!"

Brett seemed to consider this as Carly maneuvered out of their parking spot and headed back to the house.

"Interesting," he said, "not the usual angle to attract visitors, but I like it. Locals are people too," he laughed again, shaking the hair from his eyes.

"Exactly! The life-blood of the place really, right?" Carly felt her excitement rise at the idea of stretching the consciousness of such a famously high-end destination. "I'm sure you know of so many cool places that aren't in the guide books, like hidden ponds for kayaking and walking trails, right? I could put short reels together…" Why hadn't she thought of this before? She'd been thinking too much like a tourist.

"Okay, I see where you're going," Brett said, nodding his head, "but we don't want to give away all the island's best kept secrets."

"Gotcha. We'll figure it out," Carly said as she pulled into the driveway. "Do you want to come in for a beer?"

"Oh, thanks but I can't tonight — another time though, alright?"

"Sure, of course. And thanks again for checking in, it was good to get behind the wheel — I was a little nervous about it."

"No worries — you crushed it," he said, unfolding his long frame from the car, "catch you later." And with a wave he was gone.

Carly was feeling lucky to have met such a genuinely nice guy. Who would also be a great resource for her. She didn't feel that electric pull of attraction, but there was an ease to being in his company that left her with a quiet sense of calm. Her fatigue lifted and with renewed energy, she poured herself a glass of wine made dinner to eat outside in the warm summer.

Chapter Eight

I**T TOOK A MINUTE** for Carly to remember where she was when she woke in a strange bed the next morning. Had she even dreamed? Nothing was coming to her. The bed was heaven, a cloud but somehow with the perfect firmness. She felt a prick of loneliness but then remembered Brett's kindness in checking in on the Land Cruiser and getting her out there in it. She couldn't put her finger on why she got friend-vibes from him, but he seemed like a good friend to have. She wished they'd exchanged numbers.

She had two more days to learn her way around the island before guests arrived on Saturday. Carly's main responsibilities would be to retrieve the guests from the ferries and flights, bring them to the house, and make sure towels and basic toiletries were stocked.

All guests would be on their own for transportation the remainder of their stay until Carly would deliver them back to the boat or plane when the weeks were over. That was the deal they'd agreed to. This courtesy had an old-fashioned feel to it, Carly thought, without being a cumbersome responsibility of being at everyone's beck and call every minute of the day. She hoped no one minded the rumbling old Land Cruiser. It was pretty, she thought, with its white-striped rustic green body. It wasn't some swanky antique Land Rover Defender but it was vintage-cool and would get the job done. And it had a name, Nessie, right there on the license plate.

As she laid there in bed, her brain darted in all the different directions her day would take her. Or, fingers crossed, that Nessie would. And soon, to the big mid-island grocery store for provisions. She'd only bought dinner stuff last night at the little Sconset Market and she couldn't afford to keep doing that. Her phone said it was only six-fifteen in the morning but her room was already flooded with pink light. There wouldn't be much sleeping in this summer, which was fine with her — she'd fill her days to the top.

Impatient to check out the island morning, Carly launched herself from the bed, got dressed, grabbed her camera and got outside. The rising sun splashed its peach glow over the ocean and the sand below. She'd missed the orange ball breaching the horizon but she was there on the edge of the lawn to catch the sun casting a gold path across the water. Sconset cottages were touched by the very first rays. A summer of sunrises stretched out before her, it would be impossible to sleep through a single one.

Carly continued down the narrow path from the house, raising the camera to her eye with nearly every step. She felt compelled to capture it all: the sun on white fences, the sea grasses waving in the morning wind, purple hydrangeas bobbing behind a faded cedar swing suspended from the ceiling of a back porch, and weathered arbors with morning glories climbing up. The contrast was dizzying — on one side, a sweeping 180-degree view of rugged coastal beauty; on the other, manicured gardens and gorgeous old homes. Every peek over a gate, each brilliant bloom preening in the rising sun begged to be photographed. She imagined how a misty fog would wrap everything in a lacy incandescent veil. Which would be a different kind of beautiful.

Countless social media posts revealed themselves to her in her mind as she strolled. No wonder everyone wanted a piece of Nantucket.

∽

Her stomach growled pulling her back to the moment. She couldn't put off the grocery store any longer. Nerves lit up her insides thinking about getting behind the wheel of Nessie again. She told herself if she stalled, she stalled. It wouldn't be the end of the world. Backing out of the little garage was her first victory.

The driveway was wide enough for her to get turned around and headed in the right direction and off she went. Navigating out of Sconset would be the challenge with summer people on foot and on bikes all around her on the narrow lanes. Once she made it to Milestone Road, she was golden. Thank God Brett had stopped by and gotten her behind the wheel. She and Nessie would get used to each other and before long Carly would be shifting, braking, and clutching like a boss.

Once she could tell third gear from first. As if rotaries weren't stressful enough. She stalled, recovered, stalled once more. People were patient and there seemed to be no honking on Nantucket. Sweet.

The supermarket was enormous and had a contemporary feel, an industrial aesthetic with a concrete floor and exposed ductwork. She'd read about the long self-checkout lines but it was still early enough and didn't look too bad.

"Hey, how's it goin,?" Startled, Carly turned in the direction of the familiar voice. Brett.

"Oh, hi! I'm good! I was thinking on the drive over here how glad I am that you stopped by yesterday to refresh my stick shift skills — thanks again for that!" She left out the part about stalling.

"How was the first night? I don't think that place is haunted, but you never know. The Davis house, a few down from you on the corner, is definitely haunted."

"Davis house?"

"Yeah, that really beautiful, creepy old one at 11 Baxter Road — it was the very first house to be built on the Bluff in 1885."

"Ooh, yes, I saw that one on my way to Sconset Market yesterday. I definitely want to know more about that. I thought it was beautiful too, in a run-down, must-have-a-spooky-history kind of way. I think I need to spend a day at the library," Carly said, moving closer to the front of the line. She took in Brett's t-shirt, board shorts and flip flops and realized she didn't know a thing about him. "What does your day look like today? This isn't really a work outfit is it," she laughed, her finger tracing small circles in the air. "Wait, I don't even know what you do…"

"I'm actually a carpenter by trade — the car thing is a side-hustle I guess you'd say, lots of vintage cars on the island. I actually have a couple days off to spend with my brother who's on-island for a wedding. Hey, we're heading to the brewery later, do you want to join?"

Carly wondered again at his ease, and also at why she didn't get butterflies when this good-looking guy who was standing close enough for her to smell some nice combo of his laundry soap and deodorant and who was asking her out. Well, he wasn't actually *asking her out*, but still. Nothing was stirring. What was wrong with her?

"Um, sure! It could be—"

"*Research,*" they both said at the same time.

"Exactly," she said, "I really need to get to know this place for guests' questions and recommendations and all that."

While she scanned her items and paid he put his number in her phone. "I'll shoot you a text when we're heading out, okay? How about we swing by and pick you up?"

Carly wasn't used to a guy being so genuinely kind, without pretense or agenda. It was refreshing. Even if she didn't feel some massive chemistry. She'd had casual relationships in the past that were fine instead of fireworks. And then there'd been Jake, her longest and most serious boyfriend. She still didn't have 100% closure with how it ended. His taking a job in another state seemed workable at first, the alternating visiting weekends adding a fun spark she thought would carry them the distance. Until it didn't. And it became clear he wasn't going to be choosing her, *them*. It had left her feeling rejected, vulnerable, and afraid to put herself out there again on the relationship front.

"Are you sure?" she asked Brett, "I mean, am I on the way? Where do you live anyway? Not that I'd have any clue where that would be in relation to Sconset but..."

"I'm sure. My parents' place is in Tom Nevers which is actually just a couple miles west of Sconset."

Sooo did he live with Mom and Dad? How old was he?

"I can see what you're thinking — *does this guy really live with his parents*? And the answer is yes, technically, although it's an apartment over the garage that I built myself. Not sure if you've heard but real estate around here is—"

"Brett, you do not have to explain yourself to me. I'd been living in my childhood bedroom just before coming here — believe me, I get it, and I'm on the wrong end of my twenties." Carly was kicking herself for not remembering to bring shopping bags.

"Well, I got you beat by two years. I'm working on it, it's not forever, you know?"

"I do. Now, judging from your empty basket there you have some shopping to do — I'll let you go." With a bag in each arm, she smiled and gave an awkward wave telling him she'd wait for his text.

Chapter Nine

WHAT DID ONE WEAR to Cisco Brewery? After a late breakfast, Carly settled in a white wicker chaise in the shade of the back porch facing the ocean. The navy and white striped cushions were deep and soft and it was the perfect time and place to scroll through her Instagram before googling Cisco Brewers.

I was Today Years Old *when I found out that when someone tells you to "break a leg" in an audition it is because they are hoping you end up in the cast. Now my head is exploding.*

The things you didn't you didn't know. Scroll, scroll, Scroll... @cats_of_instagram, @animalsdoingthings, @pubity reels, @barstoolsports, all the photographers she followed, life coaches, fashion, food — wait, WHAT? *Engaged??* Jake Miller getting *married*? What the absolute *fuck*?

Everything went white around her. Her self-involved, *it's not you it's me*, we-should-just-be-having-fun-in-our-twenties EX?? Her heart struggled to beat and then roared in her ears, blood compressed like motor oil in her veins. Was she going to throw up? How could he still have this effect on her? This visceral response, this fresh sense of complete rejection that made her wish she didn't exist.

Ping. A text from Brett. Asking how 12:30 sounded, as though her heart hadn't just disintegrated into dust.

Carly had all she could do to respond *ok*. She had less than two hours to get it together, to cycle through the range of emotions she was plowing through. Her boyfriend of three years was getting married. He NEVER posted anything on social media! Why now, *why her*? Why hadn't Carly unfollowed him? *Did Paige know?!*

Paige, one of her best friends since dating Jake, marrying Jake's brother. They'd even kidded about getting to be sisters-in law one day if things had worked out with Jake! They were still besties — Paige *had* to know this — how could she have kept it from Carly? Of course she'd have wanted to protect her but *this*, finding out like this was worse.

She sat there, paralyzed, as little movies of their years unspooled in her mind. It was torture and she couldn't stop. Paddleboarding on Lake Sebago at his parents' summer place in Maine, winetasting in the Finger Lakes in New York, climbing Mount Washington during a flash thunderstorm, music festivals — Boston Calling every single Memorial Day weekend — the Glass Animals, Milky Chance!

But he couldn't get past her not wanting to look for apartments in Pennsylvania where he was, claiming she wasn't prioritizing their relationship over her nomadic lifestyle. That with her remote work, she could live anywhere. What a load of crap that was. He was a giant child. He was the one insisting that their twenties was the time for living it up, not locking anything in. He'd ended things over a year ago. She didn't care anymore— couldn't care! But who was this woman? What did she have that Carly didn't? She forced a deep breath in through her nose, then sighed it out. Again. Screw him. It. Did. Not. Matter.

Ugh, would people start texting her about it? *Did you hear? Can you believe it?* Not for the first time, she wanted to pitch her phone under the wheels of an eighteen-wheeler — release herself completely from the unwanted barrage of information. Useless, painful information!

But her phone was basically her life. Her job, her main source of communication, tying her to everything. It was the worst and the best thing ever to exist.

She googled Cisco Brewers on Nantucket. *The brewery's setup feels like a mix between a working farm and an outdoor beer garden. Gravel pathways meander through the property where you'll find picnic tables and food trucks. There's often live music with local bands performing everything from acoustic and folk to indie rock, and reggae.*

Sounded amazing and the perfect way to spend the afternoon. Day-drinking would do it. Sundress or shorts? The usual dilemma.

Brett and his brother rolled into the driveway at twelve-thirty sharp and Carly was ready and waiting for them out front. A quick wave of nerves washed over her wondering about the brother — would he be cute, single? That familiar inner conflict stirred again — craving the kind of connection worth sharing everything, at odds with feeling afraid, wary of loving and losing all over again.

Brett got out of the passenger side of his brother's old two-door Jeep Wrangler to let her into the seat behind him. It wasn't graceful squeezing back there and she was glad she'd decided on shorts instead of a cute dress.

"Hi, I'm Evan," Brett's brother said, turning in his seat to shake Carly's hand, "good to meet you." Unlike Brett's floppy wayward hair, Evan's light brown hair was a tidy fade, longer on top but perfectly swooped. His Ray Bans hid his eyes and his smile was almost too perfect — she felt equally interested and on alert. Dudes that good-looking threw her off.

"Thanks for picking me up, I really appreciate it," she said.

"So Brett tells me this is your first time to Nantucket?" Evan said, navigating out of Sconset.

"Yup. I'm more of a mountain girl but this is beautiful. What a place to grow up."

"Growing up here is nothing like summering here," Evan said, "and I for one couldn't wait to get the hell out of this sand trap."

"Interesting." Carly was surprised by his response, although it made sense. "Is it weird or awful that so many people are here on your little island in the summer?"

Both guys laughed at that. "Yes," Evan said, "it can feel pretty isolated here in the off-season, that's for sure. But then the massive swarm of summer people — it's overkill, you know?"

"I bet. But you need the tourism and all that, right?"

"We do. That's the main industry of the island — since the late nineteenth century," Brett added.

"Oh here he goes with his history," Evan said, "don't encourage him."

"No, I love it," Carly said, "and wow, I didn't realize that. So when the whaling thing died out then? That's smart. It certainly seems to have become a world-class destination — which seems totally crazy to me for a little New England island."

"Right?" Evan said, looking at her in the rearview mirror, "People are crazy."

Carly leaned forward in her seat to be able to hear Evan over the wind whooshing in the topless Jeep. "So where do you live now? What do you do?" Brett seemed distracted by something on his phone so she didn't feel rude directing her attention to the brother.

"I live in Boston and I'm in sales at a company called Datadog," Evan said, "It's a platform of products that help companies build, test, monitor, debug, optimize and secure their software. Hey — are your eyes glazing over back there?"

"Guilty," Carly laughed, "I honestly don't know what anyone's jobs are these days. I mean Brett's a carpenter, that I can picture, but all that stuff in the cloud, yeah, no."

"Ah, but you got the cloud part! We're basically a cloud infrastructure monitoring service built by engineers for engineers, enabling digital transformation and monitoring for our customer's entire technology stacks. It can be used by companies of any size and within a wide range of industries — Google Cloud Platform and Microsoft Azure to name a couple."

"Oh boy — good for you, I'll take your word for it! Do you come back here often?"

"I try to get in a couple weekends in the summer and Thanksgiving and Christmas — that's really enough for me," Evan said, "Brett here, on the other hand, is a lifer."

"You say that like there's something wrong with it," Brett said, "not everyone wants to sit on their ass all day in the city selling stuff to people."

"You forgot to add *for ridiculous amounts of money*," Evan said, "and hot Boston babes."

"You don't think builders and tradesmen make ridiculous amounts of money here, bro?"

Carly felt like the little sister in the backseat. It was comforting and strangely normal. And weird, since she'd only known these guys for like five minutes. They parked the Jeep and started walking. "Is this the line to get in?" she asked, changing the subject and noting the snaking crowd of people backed up to the parking lot.

"It moves pretty fast," Brett said, as they pulled into a spot, "it'll be worth it."

Chapter Ten

Cisco Brewery was everything she'd read about and more. Carly wondered if she would ever get used to it — happy beautiful people with their happy beautiful dogs everywhere living their best lives. She felt buzzed before she'd had a sip of anything. She snuck a few shots with her phone trying to capture the energy, an Instagram carousel already staging itself in her mind.

Once they were in the thick of things, and sporting their neon old-enough-to-drink bracelets, Brett seemed to disappear and Evan turned to her to ask what she wanted from the bar. "I'll get the first round, what do you like?" he said, pushing his sunglasses up on his head. Blue. His eyes were the most ridiculous blue. Cobalt like the sky in October.

"Um, surprise me?" she said.

"Is that a question? What do you like, woman?" he said, with a completely disarming half-smile.

Carly tore her eyes from his to give the chalkboard of drinks over the bar a quick look. "I guess I'll try the Pineapple Express," she said, "and where did Brett go?"

"Probably to see if his girlfriend is here yet — hey, I'll be right back." And leaving that tidbit dangling, Evan was off to the bar where a line had formed. Of course Brett had a girlfriend, the brother-vibes she got from him...it totally tracked.

She took in the scene. Yes, a farmy beer garden was a good description for the setting and the mood. But with a big dose of *bougie*. She wished she'd remembered her sunglasses so she could be checking everyone out without standing there looking like a lost child in a department store.

"Carly," Brett called out heading her way, "where's Evan? Sorry for ditching — I had to find Marin and Lindsay. Meet my girlfriend, Marin, and her friend, Lindsay."

"Oh, no worries," Carly said, facing the girls, "it's nice to meet you, I'm Carly." She turned back to Brett to tell him that Evan was getting drinks. Brett had a spark in his whole demeanor that Carly hadn't seen since he was showing her the Land Cruiser. Everything about him leaned toward Marin, a love aura. She had to admit she was relieved on some level that she wouldn't be on the receiving end of it — friendship was a less fraught ship to navigate.

"Cool," Brett said, "anyone else hungry? I'm starving."

"Ooh I'm dying for a lobster roll," Marin said, "you wanna split one, Linds?"

God, both girls looked so cool in their flowy palazzo pants and cropped white tops.

"Hell no, I want my own — you treating Brett?" Lindsay said, laughing.

"Sure, since it's the first one of the season," Brett said.

"I'm kidding, Brett, I can buy my own — but thanks."

"What do you think, Carly, what are you in the mood for?" Brett said, just as Evan was handing her a drink.

"I'm all set for now, but thanks," Carly took a deep sip of her Pineapple Express wishing again for the veil of sunglasses to hide behind. "This place is vibes," she said looking around, "and this drink — wow — oh, my God, thank you Evan."

"Of course," Evan said, turning to the band onstage. "Oh wow, Buckle and Shake is playing too, excellent."

"They're at the Chicken Box this weekend — can't wait!" Lindsay said, "a bunch of us are planning on going, how about you guys?"

Carly wasn't exactly sure if the *you guys* extended to her, but she'd heard about the *Box*. And she probably shouldn't start off with that level of partying the first weekend of guests. As the group headed over to the food trucks she sipped her drink, her head on swivel mode.

There seemed to be a collective sway to the tunes and a general sense of supreme chill. The dogs wore as much merch as their humans, it was adorable. She took out her phone to follow the brewery's Instagram account. She would definitely recommend this place to her guests.

"So, what exactly do you do?" Evan asked, taking a huge bite from his Nantucket Bay Scallop roll. "Brett said something about a guest house? Not an Airbnb?"

"Yeah, and no. It's not your typical vacation-rental-by-owner, but kind of. It's a big old house that has historically been rented out by the room per the wishes of the original owners. So what started out years ago as a sort of boarding house to give struggling artist-types an affordable alternative has kind of morphed into a set-up for like-minded couples or singles to be able to stay in a gorgeous Sconset house on the bluff for less money. With the catch of sharing the common living spaces like the kitchen, living room, back porch and yard. Does that make sense?"

"Sounds very bohemian, and yeah, I can see it I guess. I mean, it's not for me," Evan said, polishing off his scallop roll with a gulp of his drink, "What if you get stuck with some crazy dude or couples having wild sex or people eat your food, drinking your booze? Or are total slobs?"

"Control freak?" Carly laughed, "yeah, no, I guess it's not for everyone. But it makes sense for a lot of people apparently. There's an application process designed to help match guests with shared expectations and a similar approach to the stay. There's been a lot of interest — more applications than the summer can accommodate."

"Well, sure, I believe it, that's a pretty posh address out there. Did you know that back in the day there were people who lived in Nantucket town who actually had summer houses out in Sconset?"

"Really? That's insane. But then I suppose it must have felt like an excursion all the way to the other side of the island if you were traveling by horse. Anyway — it's just a summer side hustle. In the real world I'm a social media content creator for Custom Escapes Travel Group. My boss thought I'd be a good match — which was actually perfect since I recently became homeless." Carly noticed Evan's eyebrows shoot up above his Ray Bans. She choked on her drink and laughed. "Not tent-on-the-sidewalk-in-San-Francisco homeless, just sort of in between residences I guess you could say."

"Gotcha. And I can think of worse places to be in between."

Carly imagined he'd be winking if she could see his eyes. He had total main-character energy, but also seemed polite and attentive. Which could all be an act and total bullshit. Not that she was thinking about him in a flirty way but, well, how could you not. He was hot. She wondered if he felt more tourist than local now that he lived off-island — she couldn't quite tell if he was scanning the crowd for familiar faces or babes.

"Do most of the people you grew up with still live here, or did they move away too?" She asked, as she saw Brett and the girls returning with their lobster rolls.

"Some leave, some stay — not sure of the exact percentage. Some love the close-knit community but some feel smothered by it and can't wait to live larger, you know?"

"I can see that. Do you think you'll ever live back here?"

"Seasonally at best. I mean isn't that the dream?"

"That's a pretty big dream from where I'm standing but..."

"Dreaming big is the only way to go."

"Oh what's he trying to sell you," Brett chimed in, " resist!"

The band launched into their cover of "Halleluiah" and by the second chorus the crowd had joined in. *Your faith was strong but you needed proof, you saw her bathing on the roof, her beauty and the moonlight overthrew you...*

"Such a good song," Carly said, the drink hitting, "and all I can see whenever I hear it is Shrek crying because Fiona is marrying Farquaad."

"Oh my God, RIGHT?" Marin said.

Carly felt a flicker of camaraderie. She needed flowy pants and gold hoop earrings. Or maybe she was drunk. Or maybe she might cry... She and Jake knew every line in that movie. Fuck that, *fuck Jake*!

"Hey, are you okay?" Lindsay asked Carly, "You don't look so good."

Carly didn't remember when that second drink came to be in her hands but there it was. And her lips got loose and her heart was hanging out all over the place. "Well, my ex who wasn't ready to be tied down just posted an engagement photo on Instagram this morning so there's *that...*"

"Oh shit," Brett said, "well that sucks."

Evan noticed an old classmate and exited their little circle. Jesus, who could blame him, she was bringing everyone down. She organized her features into a less depressed version of herself, threw back her drink, and asked who was ready for another round.

"Maybe now would be a good time for that piece of pizza — that's what you wanted, right?" Brett said, steering her in the direction of the food trucks. Carly suddenly felt foolish and lucky at the same time to have met these people, to maybe have some friends here. She wanted to express that in some way, but she was feeling all over the place and it would come out all mushy and stupid.

"Yes. Pizza please. Let me buy. You want a slice? Oh wait, you just had a lobster roll."

"I could have a slice."

"Okay good," she said, smiling up at him, "Marin is a lucky girl." Her eyes filled up again and poor Brett looked like he didn't know what to do. She was shutting herself off!

Chapter Eleven

CARLY SPENT THE MAJORITY of Friday editing photos and finalizing some content for work and trying to forget about tears spilt at the brewery. She was officially done with Jake. Of course she'd *been* done with him, but apparently she hadn't realized she was holding onto some shard of hope that someday he'd come back, saying how stupid he was to have ever let her go. No. Over, capital "O".

Thank you, NEXT.

She walked through each of the three rooms upstairs to be certain everything was in place There was the Robin's Egg room, the New Dawn Rose room, and then the Sea Glass room. The crisp white bedding was complemented by walls painted in the softest shades of blue, rose, and seafoam.

Each room was furnished with the same Belgian pine pieces as Carly's first-floor bedroom, all with a soft honey finish and cottagey feel. She felt like she'd never be able to design rooms of a home from scratch, but that she knew what she liked when she saw it. And everything in this house felt perfect. She felt confident it would have the same effect on the guests.

Saturday would be a busy day with three separate pickups; one from the steamship, one from the Hy-Line on Straight Wharf, and one from the airport. She hoped she could count on Nessie to not overheat or to do any other weird thing Carly would be powerless to remedy.

Anticipation was always so much more fraught than the actual thing. She just wanted it to be Sunday already — with the guests settled in, going about their days leaving her to hers. But suddenly there was this hill of anxiety thinking about everyone sharing the space. She'd loved the idea of it — sounded like the college days, meeting new people, bonding over pizza and a keg. But the reality of six established adults, strangers, sharing a house? Personalities clashing, chaos and control issues — a recipe for mayhem.

Taking her tall glass of iced tea outside to the porch staring out at the sea, Carly wondered about her Sconset neighbors — were they families that had been coming to Nantucket forever? Were they old-money people or new? Was anyone renting?

"Helloo?" a woman's voice called out from next door beyond the privet hedge. Carly stood and walked to the edge of the property, curious if the hello was meant for her. As she rounded the corner of the hedge she just about banged into a striking woman of indeterminable age with greenish-blue eyes and what could only be described as some contemporary version of Farrah Fawcett hair.

"Oh, hi there," the woman said, "I hope I didn't scare you darlin, you wouldn't have a couple of eggs to spare would ya? Oh, where are my manners — I'm Antonia Davenport, your next-door neighbor!" Antonia thrust her small hand out to shake Carly's, its strength took her by surprise.

"Hi, I'm Carly, it's so nice to meet you!" Carly found herself truly meaning it. "Sure come on over!"

"Well now, isn't this the most beautiful piece of property you've got here, just look at those roses climbing up the whole side of the house — just gorgeous. And those hydrangeas — how do you get them to bloom pink and lavender in the same shrub?" Antonia had stopped to take it all in, shielding the sun from her eyes with her bejeweled hand and spinning in a slow 360 degrees for the whole view. She let out a low whistle, the kind men use when struck by something beautiful.

"Thank you," Carly said, curious about this self-possessed woman, "I mean, yes it's so gorgeous only it's not *mine*."

"I hear you, sugar, just a renter like me then, huh?"

"Something like that," Carly said, scooping her long hair up into a messy bun with the hair-tie on her wrist. "Would you join me in a glass of iced tea?" she asked Antonia.

"Oh, I couldn't impose, I was just doing a little baking and realized I didn't have enough eggs. I thought, hey, why not be neighborly and come on over, you know?"

"Of course! Welcome!" Carly was equally surprised and delighted for the company. Antonia had a way about her. She looked like the results of a Pinterest search for *not your grandma's southern belle*. Standing there in her crisp white blouse tucked into tailored, high-waisted shorts and pink espadrilles, she looked about her mother's age — but with an effortless grace and openness Cynthia didn't radiate.

Antonia followed her inside the house admiring the hardwood floors, the fieldstone fireplace, the deep cozy couches, and just every single thing. "This is quite a place for a young woman — do you mind if I ask what it is you do, Carly?"

Carly grabbed a bag of Pepperidge Farm Mint Milano cookies, handed Antonia her iced tea and led the way back out to the shady porch to get to know each other.

Chapter Twelve

"**W**OULD YOU LOOK AT this gorgeous flagstone under my feet," Antonia said.

"Is that what it is?" Carly said, "I would have said bluestone, but what do I know?"

"They're very similar — but see these shades of gray, gold and blue? That's how you know. Bluestone is, well, more just bluish and gray shades. Both make such a lovely natural stone flooring. Anyway — tell me about this place, it's really something." Antonia sat back deep in the cushions of the wicker chair, took a sip of her tea and reached in for a cookie.

"Well, you might think it's a little weird, but I'm kind of managing a group of guests who will be renting this house, separately but together." Taking in Antonia's look of confusion, Carly did her best to explain the boarding house situation that was *Driftwood Dream's* past, present, and hopefully future. "Guest house is probably the best term. And *managing* is probably too strong. Ha!"

"Such a cool old-fashioned idea, I love it! Much more affordable. So does that make you the housemother? Like Mrs. Garrett from *The Facts of Life*?" Antonia snorted a little when she laughed covering her mouth with a manicured hand.

"I'm sorry Mrs. *who* from the *what*?" Carly was laughing too but for no other reason than Antonia's laugh felt contagious.

"You mean to tell me you've never heard of that eighties sitcom about the girls' boarding school with Tootie and Blair and Natalie and Jo? Come on — it was a classic!"

"Before my time, lady, that's my mom's era for sure though."

"Damn, I always forget how old I am..."

"How old are you? If you don't mind my asking," Carly felt an unexpected comfort with this woman she'd just met—something about her put her at ease. Maybe it was her effortless Southern charm, the warmth in her voice, or the quiet confidence she carried. That was something Carly envied. Or aspired to anyway.

"Double nickels. But I don't feel any different than when I was thirty five years old."

"*Double nickels*?" Carly said, "Oohh, I Get it, fifty-five, ha! Cute."

"Right? But I still think of that number as applying to my *parents*! Certainly not to me — I just don't feel it at all."

"Well, you definitely don't look it. I'd have guessed forty-something? Maybe late thirties?"

"Aw, well thank you. The way I see it is you either grow old or you die young."

"I guess you're right — I never thought of it that way. Do you have kids? Are you married? Am I being too nosey?" Carly said, putting her bare feet up on the little table in front of their chairs.

"Well, I'm the one sitting on your porch so that might make me the nosey one," Antonia said, looking out across the lawn to the ocean beyond. "I have one daughter, probably about your age, Kaitlyn, she'll be thirty-two on Christmas Day." Antonia's sunny expression clouded briefly then cleared. "She moved clear across the country once she graduated from college to work with her daddy. Boulder, Colorado. GORGEOUS. But far enough away that I don't get to see her but a few times a year."

"Aw, I'm sorry. But Colorado isn't *that* far... Okay, it is getting-on-a-plane far, I get it, but still. So, where do you live then? Not with the dad? Oops, sorry, none of my business."

"Nope, not with the dad. Beau. I *was* with him once upon a time though. But I was only twenty one on our wedding day. Too young. And then I was a mom at twenty three. I wanted it all; the husband, the child, and a floral design business. But you can't always have everything all at once, you know? Something had to give. And I let Beau slip right through my hands. It's a longer story than that, but you get the picture." Antonia looked about as far away as her daughter was from Nantucket.

Carly leaned forward in her seat. "I'm sorry Antonia, you look so sad now and that's my fault. I apologize for prying — should we tip some Tito's in our tea?" Carly had so many more questions.

An airy laugh bubbled out of her new friend. "A girl after my won heart! Hey, I've got some stinky cheeses over at my place, with some olives and fresh figs — why don't I make a plate and bring it right back here? I'm in love with this spot! We can eat and drink and people-watch the people watching *us* as they walk by — is it okay I'm inviting myself right over? Or is it too much like hanging out with your mother?"

"It's *so* okay, and no, you're not like my mom at all. She's, I mean she's great, in that sort of linen trousers, styled bob, buttoned-up kinda way. Just not relaxed, in that shorts, gold bangles, pink nails and long feathered hair kind of way."

"Oh darlin, you are good for my ego. And you are about as different from my daughter as I can think of — so serious with her high-tech job, some type of information security analyst — do not even ask me what that means. I mean who knew that Boulder, Colorado was considered the Silicon Valley of the Rockies?"

"Sounds like she and my mom would get along." Carly had a sudden image of the four of them sitting there together — weird. "I'm excited for our charcuterie board party now — beats cooking dinner for one, right?"

"You read my mind, give me twenty minutes," Antonia said, winking at Carly and disappearing around the tall hedge.

Chapter Thirteen

CARLY AND ANTONIA ATE and drank and talked and laughed until the sun was low in the sky somewhere behind them. Carly shared what she knew of the guests arriving the next day. "First we have the Turners — Murphy and Hazel — college sweethearts, parents of two, celebrating their fortieth birthdays without the kids."

"They'll either have the best time together or miss their children too much to enjoy it!" Antonia said.

"Hmm, I didn't think of that. Okay, then there's a younger couple, not married, thirty-somethings, Burke and Remi. If I remember correctly he's a retired ski champion? And I forget what she does, but she did confide to Keith, the owner, that she thinks he's going to propose, and wanted to make sure this place was as beautiful and romantic in person."

"Yikes, I sure hope she's right — can you imagine?"

"I hadn't thought of that. I mean I'm not personally responsible for that kind of a guest expectation, but I do want everyone to have a good time, you know? I'm just here to do light housekeeping in between the rounds of guests, keep towels stocked, be a resource, and generally share the space right alongside them. And this place will surely not disappoint."

"You got that right, just gorgeous. There's a fourth room, right?"

"Yup, in that room we have August Wilder, Colorado rancher on some hiatus before he takes over the family business — something like that."

Antonia's eyes got big and round. "You got an honest to goodness cowboy comin' to stay here with y'all? Tell me he's *single*, girl!"

Carly burst out laughing, "No! No, no, *no*, it's not like that. He's actually a buddy of the guy, Keith, whose grandmother owned this place. She passed away a few years ago and Keith decided to breathe new life back into *Driftwood Dream* returning it to its former glory and purpose. So, Keith hooked his friend, August Wilder, up with Nantucket as some place as different from the Rocky Mountains as possible."

"Well, isn't that just fascinating, you've seen *Yellowstone,* right?" Antonia said.

"Seen it? Obsessed. I'm currently binging the whole series for the second time. I used to ride when I was a kid, with my grandmother. She was such a badass. Went on legit cattle drives when she was in her 60's! In Wyoming and Montana — I'm talking in the saddle from sunup to sundown — herding actual cattle, sleeping on the ground in tents, eating around a fire. Bad-ASS."

"Whew! She sounds like an incredible woman."

"No one like her. We were very close. I was so young when she made those trips, and only eleven when she passed away. I'd have so many questions now. I wish she was here to tell me the stories... I really need to get out west."

The setting sun painted the sky in swaths of peach and violet and darkened the sea. It was quiet but for the low hush of the waves rushing in and rolling out in the distance.

"Does it ever stop feeling like we're in some beautiful painting?" Carly said.

"Beats me. I haven't been here much longer than you. I think we feel pretty seduced by everything all in bloom, lush and bright with color. I'm having a hard time picturing it all in the barren gray of winter."

Carly did an exaggerated shudder with her whole body. "Oh, let's not go there — winter is too long in New England. Endless! But you wouldn't know anything about that you Georgia peach. Where did you grow up"

"You got it, born and raised in Marietta, Georgia. It's about a twenty-minute drive northwest of Atlanta. It's real close to the Chattahoochee River — I'm sure you've heard of that — and we're in the foothills of Kennesaw Mountain, which is a very historic Civil War battle site."

"Wow, your accent really comes out talking about home."

"Girl, you makin' fun of my drawl?"

"Not at all. I love it, it's comforting in some way I can't put my finger on. And yeah, I'm embarrassed to say I know next to nothing about southern history, but it sounds like an interesting place. How'd you end up on Nantucket?"

"I sold my floral design business just this past spring and decided to treat myself."

"Sconset waterfront — nice splurge, good for you. Will anyone be visiting you while you're here?"

"That might be a conversation for another time... This has been so lovely, Carly, I thank you for this. Now I'm gonna head on home and give you some time to yourself. Busy day for you tomorrow with all your guests coming in one after another. Can I help you in any way?"

"Aw, that is so sweet, thank you for offering, but I think I got this. I'll let you know though, it's so nice to have a friend! I think I was feeling a little lonely. I mean I've met a couple people but it feels like they're already a group, you know? I was getting fifth-wheel vibes hanging out with them at the brewery yesterday. Of course it did not help that I got too buzzed and then all blubbery. Ugh — my ex got engaged and it just hit me and—"

"Whoa — how did we not cover any of *that*?"

"I think it's called *repression*. It's buried now and it's staying that way." Carly knew ignoring it wasn't the same as dealing with it. But for now, it was all she could do. "Oh my God, I just realized that by tomorrow there'll be five other people here — goodbye quiet evenings on this porch?"

"Oh, you never know — they'll want to explore, go into town in the evenings. Or maybe everyone will get along and it'll be fun. OR you come over to my place."

"Definitely! One day at a time, right? Wow, this has been amazing, Antonia, I'm so glad we met."

"Me too. Bring it in, give me a hug. Get some sleep and we'll talk tomorrow, okay?"

"You got it." Carly watched her new unlikely friend disappear from view then she locked the house up for the night. When she was snug in her bed, she reached for her laptop and promised herself just *one* episode of Yellowstone...

Chapter Fourteen

CARLY WOKE WITH A jolt, sitting straight up in the bed thinking she'd overslept and was already late to pick up the Turners. Her room was so light already she figured it had to be eight o'clock at least. Nope. It was barely six a.m. She laid back down and took a deep breath. She reached for her phone and checked for missed messages then emails. No social media. It was way too early for that. She wondered for the hundredth time that if social content weren't her actual job, if she'd delete Instagram altogether. She knew a girl who did that every other week. But just because you couldn't see it, didn't mean it wasn't happening.

Even though she'd finally blocked Jake, he was still getting married. Probably buying a house in the burbs and would have two point five beautiful children.

She was twenty nine not thirty nine, she had time! Just because it felt like everyone she knew was getting engaged and thinking about babies didn't mean that had to be her timeline. And it wasn't that she necessarily needed *marriage*. Yet. But she'd be lying to herself if she said she didn't want to find a true love someday, be a part of a couple. Someone to share experiences with, the big and little things like, *babe, the temperature gauge in my Jeep is really pushing H but I just had the radiator replaced — what do you think it is?*

"What should I wear to pick up the Turners?" She had to quit talking out loud to herself. White shorts, a cute top, and flipflops would be fine. Except flip-flops and the clutch? Disaster waiting to happen — Vans slip-ons would work. Still in bed, Carly pulled up the guest profiles again to make sure she had everything right.

Hazel and Murphy Turner were arriving on the Steamship at eight-forty-five that morning. They were coming from Topsfield, Massachusetts, which would have been a seriously early-morning start for them. Should she have iced coffees for them? She hadn't really thought through the whole concierge piece, because she was not to be their personal concierge — but it could be a nice touch. Keith had set her up with a credit card for incidentals, saying he trusted her judgement.

Googling coffee shops she found Island Coffee Roasters right there by Steamship Wharf, hopefully she could park there and walk to get the coffees. The car. Anxiety rippled through Carly picturing herself navigating the cobblestoned streets through town and all the people. She should have practiced more.

Murphy Turner: Forensic Analyst for an IT firm, forty years old, married to Hazel Murphy for fifteen years. Hazel Turner, second-grade teacher, will be forty on July tenth, they have two children who will not be accompanying them. From their photo they looked like the most normal family on the planet. Murphy was average height with medium brown hair and an easy smile standing beside Hazel with chestnut hair pulled back and a happy smile that matched her husband's.

Arriving on the two-fifteen Hy-Line fast ferry were Burke Reed and Remi Hayes. They were renting a car from Nantucket Windmill Auto Rental and would need a ride to the airport to pick that up.

Burke: age thirty-five, single, retired alpine ski racer, currently employed by Takeda Pharmaceuticals in the sales division.

Remi: age thirty-three, single, former pharmaceutical salesperson, currently pursuing women's figure competitions.

Oh boy. Carly had a loose idea of what that was and that it was an actual division of competition in bodybuilding — more about lean physical symmetry and posing confidence than extreme muscularity. There was no photo with this application but she had a feeling these two might be looking for temporary gym memberships on-island. Maybe they'd done their own intel, but Carly could look into that as well. At least the fridge was big enough — there would probably be a lot of organic produce, kombucha, and overnight oats.

Or maybe they were just regular people who were super athletic and ate ice-cream and Cheez-Its like everyone else.

Arriving from Denver by plane at six-thirty that evening was August Wilder. Thirty-six-year-old range conservationist at Wilder Ridge, engaged. Did this come under the heading of *cowboy* or had she gotten caught up in her own fantasy? She supposed the category of cowboy was a broad one, especially in these environmentally sensitive times, and that if this August grew up on a ranch then he sure knew how to rope, ride, herd, and a whole lot of other stuff. There was no photo with this profile either.

Half of her hoped he was an awkward, bow-legged, tongue-tied hick in a plaid shirt with a bolo tie who only looked good with his cowboy hat on. The other half of her hoped for the Stetson guy or the Marlborough man without the cigarettes. Or Rip from Yellowstone... because 'every girl needs a little Rip in her jeans.' *He wasn't single.* None of it mattered.

Carly felt herself teetering at the edge of the rabbit hole again — afraid she might never find *the one.* She couldn't ignore the contradiction — craving that forever love, yet instinctively pushing it away. Maybe it was fear. Maybe doubt. She wasn't sure lasting love even existed, at least not for her. Jake proposing to someone else less than two years after he said he wasn't ready for that kind of commitment had her questioning everything.

At what point should she consider freezing her eggs? Was there other drastic reproductive crap available to single women now?

She needed to get out of bed and out of her head. Maybe she'd learn a thing or two from the Turners. They seemed solid — married in their twenties, raising two kids, and still into each other enough to want to spend two weeks alone together on an island. How did they know the other was *the one*? How was anyone ever sure of that?

She used to believe more easily in it. But then her best childhood friend's parents broke up after thirty-six years of marriage. They'd always seemed so perfect for each other — a solid team in every way — role models for a successful marriage and a gold-star family if ever there was one. Then the kids all grew up and away and they didn't seem to know each other anymore. It all seemed so unfair. And now the same thing was going on with her dad's sister, Carly's favorite aunt, and it was all just so unpredictable and devastating.

How was anyone supposed to keep a marriage from being the one where you're both just ghosts on opposite sides of the kitchen, aware of the excess weight, the subtle meanness and misunderstanding? Trying to remember how it had been before? What if the loud chewing, the toothpaste in the sink, and nail clippings on the floor became the tipping point — how did you stop those things from taking up all the space?

What if she clouded every future relationship with the past?

You couldn't just go brand new into relationships every time — you had to pay attention. There were signs, red flags. And what about the *sunk cost fallacy*? Where you hang on because you don't want to 'waste' the time you've already invested. Three years with Jake was significant — they were in it — beginning to talk about getting an apartment together, his out-of-state job only temporary. Until it wasn't. The long-distance relationship had lost its shine and Carly wondered if she should have cut her losses sooner. But three years felt like a lot to have committed. She didn't want to have regrets, she just wanted to be smarter.

She wished she could pull off casual. Hookups for fun. But that wasn't her style. She was responsible, attentive, deliberate, strong, kind, and probably a hundred other things. Why wasn't that enough?

Chapter Fifteen

CARLY GOT NO SMALL amount of attention cruising into town in the vintage FJ55 despite the fact that antique cars and trucks were not unique on Nantucket. Restored Broncos, Land Rovers, and old wood-paneled Jeep Wagoneers were all part of the scene, but she felt more conspicuous than she was comfortable with. And like an imposter. She kept her sunglasses on and powered through.

The ride down to the steamship wharf was smoother than anticipated and she was ecstatic about that. She stalled once at the Milestone rotary, nothing new, recovered and didn't let it get to her. She even found a parking spot at the dock and was able to walk to Island Coffee Roasters for the iced coffees. And even if she'd gotten it wrong with the milk and sweetener, it was the thought. At exactly 8:45 the Eagle pulled in.

She put the coffees in the car and retrieved the sign she'd made with the Turners' name on it. She wondered if she'd recognize them from their photo. They had no idea what she looked like and she was grateful that Keith had suggested she whip up some type of placard. She was nervous watching families and dogs disembark wondering if Murphy and Hazel were going to be as chill as they seemed, or if they'd have all kinds of demands and never be satisfied. She chased the thought away — people like that wouldn't be sharing a house with strangers.

Carly scanned the crowd of people descending the ramps for anything familiar. All the hats and sunglasses made it a challenge. But there they were, she'd have bet on it. The woman in a wide-brimmed sunhat visor with her chestnut mane pulled back, an easy smile, holding the hand of a dude in a Patriots ball cap. Both were of average height and average weight, he had a backpack and she carried a straw tote. Their matching smiles reflected their carefree joy — as opposed to the couples with children, pets, bags, boards and fatigue.

She noticed them scanning the crowd below looking for her so held the sign up higher. Hazel caught it right away and waved, elbowing her husband, pointing Carly out. Adorably nautical in her sleeveless navy and white striped top and white shorts, Hazel's fair skin was already pink from the boat ride. Murphy looked like every other dad-dude in khaki shorts and a faded blue t-shirt and sneakers. He must have just gotten his hair cut for the trip — Carly noticed stripes of lighter skin at his temples and back of his neck. She softened toward them.

"You must be Carly, hi!" Hazel said, surprising her with a robust hug before stepping back, seemingly aware of pushing the limits of personal space. "Sorry about that, did I get you in the eye with my hat? Ohmygod I just cannot *believe* we are actually *here*! It's just, I mean look at all those cute little boats bobbing in the harbor, and those homes on the cliff coming around the point, I mean it's not real!"

"She's not too excited, right? Hi, I'm Murphy Turner. Thanks so much for picking us up this morning." And noticing the Land Cruiser he let out a low whistle asking if it was her car. "This is gorgeous! I love my Toyota Sequoia but *this,* wow, what a throwback, very nice."

"You must be exhausted catching the six-thirty boat this morning," Carly said to Hazel, who was still looking all around, taking it all in. "I have some iced coffees in the car." Carly opened the driver's side to retrieve one of the coffees, already sweating with condensation, and handed it with a napkin to Hazel.

"Oh how thoughtful, you didn't have to do that!" Hazel took a deep sip from the straw, "But I am so glad you did, this hits the spot."

"My pleasure," Carly said, while Murphy lugged their bags over fitting them into the back of the car. "Is there somewhere you'd like to stop on the way back to the house? Like for food or wine or beer or whatever?"

"Ooh, I hadn't thought that far ahead," Hazel said, "we don't want to put you out. Since there are bikes for us to use, we figured we could just take those to get what we need, right honey?" she said, turning to her husband, "or the Wave — isn't that the name of the shuttle bus?"

"You can absolutely do that," Carly said, "the shuttle stops include Nantucket Town, Sconset, beaches, the airport, and grocery stores and restaurants. Or you could always Uber or sometimes a taxi is quicker or even cheaper depending on the time of day."

"Sounds good," Murphy said, "but if there's a liquor store on the way, it would be awesome if we could pick up some beer. If it's not too much trouble."

"Oh honey, we can—" Hazel started but Carly interrupted.

"Not a problem at all and I totally hear you. We drive right by Hatch's Package Store. Vacation starts now, right?" She flashed a conspirator's smile. "Okay, who's riding up front with me? I don't want to feel like your chauffer. Even though I guess I kind of am, ha!"

"Oh, Murph, you go ahead. I know you're dying to get a closer look at this boat. It is very cool, I'll say that — and a stick shift, good for you, Carly, I never learned to drive one."

Clouds seemed to roll in out of nowhere blocking the sun and Carly pushed her sunglasses on top of her head. She checked Hazel in the rearview mirror as they navigated the bumpy cobblestoned section of Water Street and across Main. "Sorry for the rough ride, you okay back there Mrs. Turner?"

"Mrs. Turner is my mother-in-law, let's stick with Hazel," she said removing her own sunglasses and giving Carly a wink in the mirror. "It's Hazel and Murphy while we're here, not Mommy and Daddy or Mr. and Mrs. Let's turn back the clock, right hon?"

Murphy turned in his seat to meet his wife's green gaze, "Are you alright back there?" Then back to face Carly, "you've never met a more dedicated mom. Can't imagine her turning that off for two whole weeks."

"I didn't say I was turning it off — just maybe it won't be my primary identity while we're here. Isn't that what we promised each other?" Hazel said leaning forward in her seat to be sure her husband heard her over the sound of the wind rushing through the open windows.

Murphy reached a hand back to squeeze his wife's leg. "There isn't a better mother out there, babe." He noticed she was already on her phone. "Don't tell me you're already texting your mother..."

"Oh stop. I'm just letting them know we've arrived," Hazel said with an easy smile.

"Because you promised me, Haze, that you would let your parents be in charge, do their thing, and let the kids enjoy them without the non-stop checking in."

"Right. And I do. Promise."

Carly took a right into Hatch's, "Here we are. I think I'll pick up some spiked seltzers since we're here. And seriously, if you're into those at all, you have to try the Cisco Brewers lineup. They have a bunch of different flavored hard lemonades like blueberry and cranberry and then a bunch of hard teas like peach, lemon, mango — perfect for the beach."

"Oohh those sound amazing — I'm sure Murph will stick to beer but I'm down to try those for sure," Hazel said, following Carly to the Cisco section. "Hey, Murph, look at all these Cisco beers! Shark Tracker, Whale's Tale, Grey Lady, Summer Rays, so many!" Then Hazel laughed as Murphy reached for his standard favorite, Mich Ultra.

"Well, you can take the boy out of Missouri but you can't take Missouri out of the boy, ha!"

Hazel stood on her toes to kiss her husband's cheek as he wrapped his arm around her. Carly smiled to herself — she could tell these two were still in love. Even after a couple of kids and a couple of extra pounds. It gave her hope.

Chapter Sixteen

Even though Carly was getting the hang of driving the Land Cruiser around the cobblestoned town and darting tourists, her whole body seemed to sigh with relief when they pulled into their driveway. She had a few hours before she needed to retrieve Burke and Remi from the Hy-Line and she thought she might walk to Sankaty Head Lighthouse in the meantime. It might be the last time the Turners would have the house to themselves.

"Oohh, it's even more magical in real life," Hazel said dreamily, getting out of the car looking up at the house. "Murphy, can you believe we are here? And oh my God, we could never afford a place like this alone — I'm glad we found this listing. What a fun idea to share it with other people.

"Sofia would go crazy for these flowers, can you picture her, Murph? Making little bouquets for every room?" Hazel said, wistfulness coating her voice.

Murphy seemed to catch the tenderness in her voice too. Wrapping her hand in his he said softly, "I can picture that. Let's text your mother some photos to share with her."

"Do you think we're allowed to do that? Cut some flowers for the house?" Hazel asked Carly.

"I don't see why not," Carly said, helping Murphy get the bags out of the back, "I mean, as long as you don't go crazy I guess. I was actually thinking the same exact thing — let's do it."

"Let me get those, Carly, you don't have to do that," Hazel said, taking her share of the luggage to the front door. Once inside the house Carly almost couldn't wait for the Turners' reaction to the sweeping view of the Atlantic Ocean that poured in from the wall of windows opposite the kitchen and living room. The open design of the house made you feel at the edge of the world.

"This is really something," Murphy said, staring out beyond the emerald lawn to the sea sparkling with diamond light. "I thought I knew what to expect, I mean the photos were terrific but this, well, this defies description." It was exactly the reverence Carly was hoping for.

"Liam would drag me out there fishing every day," Murphy said, as if he were picturing the scene beside his son.

"It's not quite as close as it looks," Carly told them, "we can go check it out once you're settled in, or whenever, but beyond the lawn is a set of wooden steps down then a sand path out to the beach. It's beautiful and serene and super private — but it's a little walk. And of course you don't need me, you can check it out whenever you want."

"Are there chairs down there or an umbrella?" Hazel asked.

"Um, no, you'd have to haul those down from the shed up here — I hope that's okay."

"Of course! It's not like we have to wrangle kids and their buckets and boogie boards and all that stuff, right?" Hazel said. Was she wiping a tear? Carly couldn't imagine not being *ecstatic* to have some time away from the kids. It had to be a lot meeting their needs all day, every day, and two weeks away from that sounded like utopia. She hoped Hazel could be more present and not spend too much time missing her kids.

"Let's unpack and let the good times roll!" Murphy said, steering his wife in the direction of their bags by the stairs. "Which way to the New Dawn Rose room, Captain Carly?"

The Turners were happy with their ocean-view room, even if it was a bit on the pink side according to Murphy. "Oh hon, pretend it's the sunrise pouring in...," Hazel said.

"Oh and it will, believe me," Carly added. "Let me tell you, the sun rises earlier here on this eastern edge of the island than anywhere in the country, it gets bright *early*!"

"Thanks for the heads up," Hazel said, "I'm an early bird anyway. Once you have kids, you know—"

"Okaayyy, enough about the kids," Murphy said, wrapping his wife in a bear hug shooting a combo eyeroll/wink over to Carly. "Let's unpack and go for a walk — check things out."

Carly backed out of the room telling them if they had any questions, to reach out any time. She changed into her Nike shorts, tank top and sneakers, grabbed her camera and crossbody and off she went along the bluff walk in the direction of Sankaty Head.

The clouds that had scudded in over the sun on the drive from town had blown away again. The sky was an unbroken blue, the light drinkable. Carly wished she'd chugged water before leaving but she'd been anxious to leave the Turners to their thing. She wouldn't be surprised if after hanging their clothes they passed out on the big cozy bed for a couple hours.

They'd looked tired. Being responsible for a family — whether or not they were with you — had to exhaust a person in ways Carly couldn't fathom. Murphy was probably looking forward to lots of wild sex with the kids an ocean away. But what did she know? Other than the fact that the forty-year-olds with two kids were undoubtedly seeing more action than she was.

Carly couldn't imagine ever getting sick of walking the bluff or along Baxter Road. She wanted to know the story behind every house. She'd done a little research and learned that one of the most famous Sconseters of the nineteenth century, Edward Underhill, was the guy with the vision for Sconset as a village. He'd been a Civil War correspondent for the New York Times in the late 1800's who, after visiting Sconset a few summers, built more than a dozen summer rental cottages on three Sconset streets. Carly had walked Evelyn Street, named for his wife, and Lily Street, named for his daughter.

His cottages were modeled after old fishermen's shacks on the north side of the village, and they came furnished, making them popular with actors from New York when the theaters took summer breaks. He was the first to bill Sconset as a summer resort. It was cool picturing this speck on a map as an actor's colony back in the day, with Broadway actors, artists, and writers renting the same cottages every summer.

The houses on Baxter were castles in comparison. Each with a story she wished she knew. How many of them were haunted... she needed to get a ghost-story book from Mitchell's Book Corner. Click, click, click — she was taking so many photographs. Would a single one of them capture the feeling, the largesse, the color and the taste of the air?

Ideas for Instagram reels and carousel posts tumbled in as Carly shot small videos and stills.

After getting every angle imaginable of the red-striped light house, Carly reversed direction, bypassing *Driftwood Dream* right into the village. She was craving an ice-cream cone from the little market and wasn't ready to return home just yet.

Chapter Seventeen

CARLY WALKED WITH HER Moose Tracks ice-cream cone over the little wooden footbridge around the corner from the market then down to the beach. The water was warm, felt like at least seventy degrees. Bathwater compared to what she was used to in New Hampshire and Maine. She took off her sneakers and tied them over her shoulder to walk in the water as far as she could until the start of the path along the bluff. She had the pristine stretch of golden-sand beach all to herself.

Sitting on top of miles of prime fishing waters, it was easy to see why Sconset began as a fishing village. But it was hard to wrap her head around it beginning as early as the 1600s. And mind-bending to imagine this rose-covered retreat for the wealthy as a rough working village of fishing shacks. And while it felt like the middle of the ocean, it was still Massachusetts.

Coming up the path to the house stole her breath every time. The string of elegant homes along the bluff, their American flags snapping in the wind, arbors heavy with blossoms offering peeks of the grandeur beyond, and secret views of a life torn from the pages of a novel.

Carly still had time before she had to head back into town to pick up Burke and Remi. Filling her knock-off Stanely cup with water, she got comfortable on a porch lounge chair and pulled up her emails to make sure their arrival was still on-schedule and that she was caught up with her other account posts on social media.

Digging into Nantucket's history had endeared the island more to her, inspiring her to create next-level content for Custom Escapes. Understanding the legacy of a place and its people deepened a person's connection to it. Her whole island experience was beginning to gain more relevance through its historical narrative. She'd gotten caught up in the trend of highlighting the more bougie side of destinations, but it was hitting home more than ever that historical context made any location more profound. Because wasn't there always a bigger story? Beyond the surface?

Carly understood that people traveling to new places had a mix of motivations, ranging from an interest in history and culture to a desire for manicured beauty with modern conveniences. And that while some people might be drawn to the historical depth of a place, there were plenty of others who just wanted it to be beautiful with a contemporary, curated vibe. Having landed in such a destination location, Carly was starting to realize how important it was for her to dig deeper on the places she was promoting — really exploring the authenticity of a place would elevate her content to a new dimension.

Looking up from her laptop she noticed Hazel and Murphy reaching the top of the staircase that lead down to the beach. They were holding hands, a good sign. And they were smiling, also good. How could they only be ten years older than she was? Well, technically eleven, but Carly kept telling herself she was already thirty — to get used to it, try it on for a while so when the day actually came it would be like, *yeah whatever.*

"Hey there, we met your neighbor down on the beach," Hazel said, "Antoinette? She's so nice!"

"Antonia," Carly corrected, "and yes, I agree! We only met yesterday but I feel like we must have been friends in another life."

"Super nice," Hazel said, "we should have her over sometime, you know, have like a big family cookout or something."

"Slow down, babe," Murphy said, "I know you are a natural care-giver, amazing and selfless, but this is your time *off* from taking care of everyone, cooking for everybody, right? Time for you and me?" Murphy looked a little uneasy, like he was already bracing for how his wife might slide into the role of caretaker and confidante to everyone around her — while he quietly hoped there'd still be space carved out just for the two of them.

They hadn't even met Burke and Remi yet, never mind the Colorado cowboy — who's to say they'd want any part of family meals? It was hard to imagine what it would all look like once everyone was there. Carly envisioned the guests wanting to do their own thing, eating out mostly — Nantucket was a splurge kind of place. She couldn't imagine them wanting to cook in much — but maybe once or twice? Carly thought it sounded like fun — things would unfold as they would.

"Oh yeah, you guys asked about the bikes," Carly said, to divert the conversation, "let's go out to the shed and I'll show you the fleet." The shed had its own hedge of hydrangeas and window boxes spilling over with wave petunias.

"Even the shed is cute," Hazel said, reading Carly's thoughts, "It could almost be a little apartment."

"Or a studio," Carly mused.

"Ooh these will do," Murphy said, of the new bikes hanging from racks. "I didn't know if we should expect web-laced Schwinn ten-speeds, but these are nice hybrid bikes. Should be great on and off-road, and these flat handlebars are much more comfortable then hunching over." He freed one from the rack, "lightweight with decent wide tires, perfect."

Carly was relieved the bikes passed inspection. She wondered if Murphy was a member of the *spandex mafia* as she called those annoying clusters of male cyclists who biked two-abreast thinking they owned the road. She hoped not.

"Well, Murph, I'm glad you approve. Not that I can remember the last time you were on a bike..." Hazel said, reaching up to squeeze his shoulder

"Oh yeah? Well what about you, Haze, and I don't mean a Peloton at the gym." He laughed good-naturedly adding, "besides, you know what they say, *it's like riding a bike.* Muscle memory and all that, right?"

"Right," Hazel said with a smile. "I'm glad some of the bikes have baskets — perfect for beach towels and or groceries."

"Or beer," Murphy added with a smile.

"Yup, and the beach chairs have those backpack straps plus a little pouch," Carly said, "so you could easily ride with the chairs on your backs and stuff some things in the pouch too. And there's a pump hanging right over there if the tires need air, but they should be all set."

"Hey, how about this," Murphy said, turning to face his wife. let's find that secret beach you've been talking about. Leave it all to me, Haze — I'll handle lunch, pack some adult beverages... Sound good?"

"Ooh, look at you go, Murph," Hazel said, wrapping her husband in a side hug, "I could definitely get used to this. I'm so glad we found this place." she said, turning to Carly, "everything is so crazy expensive. We've been wanting to come to Nantucket for a while but it was always out of reach — paying off student loans for forever then having kids — there was always something smarter we were supposed to be doing with our money. But, we decided it would be our gift to each other for our fortieth birthdays and we just went for it."

"And you made the cut! Keith had a lot of interest in this place. I know his goal was to align lifestyles, vacation expectations, and interests as much as he could from the profiles. You're the first round — I guess we'll see how successful he was, right?"

Carly checked the time on her phone and decided she needed to eat lunch before heading back into town for Burke and Remi. "First come, first serve, with the bikes here so help yourselves. The guests coming in this afternoon are renting a car so who knows if they'll be interested in the bikes. But you can park yours off to the side over here and I'll let them know they can choose from the ones still hanging, sound good?"

"Sounds like a plan, thanks again Carly," Murphy said. Then to his wife, "We should try these out, take them for a spin out to the lighthouse, okay?"

"Sure. I mean how different can it be from a stationary bike, right?" Hazel laughed nervously.

"You'll be fine," Carly said, "just find your balance and keep the thing moving."

"Right? That was the hardest thing to get the kids to do," Hazel said, "if you go too slow you tip right over!"

"Truth. Have fun." Carly wondered if once you were a parent, every single thing you did was framed by your kids' experiences. Were you ever just yourself again? Seemed like a total identity crisis.

Didn't you have enough of those as a single person trying to exist in the world these days? Hazel and Murphy's lives seemed a world away from hers.

Chapter Eighteen

CARLY SHOULD HAVE ALLOTTED more time to get into town on a Saturday. Vacation rentals ran Saturday to Saturday — she definitely should have factored that in, not only for traffic but parking. An incoming email further delayed her, since it was arrival day, she didn't think she could ignore it. She wasn't expecting any contact from Colorado unless there was a problem, so when she saw August Wilder's name in her inbox she figured she'd better open it.

Keith had handled all the guest correspondences up until now so this was weird. Was Keith late for a golf game and handing this guy off? It looked like August's flight had been cancelled and he'd be arriving at eight o'clock instead of six-thirty, no big deal. Carly didn't know what to make of his tone though, the brevity. Was he going to be some entitled dude who didn't want to be on this sabbatical to begin with? Or just irritated by the delay.

The whole thing was weird. Since this guy was Keith's friend, he'd given Carly more details and backstory. August was the son of a millionaire rancher who was requiring him to spend two weeks, two thousand miles away from the family property to gain some distance and perspective on his future. Seemed so old school. And of course all she could picture was the Dutton Ranch from Yellowstone. Ridiculous, but still.

Who would this guy be most like in that cast of characters? She thought about it on the drive into town.

A male version of Beth Dutton? Everyone loved Beth, she was so badass but also intelligent, loyal, ruthless, and emotionally scarred. As John Dutton's daughter, she was fiercely committed to her family's legacy, unapologetically manipulative, but with a soft side that bowled you over when you least expected it. And her devotion to Rip was swoon-worthy. Their love story epic.

Or would he be like Kayce Dutton, the youngest son? Former Navy SEAL, torn between loyalty to his family and his desire for a peaceful life with his wife and son. Or maybe he was like Jamie Dutton, John's adopted son and a lawyer, a brilliant but tormented outsider, torn between loyalty to the family that raised him and the identity he'd never fully been allowed to claim.

Carly hoped this August Wilder was nothing like Jamie — a man struggling with his ethical compass and so driven by insecurities and need for validation that it is ultimately his tragic undoing.

Of course he could be some combination of all of them *or* exactly like none of them. She looked over at the *Burke and Remi* sign in the passenger seat — and wished she'd thought to search them on social media. Except she was still boycotting. Outside of her work content, of course.

It was dangerously close to the one-forty-five arrival time of the Hy-Line as she circled the grocery store parking lot by the dock for a second time. Sweat prickled along her hairline and under her arms. It was musical chairs, she kept her eyes peeled for backup lights and prayed she was next in line. The stress was a thing she could taste.

She whipped into the diagonal space and ran for Straight Wharf just as the boat was docking. She had an image of what she thought this couple would look like but she could be completely wrong. She tried to delete her picture and just hold the sign up high.

She was trying to be open. But Burke just had to be some sandy-haired stud in short shorts and possibly a too-tight Under Armor golf shirt. And definitely Ray-Ban aviators. Remi would have dark hair, the kind that looked like mahogany when the sun hit it, tied back in a severe ponytail, wearing some kind of pricey athleisure wear, and trendy thick-framed tortoiseshell Tori Burch sunglasses. Not that she was judging. God, she was judging. But bikini competitions? Come on.

Carly was half-right. The Remi half, who was pulled almost exactly from Carly's imagination, down to her head-to-toe Lululemon and chunky platform Pumas that screamed edgy streetstyle. Burke, on the other hand, was not the douchey ex-pro athlete she'd conjured. She got the sandy-hair and aviators right, but he was disarmingly boyish in wrinkled shorts, faded Soundgarden t-shirt, and flipflops that had seen better days. They looked the part, a good-looking pair of fit humans, but something about the dynamic felt forced.

"You must be Carly," Remi said, tipping her sunglasses down on her nose looking her up and down. She could have kept them on to do that, Carly thought.

"I am. Welcome to Nantucket," Carly smiled and reached a hand out to shake Remi's first then Burke's. "I'm parked just over there, we can walk over once you get your bags." Rats, she'd forgotten to get coffees. But then she shook it off because something told her that she wouldn't have gotten that order even remotely right. "Do you guys want anything from Provisions over there across from the Gazebo? They have great sandwiches and any kind of coffee…"

"No, we're fine, just get us to the airport for our Jeep rental. Please." Remi said.

Oh, so it was going to be that way. It was hard to know what Burke was thinking behind his sunglasses as he turned to get the bags. Remi clucked her tongue and followed after Burke, "He'll definitely get at least one wrong bag…"

Don't judge, don't judge. Burke looked like a sherpa returning from the luggage carts with bags cris-crossed over his body and one hanging from each hand. "Here," Carly said, " why don't you let me take one."

For someone who made being fit her career, Remi was hauling startlingly little to the car. But then again, bikini models probably didn't stay in shape for the strength of it. God, Carly could not get behind that. Not that it was her business to have an opinion on it, or Remi, one way or the other.

Burke let out a wolf-whistle as they approached the Land Cruiser. "Are you kiddin' me? This is your rig? So sweet."

"Wait, really?" Remi added, and not in a good way, "How old is this thing?"

Carly stopped herself from sighing and from meeting Burke's eyes. "It's property of the house, so, not technically mine, but for my use while I'm here. It's a 1972 Toyota FJ55 Land Cruiser — a cult classic I'm told."

"It absolutely is," Burke said, "My dad's brother restored one of these — a two-door though, very cool. How does she run? I bet she handles the cobblestones like a tank."

"Wonderful," Remi said, "every girl's dream. I was picturing a cute new convertible Bronco."

"Is that what you rented?" Carly asked, sensing Remi's vacation might be starting out on a disappointing note. She slid into the front seat peeking at Remi in the rearview mirror. And there she was again, tipping her sunglasses to the tip of her nose to meet Carly's gaze.

Remi clucked her tongue, sighed and said "no" in that way that gave it two syllables, "*No-ah*. That's what I *wanted*, but Burke had already committed to a Wrangler at the airport rental place and they don't *do* Ford Broncos. Whatever — how far to the airport, I'm going to need my protein smoothie soon. Oh fuck, Burke did you remember to pack the spirulina?"

"We can probably be there in about fifteen minutes," Carly said, "but while we're here, did you want to pop into the grocery store? The mid-island market gets more crowded than this one."

"What do you think, Rem?" Burke said.

"I think I'm definitely not in the mood for that," Remi said, "we'll just eat out later, right?"

"Whatever you want, princess," Burke said.

If there was sarcasm in *princess*, Carly couldn't quite tell. Everyone knew love worked in mysterious ways. "Ooh, I just remembered, there's a great little restaurant in the airport, Crosswinds, it's super reasonable, breakfast, lunch, and dinner and a full bar. If you guys are hungry like right now..."

Burke and Remi responded at the same time.

"Sounds great, I'm starving."

"Ew, the *airport* restaurant?"

"Thanks anyway for the tip," Burke said to Carly from beside her in the passenger seat. Then turning to Remi, "Sure you don't want the front seat, babe?"

But she was already fixated on her phone, fingers flying. Carly knew they were from Connecticut and basic facts about them, but was unsure how much conversation she should make without overstepping. "So, a retired ski racer, huh? That's intense," was what came out.

"Don't be too impressed, not that big a deal," Burke said. "It was in my DNA, I guess you could say — Dad raced in the eighties — until I fucked up my back and game over."

"Sorry about that, yikes. Must be hard to just change course, right?"

"Well, it's not like you plan on crushing gates doing fifty miles per hour forever."

"I guess. I mean I can't even imagine that kind of speed on two boards strapped to my feet. At least you're not in a wheelchair, right? That could have ended worse."

"You are a thousand percent correct."

"I used to go skiing with my brother," Carly said, "He was totally into it and I thought, anything he can do... Our parents weren't skiers but he'd take me up to Killington in Vermont with his buddies and

Sugar Bush and I think he thought I would just learn by osmosis. But it was more like survival. I don't know how I didn't die. I did okay, but those double-black diamonds weren't for me." Carly was loosely aware of filling the space with her rambling but she couldn't seem to help herself. "Yeah I was kinda like *peace out* after taking a few headers on some glade trails, but Grayson, that's my brother, he lives for it. Skied for UNH and now he's the head Nordic coach there."

"At the University of New Hampshire? Division One, good for him. Wait — I might know him. Grayson…?"

"Yup, Grayson Hill."

"Hmm, I think I raced against him in undergrad!"

"Where'd you go to college?" Carly said, peeking in the rearview to see if Remi was still immersed in her phone and not pissed at either the rough ride or the conversation going on without her.

"Dartmouth. He might have been younger than me though maybe?" Burke said.

"He's thirty-three?"

"Yup. I got a couple years on him then. Cool. So he's coaching, huh? A professor too then?"

"Um, sorry to interrupt your little party up there," Remi interjected, "but I feel like I'm gonna puke back here — are we there yet?"

Chapter Nineteen

AS EASY-GOING AND kind as the Turners were, Burke and Remi were a more complex dynamic. Driving home alone from the Jeep rental place, Carly caught glimpses of tension in their connection and wondered how long they'd been together. Lately she'd found herself becoming a detached observer of relationships — curious about what made the good ones work and tuned into the cracks of the ones that didn't.

Burke came off as beyond cool on paper, equally so in person. She'd absolutely expected arrogance but he was so chill, easy to talk to. It occurred to her that maybe he felt easy because he was off-limits. She didn't have to waste time or emotion wondering what impression she made on him. She could be a hundred percent herself and talk about anything or nothing at all. Remi, on the other hand, stressed her out.

Granted, she'd spent less than an hour in their company and traveling could be exhausting, but still. She seemed a little high maintenance. Carly knew she was making assumptions about anyone who made a career out of posing in a bikini on a stage but she couldn't seem to stop herself. Ok, so to do what she did she had to be super disciplined. But did it count if it was for vanity purposes? What exactly was the point of figure competitions? Or was it bikini competitions? It seemed more about appearances than skill — that was hard to get behind. Wasn't it just lucky genes? Or a great plastic surgeon? And it turns out she was an influencer too. Carly wasn't sure it was the best lifestyle choice to be talking anyone into.

But Keith seemed to think they were a good fit for the house, so Carly tried to reserve judgement. If nothing else, maybe Burke and Remi would be an example to Carly of what doesn't work in a relationship.

As she pulled onto Baxter Road, Carly felt a rise of some unnamed hope. When she examined it she realized it had to do with Antonia, and wanting to hang out with her again. They'd had such unexpected fun the other night and Carly was craving more of it. She knew Antonia was more her mother's age than her own — did that mean she was missing her mom? Maybe it was more of a cool aunt vibe with Antonia, or maybe she missed having a friend, a confidante.

How were the Turners doing...had they biked to get some groceries? Maybe just around Sconset or to Tom Nevers, two miles down Milestone Road. She needed to stop concerning herself with it all. It wasn't so much that she was worried about them, but in some way felt responsible for them, or at least their good time. Carly had to release herself from this. She needed to have more going on for herself.

Should she bake cookies? Oh God, that was total house-mother territory and not a part of her job description And someone like Remi might not only reject that but probably be insulted. *As if* she would ever put any of those simple sugars, seed oils, and saturated fats into her body. She needed to quit projecting, Carly was her own worst enemy. And if she wanted to make a batch of Tollhouse chocolate-chip cookies, even if just to smell them baking, she would.

It felt like a homey thing to do. And she wanted to make the house feel like a home, for herself if for no one else.

She could bring a plate over to Antonia's and they could sit on her porch — maybe be able to eavesdrop on all the goings-on at *Driftwood Dream* but from behind the privet hedge. She liked having a plan. But what if Antonia already had plans? They should exchange numbers.

Ugh, that plan would have to wait — there'd be cocktails involved — she couldn't be late to pick up the cowboy, or space it out completely. She'd go next door later and see what was what.

The house was quiet. Carly didn't notice bikes in the driveway — would they have parked them back in the shed? Then she saw the wavy fall of Hazel's hair against a wicker lounger on the deck. Her first instinct was to go out and say hi — but was that intrusive? It felt rude to ignore people all living under the same roof — how was this going to work? What was the call? She was already overthinking every damn thing. Things would unfold in their own time. And each group of guests would bring its own nuanced preferences and dynamic.

She pictured the guys all getting along great. Shooting the shit, talking finance or baseball, or who the Patriots had coming down the pike for a decent offensive line. But then would that piss off the women and turn into beer on the porch with the boys instead of couples time?

Not her problem.

She almost wished she were the type to unroll a yoga mat on the lawn at sunrise enticing the other ladies for a morning flow. But that wasn't her. She could climb tall mountains, run for miles, cook every meal over a campfire alone in the woods, and she could cast a perfect fly-fishing line. Yoga, though, *that* would be more useful in this situation.

"Hey darlin'," Antonia said, from her porch swing seeing Carly approaching from across the lawn. She held a hand up to shield her light eyes from the sun and patted the space beside her on the swing. "To what do I owe this pleasure, beautiful girl? Come sit."

For reasons Carly couldn't quite pin down, Antonia's warm greeting and big smile were restoring. She didn't overthink the age gap or wonder if she was subconsciously seeking a mother figure — she just let herself appreciate the comfort of having a friend, someone steady and present. There was a trustworthiness about Antonia, a quiet authenticity that felt dependable and selfless.

"Hi, I'm glad I caught you," Carly said, taking a seat next to her. "I was going to come crash your place with a big plate of chocolate chip cookies later, to give the guests time in the house without me, but then I remembered I have one last pickup at eight o'clock since his flight was delayed."

"So, wait, the cowboy was delayed? Well shoot, I was gonna crash *your* place to get a peek at everyone, Oh I'm just terrible aren't I?" Her laugh was a silvery windchime.

"Not at all, I would love that actually. Why am I being so weird about this? Being there with them? I mean it's not like I'm supposed to be entertaining them or anything…I guess I just feel responsible for their good time or something. My role here is pretty loose beyond basic upkeep and towels, but it's my home too for the summer."

"It's a unique situation for everyone, most likely, and you'll all figure it out," Antonia said, turning her petite body to face Carly, "Even with Airbnb properties, if the owner is on the grounds wouldn't that be in a separate area or garage apartment or something?"

"I actually know the answer to that. Whether or not Airbnb owners stay on the property depends the host's preferences. There are two main types of Airbnb rentals: Entire Home or Apartment options in which the host typically does not stay on the property, and guests have full privacy and exclusive use of the space. But then there's Private Room or Shared Space options where the host does often stay on the property in a different part of the house. Guests share common areas such as the kitchen or living room with the host."

"Gotcha. And this isn't an Airbnb at all, right? But more an eccentric old lady's guest house tradition?"

"Right, so I'm making it up as I go along. I don't want to intrude on them but—"

"Hey now, it's your house as much as it is theirs while you're all here. You should not feel like you have to hide or make yourself scarce — that's what they signed on for right?"

"I know, you're right. I guess I'll get used to it, we all will, it's just strange for me. It's still new. Almost feels like college apartment life — except that we were all the same age — and we chose each other!"

"Oh stop," Antonia said, nudging Carly's leg with her own, "It's not like they're geriatrics — all mostly thirties, right?"

"Yes, except the couple celebrating their fortieth birthdays, the Turners. I mean they have *kids* — different stratosphere." Carly pushed off her toes a tiny bit to give the swing a push.

"You're doing just fine. You are accommodating and resourceful and kind. I can tell you really care if they are happy, and that their good time is important to you. You guys will find a groove."

"Right and just when we do, they'll leave and I'll have to start over with a whole new houseful!"

"Oh, come on now, don't go borrowing trouble..."

"You know — my Gram would say that all the time," Carly said, tucking her knees up under her chin as they swayed in the swing.

"Words to live by, sweetie. Hasn't anybody ever told you that most of the things we worry about never even happen?"

"Yeah, See? Worrying must work then!"

Carly's phone pinged with an email notification. "Oh for fuck's sake, now Colorado is coming in on an *earlier* flight. In like an hour!"

"Perfect!" Antonia said, slapping both her legs with satisfaction, "then our little porch party is a go."

"Except now I won't have time to bake the cookies," Carly said, pulling a sad face.

"Well then, lucky for you that one of my specialty cocktails is called the Chocolate Chip Cookie!"

"You have got to be kidding me..."

"I most certainly am not. We'll do Baileys Irish Cream for a creamy base, add Kahlúa for those coffee and chocolate notes, we can add vodka for an extra kick," Antonia said elbowing Carly playfully, "chocolate syrup for sweetness and richness and whipped cream and chocolate chips on top!"

"Oh. My. God. That sounds amazing, I can't wait," Carly checked the time again, "Should we get a pizza or something?"

"Absolutely not," Antonia said, "I'm making lobster salad and there's more than enough for two. Any opposition to celery? Or Avocado?"

"Nope. You're my hero. Are you sure you didn't have plans, Antonia? Don't lie..."

"Go pick up your cowboy. And I may be a lot of things darlin, but a liar ain't one of 'em. Now scoot."

They stood up from the swing at the same time and Carly leaned into Antonia's small, sturdy hug before heading back to *Driftwood Dream*.

Chapter Twenty

THE TURNERS WERE ENJOYING the back deck when Carly headed out while Burke and Remi settled into their room. She was grateful that she didn't have to be social program director and that the guests were on their own as far as meeting each other finding a way to be together in the house. She wondered what scene she would return to, and if the others were curious about the new arrival.

She felt all turned around on her way to the little island airport. The route was simple enough, it was more all the back and forth of the day. She was glad her chauffeur duties began and ended here, until the return trips to boats and planes.

What did August Wilder have planned for transportation during his stay? There hadn't been any mention of a car rental that Carly recalled. Did he plan to Uber everywhere? His father was a wealthy man — did that extend to him? Did he rent a horse? Were there horses on Nantucket?

Carly parked in the small lot and walked to arrivals with her *August Wilder* sign. No one else around her was holding any kind of sign and she felt silly. Though Saturday was the busiest travel day to and from Nantucket, the airport was so much quieter than the boat docks. Anxiety rode the edges of her skin as she waited for the plane to deboard.

Her fingers hesitated over her phone in a spontaneous decision to email Keith asking for more information about this guy, a basic physical description at least. But there was no time.

Would he strut over to her with a *howdy*? Would he be in boots and a hat? She hadn't seen anyone on the island who would fit that description. Flip-flops, sneakers, and loafers was pretty much it. This guy would be a fish out of water.

"Pardon me, Carly Hill?" She swung around at the sound of her name. Who around here knew her full name? And if she had to describe the tone, it was somewhere between impatient and annoyed. Which was a shame because she was looking into the coolest eyes she'd ever seen, the color of sunlight passing through a glass of whiskey.

"Yes?" she asked, because who *was* this man? Gorgeous in such an easy and immediate way. His mink-brown hair fell to just above the collar of his black t-shirt tucked into faded jeans. A woman rushed up behind him and handed him the cowboy hat he'd left on the plane. That's when Carly noticed the boots. August Wilder. Just holy shit...

"Oh, hi! You must be Mr. Wilder." God, she sounded way too excited. Lust at first sight was real. "Here you are, welcome to Nantucket." His features were a frozen landscape, his expression unreadable. His skin was a rugged bronze from a life lived outdoors in the mountain sun, he was a perfect combination of height and muscle.

"Is there something amusing Ms. Hill?"

"Oh boy. We need to start over. I'm Carly, it's nice to meet you," she said, extending her hand. It was sweaty, bordering on clammy. She almost wished he were just a country boy in a plaid shirt — or that she'd worn something cuter and with a swipe of mascara.

"Good to meet you, Carly. August is my grandfather. Call me Gus." He returned her handshake with a solid grip, conveying an unspoken appreciation of her own strong grip.

He had a presence she sensed right away — one that commanded attention. Some combination of power and confidence that didn't feel like arrogance.

"Are we ready?" he asked, picking up the leather duffel at his feet and pushing his cowboy hat down on his head. It was cream colored, with a narrow leather band and side vents, a summer version. Sexy as hell.

"Right this way," she said, turning and heading to the car. She suddenly felt self-conscious about the antique she was driving, this guy seemed a little high-end. Her Yellowstone comparisons were coming back to her — but she couldn't pin him down.

He bordered on abrupt, but it had probably been a long-ass day. And, she had to remember, he wasn't exactly there by choice. She needed more details on that situation — and why a man of age thirty-six and on his way to the altar, would be under the thumb of his father. She knew too much. And not nearly enough. Damn you, Keith.

"This is us," she said stopping behind the car, busying herself with opening the back to avoid his expression.

"So this is what I'll be driving? Cool — it has a certain charm," he said, loading his bag in.

"I'm sorry, what?"

"The car — Keith said it was mine to use while I'm here. What year is this, I don't think I've ever seen a Toyota quite like it."

Carly was too stunned to speak. *Keith* said...? Well, it would have been really nice of Keith to tell her about this cozy arrangement. She wasn't sure how to respond, how this was going to affect her days — would she be asking Gus for permission? Begging rides with him? How could Keith have forgotten to mention this? *Ugh,* it would have been easier if he'd been a dick about riding in the old tank and rented his own car.

"Umm, Keith didn't say anything about that?" She was feeling so flustered she stalled pulling out of the airport twice, confusing third for first again.

"First time driving stick?" he said, biting back a smile.

"Hysterical, really. So, you haven't rented your own car?" she said, trying to keep her voice even and polite while her mind scrambled to picture how this would work.

"Why would I do that when I have this? Access to a vehicle was part of the deal."

She was glad he didn't call her *sweetheart* or *doll* but still, the words he was speaking weren't computing. She didn't want to say too much until she'd spoken with Keith and she wanted to focus on her driving and not stalling.

Was it a huge deal if they had to share? She was probably freaking out over nothing. "I guess we'll figure it out, no big deal," she said, trying to convince herself. "I was going to ask if you wanted to stop off for food or anything but it looks like you'll be able to drive anywhere you need to." She was definitely taking his hotness out on him.

"Is there a problem, sunshine? I don't want to cause you any distress."

And there it was. Sarcasm? She really couldn't tell. "No problem, cowboy."

He laughed then, a throaty sound that made goosebumps rise on her skin.

Chapter Twenty-One

Walking into the house hearing tunes cranked made Carly smile. Jason Aldeen's "My Kinda Party," perfect. But where was everybody? She was giving Gus a basic tour when she spotted the Turners and Remi and Burke spread out between the back porch and the chairs on the lawn.

"Beautiful spot," Gus said, stepping out back onto the flagstone porch, "evening, everyone." Gus removed his hat and was wearing some smile Carly had yet to see.

Introductions were made and Carly noticed that everyone seemed relaxed and with a drink in their hand. Even Remi, although it could have been water, wine with an abundance of ice, or straight vodka — who knew? It was a movie scene in the purling dusk, silver edged, and it looked too good to be true. She was ready to show Gus his room and be on her own time. She was dying for a cocktail with Antonia next door and her stomach growled at the thought of that lobster salad.

She was glad when Gus turned to come in so she didn't have to break into his good time. "Your room is up this way," she said, her bare feet making no noise on the smooth pine stairs. His was the only bedroom in the front of the house and without an ocean view. She wondered if he knew that, if he'd care. The room was larger than the others, but he was there alone. If it were her, she'd choose a smaller room with an ocean view any day. Maybe he didn't get a choice, or there was some kind of room lottery. She started to feel guilty for her large room *and* ocean view, but shut it down quick.

"The Sea Glass Room," he said, reading the little sign on the door before pushing it open, "looks good, thank you." He'd barely looked.

"You should have plenty of towels under the sink in your bathroom — if you run out there's a linen closet out here in the hall and the washer and dryer are on the first floor for guest use. Oh, and there's an outdoor shower on the south side of the house if you're interested, tucked in by the garden. Cedar plank stall, can't miss it.

"An outside shower, as in open to the elements?" he said, setting his bag gently down on the floor by the closet."

"It's a luxury around here. Don't knock it until you try it, trust me." She offered a small smile and backed away, anxious to be anywhere but in the small space he took up so much of.

"So, the keys to the Land Cruiser?" he asked, setting his hat on the bureau as she was turning to go. She couldn't pinpoint why this got under her skin. Why was it pissing her off so much? Was it the expectation, his entitlement? It wasn't exactly his fault if his good old friend Keith had offered it up.

"In it," she said, "and it needs to be returned to the garage every time. As you probably noticed, or maybe you didn't, it's been meticulously restored. The salt air will do a number on it — corroding everything."

"Yes, ma'am," he said. Again the question of sarcasm. Either way, she was all set with him for now. He was tall and imposing standing there, everything about him dark in the low light. He had a quiet intensity, probably used to being in charge. It wasn't an unattractive quality, but something about him unnerved her. She tapped the door casing on her way out as if to convey *we're done here.*

Carly grabbed a hoody from her room and headed over to Antonia's. She called out a cheerful *have fun* to the group on her way across the lawn but couldn't tell who exactly was still there. Lainey

Wilson's "Watermelon Moonshine" was playing and a ping of thirst hit the back of her throat anticipating Antonia's signature cocktail. She was past due. She started to question whether or not she should have told them where she'd be, but decided against it not wanting to set that precedent. They had her cell for emergencies.

"Hey Carly!" someone called out before she'd made it around the corner of the lawn. She'd been so close. She turned back.

"What's up?" She noticed Murphy and Burke each with a beer and a smile like they were frat bros, and then Hazel, pacing at the end of the porch with her phone to her ear. No Remi and no cowboy.

"What would you say is the best beach for surfing here?" Murphy asked, with a smile riding up into his eyes, "Burke here says he can teach me how to hang ten."

"Whoa, nobody said anything about hanging ten, bro — maybe we could get you up on a board though — ride a few waves. I mean, maybe you'd catch a couple," Burke laughed, "not making any promises big guy."

"You calling me fat?" Murphy said, good-naturedly, "I've earned this," he said patting his belly.

"Nah, man, you're cool, I'm just saying, it's not as easy as it looks. And you know, men of a certain age..."

"Now you're calling me old? Dude, are you serious I'm turning forty not fifty — you're not as far behind me as you think," Murphy said, "trust me."

"And what's wrong with fifty?" Antonia said, out of nowhere, coming across the lawn to the porch. "Sorry for eavesdropping but I've been waiting for my girl here forever — what, did you kidnap her?" Then turning to Carly, "did they make you a better offer? A better drink than the Chocolate Chip Cookie?" Carly wilted with gratitude as Antonia handed her the mudslidiest, most delicious looking drink ever.

"And who is this gorgeous creature?" Burke asked.

Oh brother. How many beers in was he? The Casanova comes out apparently.

"What I mean to say is good evening, I'm Burke, and you are...?"

"Ah, does that make you the cowboy or the ski racer?" Antonia asked.

Burke looked down at his board shorts and t-shirt then back up at her grinning, "do I *look* like a cowboy to you? Have a drink with us."

"So that makes you the downhill daredevil then, right?"

"It's like you already know me. And a southern belle to boot," Burke whistled, "come on, one drink."

While Antonia looked to Carly for direction, Carly was looking for Remi or even Hazel to insert themselves into this escalating, alcohol-infused plan. How many drinks in were they? Remi was hoping Burke would propose on this trip and Murphy hoped to reconnect with his wife. Partying with her and Antonia was not an auspicious start.

"Who needs a drink?" Gus called out from the slider.

Was this really happening? He was still in jeans but had a white t-shirt on now. It changed his whole look.

"I sure as shit do," Remi said, materializing beside Gus on the threshold to the porch looking out, "what in the fresh hell is going on out here?"

"Well, *now* it's a party," Burke said, winding his arm tenderly around his girlfriend's waist.

He was smooth. It would have been the perfect moment for Antonia and her to make themselves scarce and head over to Antonia's place for the lobster salad, maybe leave the guests to their bonding.

"One drink," Antonia said.

Or maybe not.

"Save a Horse Ride a Cowboy" came on right after "You Look Like You Love Me" and Gus was taking orders for his famous Snakebite — whiskey and lime juice, what could possibly go wrong? It felt like her heart was giggling. Carly didn't think she'd be tasting that lobster any time soon, and she wasn't sure she cared.

It dawned on her that she was enjoying herself, getting these glimpses into other people's lives, their choices and connections. She might learn something if she paid attention. She could see pieces of things she longed for: the comfort of stability laced with the spark of surprise, devotion without confinement, the ease of being understood paired with the thrill of being challenged. There was a lot she didn't know yet, but the not-knowing was starting to feel full of possibility. What Carly was starting to understand was that all she wanted was what everyone wanted — a place and a person that felt like home, to be moving forward in this life instead of standing still.

Chapter Twenty-Two

T HE HOUSE WAS FULL and Carly decided her heart was too. Meeting everyone face-to-face, seeing the real people behind the bios was a game-changer. People were complex and distinct, complicated, and unpredictable — each with their own layers. But strip it all away, and it felt like everyone, including her, longed for the same thing: connection.

The anxiety Carly had let weigh her down started to lift off of her like dandelion fluff. She had a sense that the group of guests would get along just fine, be respectful of each other and the property, and maybe even hang out together over the course of their stay. Keith had given her the freedom to let her role ebb and flow with the needs that arose among the group and within the house and grounds. And since she was up before anyone else, she was excited to hop on a bike to the Sconset Market for their fresh-from-the-oven blueberry muffins to treat everyone on their first morning on Nantucket.

One by one, they drifted out of their rooms with that vacation look in their eyes, finding their way around the kitchen and coffee maker — only to be floored all over again by the view spilling in through every window. Carly assured the guests that she'd be reachable via text if they had questions or concerns and left them to their day.

She was excited for a run along the beach before she'd head out to collect experiences and photo content from off-the-beaten paths of the island. The Nantucket Conservation Foundation had an online properties map as well as individual trail guides— she was eager to start exploring. Brett had to work and couldn't join her but he'd shared with her his favorite trails. By day's end she'd have a lot more to share with not only her guests but also with the thousands of Custom Escapes Instagram followers. And knowing she could access the entire island by bike alleviated her original stress about sharing the car with Gus. It would take longer to cycle to the different trailheads, but she had all summer.

Her phone stayed remarkably silent across the day. And knowing she wasn't needed anywhere else for the afternoon allowed her to soak in the sunny windswept day through the hundreds of acres that made up Sanford Farm and Ram Pasture. She was treated to amazing views of North Head and Hummock Ponds, sandplain grasses swaying in the wind, and a surprise peek at a gorgeous undeveloped beach at the southern boundary beyond an historic barn in the middle of the property. Carly was giddy with the images she captured of what felt like a secret world, and realizing there were at least a dozen other properties to venture and share.

By early evening, everyone had made their way back from their individual adventures, contentedly spent and eager to unwind with a drink on the back porch and trade stories. The camaraderie among them was a tangible thing, and their insistence that Carly join them gave her a sense of belonging she didn't know she'd been missing.

It wasn't exactly the cast of *Breakfast Club*, but a cast of characters nonetheless. A jock, a bikini model, a mom, a workaholic husband, and a cowboy. Carly hoped that didn't make her the basket case.

It was starting to feel like those first nights of freshman year in college — total strangers living together — bonded by tunes, booze, and the pull of inclusion. And with the built-in safety that it was fleeting only amplified the rush.

Gus was making another version of his summer snakebite and before she knew it he was handing her a second drink. She took the glass of whiskey, letting the heat trail down her throat and settle softly in her stomach. She tried to ignore the zing she felt when his fingers brushed hers. She was buzzed, leaning into the sense of calm at things clicking into place. She wasn't used to whiskey but she didn't hate the golden fire that lingered inside her.

She stepped away from the group to take it in. Hazel had finally pocketed her phone and joined the fun. She'd mentioned that her kids weren't used to her being away from them and were clinging more than usual. Carly couldn't truly know how that felt but she hoped Hazel would find a way to let go a little and let her parents handle it — she found herself wanting a win for Hazel and Murphy.

Carly was invested. She couldn't try to pretend otherwise. It was like she saw all these new people in her life as the potential stages of her own life. She was rooting for them, wanting everything to work out for everyone. Because that meant there was hope for her. To find a person to love and be loved by, to build a family and not lose sight of the most important things about that, work that helped her grow, and a home that made her smile to wake up in every day.

She still wasn't sure about Burke and Remi— they both seemed to prioritize themselves more than each other. How did that work? It seemed at least lonely, and at most boring. Burke appeared to thrive in the company of others – he was open, happy, and he listened when someone spoke. But was there something beyond that — an underlying sadness possibly? That seemed veiled by his sociable facade. But what the hell did she know? Her head was swimmy with booze and she wished she'd stop trying to figure everyone out.

She wondered if Remi could ever turn off the calorie counting, stacking the protein grams in her head, and calculating where on the glycemic index everything fell. She mentioned that her next competition was at the end of August — did that mean she had to keep up the crazy until then? Or was it her whole life? It didn't feel super sustainable to Carly, but maybe it worked for Remi. And maybe Burke's chill balanced her hyper-focus.

Gus...she didn't know what to make of that guy. He seemed, on some level, unknowable. But that was her baseless and premature judgement. What exactly was the relationship with his father like? Was Mom alive? Did he have siblings? Was he the eldest son and the reason he was poised to take over the ranch? Did Dad disapprove of the fiancée?

So many questions that were one-hundred-percent none of her business. She had her own questions to navigate, her own what-ifs still tangled and waiting. Like would this new geographical distance of her mother bring them closer or make the space between them feel permanent? Losing her little brother had done a number on the whole family, wrecked them each in their own way. She hardly ever allowed herself to revisit that tragedy — but had it defined her ultimately, shaped her more than she realized? Leaving her uncertain how to love fully — or be loved back?

Her instinct had become to swim away from such depth, to stay where things were light, unanchored, fleeting. This realization crashed in with no warning, no cushion. It slid into place, sharp and sudden, like a key in a lock.

She swam to the surface — reaching for things to look forward to. Like seeing Antonia and getting her take on everyone. And to the lobster salad they'd decided to save for tonight.

∞

"Hey there, why are you standing over here all by yourself?" Antonia said from out of the shadows as if Carly had conjured her. "You've got quite a group here don't you — are you more relaxed now that they're all here and you don't have to be Julie McCoy the cruise director?"

"I'm sorry, the who?"

"Aw, come on, from *The Love Boat.* Your mom never talked about that show?"

"Oh yeah...she told me about babysitting on Saturday nights when she was in high school — the lineup of TV from *Love Boat* to *Fantasy Island* straight through to *Saturday Night Live*, sneaking boyfriends over, scarfing down the family's Pop-Tarts stash... The eighties sounds like the place to be."

"Yes! I feel bad for you Millennials... You missed out on letters, phone calls, just hanging out, and the *Love Boat*. No social media!"

"I can definitely see the allure," Carly said, trying to imagine life without any social media at all. She really couldn't.

"I'm not so sure we appreciated how good we had it...the simplicity of it. Anyway, so, Julie McCoy was the face of the Pacific Princess, the love boat — she was the glue — connecting the passengers, helping them with the crazy romantic entanglements that unfolded onboard."

"Okay...that doesn't sound awful."

"Fun, right?" Antonia winked. "Now come on over here and talk to me. There are some fine looking men here."

"*Unavailable* men. So I'm not sure what you're up to but, no."

The air was silken and Carly could taste the ocean. The night hummed with energy, the start of something, a shift. Her heart was still a clenched fist, after seeing Jake's engagement plastered all over Instagram, but the synergy of this group started an unfurling in her chest.

"Hey there Carly, I hope I'm not interrupting," Hazel said.

"Not at all, Hazel, what's up? Are the kids okay?"

"Oh, don't even get me started, they're aging me in real-time. Is it okay to use the outdoor shower at night? I mean is there a light?"

"That's my favorite time," Antonia chimed in, "all naked under the stars..."

"Who's getting all naked under the stars?" Burke had suddenly appeared. His hair was more tousled than it had been and his eyes were glassy — was he smoking weed in between beers? He seemed like a guy with secrets.

"Alright, alright," Antonia said, leading Burke back to the porch where Remi was sitting with her mystery beverage, "let's you and me see about getting some food — have you eaten anything, handsome?"

"Oh boy," Carly said. Then turning back to Hazel, "it is absolutely okay to shower outside whenever you want. Come, let me show you where the light switch is." Carly was tempted to pry further into Hazel's situation but wanted also to respect boundaries. It was just that it seemed so much easier to see the cracks in other people's relationships than it was in her own. Had she been able to see her chasing-the-next-zip-code lifestyle through Jake's eyes, would she have changed? Looking back, was it really just avoidance dressed up as freedom? But she felt like she could give Hazel clear advice:

Try to see yourself as more than your children's mother — your kids are FINE. Pretend you and Murphy just started dating, try to remember how you would find ways to accidentally touch him and linger there, the fire that came with just your thigh resting against his. How slow the kissing was, how it left you boneless.

But what did Carly know about being forty years old? Or about being with one person for twenty years, and a parent for eleven of those? Maybe couples never really got back to that blaze. Maybe it all just got redefined.

Chapter Twenty-Three

WHEN CARLY RETURNED FROM getting Hazel squared away with the outside shower and its quirky faucet handles, she noticed thick pillar candles in hurricane lanterns were lit, throwing their amber light over the stone steps and on the end tables on the porch. Through the French doors she saw Antonia and Burke in the kitchen putting some kind of snack together. Had anyone eaten? Were people drunk? Where had Remi disappeared to — and Murphy for that matter? Maybe he'd surprised Hazel in the shower to remind her of why they were there.

"I would have bet money that nothing beats a Rocky-Mountain night sky," Gus's voice startled her from an Adirondak chair on the shadowy lawn, "but this..." he said waving an arm across the winking diamonds overhead, "is impressive."

Carly took a seat beside him, leaning all the way back to look up. "Well, there's no light pollution out here in the middle of the ocean, and it's not humid tonight, maybe that's why?" she said, sounding more like she was asking. "What exactly makes the Rockies' night sky so incomparable? I mean, talk to me like I'm four, don't get all sciencey on me."

"*Sciencey* huh? Well, I don't know how sciencey the high altitude is but it makes for less atmospheric interference. You're actually physically closer to space at higher altitudes. Which means less air the light has to pass through, making celestial objects appear more vibrant and distinct," He paused to look over at her before continuing, "and then there's the thin air, less moisture which gives you the brighter, crisper views."

"Makes sense," she said. She was low-key impressed. "I've never been out west."

"Really?"

"Never been further west than Kansas City."

"For?" he said.

"College club volleyball nationals tournament." How had it already been almost eight years since she'd graduated college? She was a senior citizen. Where would she land? With the perfect buzz, and wishing she had a drink in her hand to keep it going, she was suspended somewhere between the nostalgia of the past and the pull of right now.

"Very cool," he said, "but Kansas City ain't Colorado, kid."

Kid? "Never said it was." She turned in her seat to face him, "But while we're on the subject, is Colorado like Montana at all?"

He let out a low laugh and said, "Please tell me you are not gonna start talking about *Yellowstone,* now are you?"

Carly was glad it was dark so he wouldn't see the blush burning her face. She was such an amateur. "Busted. I mean what can I say? I'm obsessed. Compared to the little Massachusetts town I grew up in, that landscape is goals. And riding horses in the sunset and the big sky and the hot cowb—" Jesus, she almost gave herself away. Cowboys were hot. How much she'd actually love to just say *screw it* at the end of summer and drive west in her old Jeep.

"Aw, sweetheart, believe me when I tell you that while ranches do provide the breathtaking views you're thinking of, the day-to-day life is a lot more isolating and a whole lot less glamorous. Just see if you can imagine it all without the thrill or high-stakes drama, family feuds, and the power struggles of those TV shows and movie plots. It's not all cattle drives and rodeos y'know. It's the reality of managing land and livestock — coordinating resources like water and grazing land." His words crystalized in the salty air between them. "What it is *not* is Rip Wheeler riding Beth Dutton out on the back of his horse to some big beautiful log cabin saying, *I built this for you*, then making mad love up against the fresh timber walls."

"Not that you've watched it *at all*," she said, her eyes as round as marbles, "that was season three, episode seven!"

Gus turned back to take in the view. Carly noticed the masculine spike of his Adam's apple when he tipped his head up to the sky.

"It's easy to poke fun at," he was saying, "with all its unrealistic drama and soap-opera-style tension — they kinda leave out the monotony. But it's hard to hate something that's brought a rancher's life into the spotlight. You know, all that newfound respect and interest in Western culture isn't all bad."

"Ah, so you *like* being seen as a smokin' cowboy stud." She needed to stop talking. She felt caught when he fixed his gaze back on her as she rambled on, "I mean, of course there are plenty of people who go for that, obviously, but..."

"But you're not one of them?"

What did it matter — he was engaged! So he was going to be a shameless flirt on top of being ridiculously attractive? This was her special power — feeling drawn to unattainable men. *Was she drawn to him?* Ugh — she was a little drunk — where was Antonia?

"Here I am," came the sound of Antonia's sing-songy voice, as though Carly had spoken the words aloud. "I hope you don't mind my turning your borderline avocados into guacamole, and opening up that big old party-size bag of tortilla chips — was that okay?"

"More than okay, thanks Antonia, it's perfect actually," Carly said, scooping a generous amount of creamy guac onto a chip. How had she lucked out with Antonia for a neighbor? Was she going to be everyone's mom? Carly wouldn't mind that at all. "This is SO good," Carly moaned, "just the right touch of lime juice."

"Sounds like you're having some out-of-body experience over there, let me have some of that," Gus said.

"Well," Antonia said, "you know what they say about avocados…"

Carly looked up at Antonia standing there, "Um, no? They're not like some aphrodisiac like oysters if that's where you're going."

"Maybe," Antonia said, "I know they're very rich in healthy fats and vitamin E, which does wonders for your energy and stamina. AND they were considered by the Aztecs as a symbol of fertility."

Gus choked on a chip and guacamole sprayed from Carly's mouth. Gus recovered first. "I'd better get to the store tomorrow after consuming everyone's provisions," he said.

"So, what's it like for you, Gus, living on a ranch?" Antonia asked, "Do you stay in like a bunkhouse with the other cowboys and share the kitchen, taking turns making dinner like they do on TV?"

Carly thought Gus might choke on another chip — but she was glad Antonia had asked. Carly was dying to know more — there was no way he lived in a bunkhouse with the ranch hands. He had to live in the big main house with the family. Jesus, she'd been watching too much Netflix.

Gus seemed to be studying them both as Antonia pulled a chair closer to join them. It was almost as if he wasn't sure how much he wanted them to know. "So, this is going to be a lot like living in a bunkhouse isn't it?" he said, "Sharing the kitchen and the fridge — will we eat together?"

Carly couldn't tell if he was being sarcastic and mocking or coming from a place of honesty and just asking. He was a smooth dude. Diverting the question and asking his own.

She could play at that. "So is that a yes to living in a bunkhouse then? Or do you live in the main house?"

His dark gaze pinned hers for a beat before answering. "The main house? You mean like John Dutton's massive weathered-log mansion with the wraparound stone porch and river-rock fireplace?"

He was making fun of her and could barely conceal his smile. She deserved every bit of it.

"It's almost exactly like that, actually," he continued, "though I have spent time living with the other wranglers, sharing space and responsibilities. It was the most fun I've ever had."

Well. She didn't know what to say to that. But she liked him even more.

"You won't have to cook for anyone else," Carly said, "but then again, that's up to you all." She wanted to say more — like something about the camaraderie and the deepening of friendships — but this wasn't a TV drama. It was five people on a summer vacation for a couple of weeks. People who would no doubt want to eat out most nights at some restaurant they'd seen on Instagram or in a novel.

She felt a prick of disappointment. Suddenly wanting to be a part of this group, making drinks and memories, laughing, and getting to be her wittiest, coolest self. A familiar tug of loneliness stirred inside.

"I think I hear that lobster salad calling my name," she said to Antonia, rising from the deep chair and shoving her hands deep into the front pocket of her hoodie.

Chapter Twenty-Four

NIGHT HAD SETTLED COMPLETELY over the village of Sconset but the light of the moon danced in ripples on the ocean beyond the dunes and stars poked bright holes in the dark. "Now, you just sit tight right here and breathe in the night," Antonia said to Carly once they were alone at Antonia's, "and I'll be right back with the perfect unoaked chardonnay which is gonna make that lobster explode in your mouth, trust me."

Carly was too tired to argue, not that there was anything to argue about, it all sounded orgasmic. It was strange but nice being waited on — she was more used to doing things for herself. It had been a full day and she felt a wave of gratitude for the unexpected friendship she'd found with Antonia. She couldn't picture her own mother opening her heart and her home to the lonely girl next door.

"Here we are," Antonia said, handing her a fishbowl glass of wine, "I promise you it's not a syrupy chardonnay, but more crisp and fruit forward."

"Are you reading my mind? Or did we have a chardonnay conversation that I've already forgotten?" Carly said, taking a gulp instead of a sip. "And I'm not sure I know what *fruit forward* means but this is yummy!"

"Good," Antonia said, setting plates of lobster salad down on the small table between their chairs. "Are you getting the green apple?

Hints of pear? I'm telling you, unoaked is the way to go. People think chardonnay is too buttery, creamy, but that's from the oak barrels. This is so much more—"

"Refreshing," Carly said, "clean. More, please."

"Slow down there, girlfriend, I don't want to have to get one of your adorable housemates to have to come carry you home. Can we talk about the hotness level over there please?"

Carly choked on her wine. "So, it's not just me, right? It's almost unnatural. Thank God they're all taken — I'm a horny mess, I don't know what's wrong with me."

"You're a young woman who hasn't even reached her sexual prime," Antonia said, "a beautiful, eligible, desirable young woman, who I can't for the life of me imagine why or how she's still single."

"Cringe. Ugh, can we not talk about this? And how desirable can I be if my ex bailed on our three-year relationship two months before were about to start looking for an apartment together? Then less than a year later asked someone else to spend eternity with him? Talk about a punch in the heart. Total stab to the ego... Oh my *God* what *is* this dressing?

"He wasn't your person. It's that simple. I know it's hard to see in the moment, but you have to trust that you're on the path you're meant to be on," Antonia said, patting Carly's hand. "And this is just a citrus vinaigrette — some Champagne vinegar, a little fresh squeezed orange juice, a little honey — you like it?"

"Like it? I'd marry it — do you always eat like this? Like, are you the kind of person who just whips up amazing, cool, delicious stuff for every meal? Even if it's just you? I'm so not," Carly said, in between groans of pleasure, devouring her lobster and avocado salad.

"I do appreciate fine things — life is too short not to treat yourself. And much too short to wait around for someone else to do it for you. I guess I learned that early on. And I'd rather have a few quality things like gorgeous linens, a few spa treatments a year, and an insane handbag that costs a fortune, than a closet full of junk."

"Preach it. *And* this amazing first-class house on the Sconset Bluff of Nantucket Island? I mean I know you're just renting it but still, good for you. It's so impressive that you've worked hard to have it all."

"Oh, don't misunderstand, sweetheart, I do not have it all. And there is a price tag for wanting it all and for working too much. Finding the balance is the tricky part...and I'm not so sure I've found that even yet. You see, if I had, my daughter would be sitting where you are right now."

Carly hated to see the light from Antonia's eyes dim, her whole self seemed to deflate, the plush cushions swallowing up her small frame. "No, don't do that, do not do that to yourself. You haven't told me much about your flower design business but I'm sure you were the best at it. And I'm sure you were the best mom too, *are* the best mom. Just because maybe your daughter has more in common with her dad doesn't take away what you mean to her, right?" Carly refilled both their glasses.

Antonia smudged a tear away from the corner of her eye, "why are we human beings such a mess? And I'm sorry — this was your pity party and look what I've gone and done..."

Carly barked out a one-syllable laugh, "*My* pity party? No. I'll gladly hand over the mic. What's making you sad exactly?"

"Mid-life crisis maybe? Except that if I'm fifty five, that means I'd have to live to 110 for this to qualify as one." Turning the sapphire and gold ring around and around her finger, Antonia looked off into the middle distance. "More than half my life is behind me, Carly. I know you can't even fathom such a thing with yours barely out of the starting gate, but let me tell you, it goes by like lightening. And I can't help but ask myself sometimes what I have to show for it..."

"Aw, you have plenty to show for it — look at all those quality things you just mentioned? And you ran a solid business, you have a daughter you adore, whom you set a strong example for I might add! And you can afford to be *here*...what more could you want?"

The look she gave Carly seemed to say, *you just don't get it, girl*. "I worked so hard my whole life — I guess I just thought I'd always have more time for Kaitlyn after just one more event, or the next thing, you know? But before I knew it she was all grown up. Just a couple years older than you as a matter of fact. But you know the song... "Cat's in the Cradle" — *there were planes to catch, bills to pay, she learned to walk while I was away....*"

"I do know that song. It's so sad. And it always gets me. You probably hear it like: *...I finally retired but my girl's moved away... I called her up just the other day. I said I'd like to see you if you don't mind, she said I'd love to, Mom, if I could find the time....*"

"Exactly. Somehow I convinced myself that everything I did was for her. But all she wanted from me was pillow forts and tea parties, to read to her, listen to her, drive her to practice, watch her games. But I was always somewhere else; working strangers' weddings, birthdays, anniversary parties and galas. And it was her father there pouring Kool-Aid into tiny cups in tiny saucers for her teddy bears and dolls." Antonia dabbed the corners of her eyes with a napkin. "My flower designs were in such high demand, I was booking out eighteen months in advance — I thought that meant I was a success, I felt like a celebrity! But why on earth did I think this would matter to a little girl? Who only wanted her mamma? I was so blinded. I'd give anything to get those years back."

They sat in silence. Carly wondering if her own mother felt any of these things...if she had regrets about working all the time, hiring babysitters and nannies. All those little things she missed that added up to the big thing — feeling cherished, wanted. Carly loved her mom, but hated the pain she carried from losing a child. She grew accustomed to the distance her mother built in, to the way one new medication after another had her consciousness bumping the ceiling like a lazy ballon.

Carly quietly considered all the ways women, moms especially, were judged. Somehow, that when moms missed a moment, it became a moral failing — never mind the hundred ways they showed up every day. She could see now that her mom had done the best she could, carrying her own grief like a second skin while still trying to show up for Carly. The distance hadn't been coldness — it had been survival. Maybe her mom hadn't always been fully there, but it wasn't from lack of love. It was just... too much pain, too little space to process it.

Carly was beginning to realize that love could look like absence sometimes — that it could be tangled with grief, work, exhaustion. And that didn't make it any less real. Carly could see that Antonia carried guilt for the years she spent building a business — but wasn't it possible that her daughter didn't remember neglect — that maybe what she remembered was ambition, strength, a mother who tried?

They were women shaped by loss and responsibility, by the impossible expectations of motherhood. But there was something powerful in seeing them now, Carly considered, not as failures—but as women who kept going.

"Have you talked to Kaitlyn about coming out here for a visit? I'm sure she would jump at the chance, Antonia."

"I have. And she's not exactly jumping...more like treading water. *Maybe, Mom, not sure that will work...*"

"That's not a *no.* We'll get her here. This place isn't exactly a hard sell. And that's basically my *job,* ha!"

"Aw, Carly, you're sweet. I appreciate your optimism. I'm so glad we're neighbors, for a little while anyway. I sure am beat trying to keep up with you all, let's call it a night — tomorrow's a new day."

They unfolded themselves from the chairs and hugged each other goodnight. Carly felt lighter walking over to *Driftwood Dream.* Having someone to share her thoughts with helped soften the clamor of her mind.

Chapter Twenty-Five

T HE MORNING'S PINK LIGHT painted her walls and the house was quiet. From her open window she could hear the distant cadence of low waves rushing the shore and retreating again. Carly wondered who'd be up first, what morning routines would evolve. Would coffee-making clash? Would everyone want to be in the kitchen at the same time? Would anyone catch the sunrise or walk to the little market for coffee? She needed to hit the grocery store, but was Gus planning on using the car?

The mid-island grocery store was open from six a.m. to midnight — surely this offered enough flexibility to accommodate her and the cowboy. They'd work it out later. For now she wanted to get her body in motion.

She had the bluff walk all to herself at that hour. There was something to watching a new day rise up out of the sea and how the light changed with every minute. The ornamental grasses lining the properties waved in the soft air and drops of dew glistened on hydrangea blossoms bobbing their pom-pom heads.

The foam on the water was tinted peach as it curled in and Carly decided to take the stairs to the beach and walk in the liquid gold. She stepped out of her flip-flops as soon as she hit the sand, it was cool between her toes. She noticed a figure down the beach who'd had the same idea, walking barefoot along the tideline carrying his shoes. Her first thought was to be irritated that she had to share the moment. But her second thought was that sharing a thing usually doubled the pleasure of it.

The closer the person got, the more her radar seemed to vibrate — it wasn't some random person catching the sunrise. It was Gus Wilder. So he was an early riser too.

"Mornin'," he said, as their paths met. He was in a white t-shirt and jeans with the cuffs rolled to mid- calf. The sun lit his dark hair softening his formidable look, hints of a burnished gold played on the strands that caught the early light. "just the person I was hoping to run into," he said.

"Really? Is everything all right with the room? The hot water didn't run out on you, did it? Because I'm pretty sure Keith said he replaced the old water heater—"

He let out a low laugh, "No, nothing like that, everything is perfect. Just wanted to check with you about the car — I need to make a grocery run and I didn't want to interfere with your schedule." The morning light turned his whiskey eyes to cognac.

"Oh, sure, thanks for checking in. I had the same thought. You know — about the car and food shopping. You could go whenever and I could get to it later — whatever works, no worries." She was rambling, Jesus. "You're up early — occupational reflex?"

"Exactly. The sun has to catch up to a rancher's morning."

They stood looking out over the water. She was trying not to picture him in chaps, boots, and a hat, setting out in the saddle along the boundaries of the ranch...with the first rays of dawn cresting a mountain, its beams piercing the horizon, until the light gathered strength and spilled gold down the mountain's face.

A cool wave ruffled in over her feet stirring her from the vision. "I'm sure," she said, "long days. But aren't you more on the management side now?"

"Yes. But even ranch managers embrace early rising and are hands-on, saddling up and riding out to check on the livestock and the pastures. We lead by example as well as needing to be able to identify potential issues early. And it's tradition, the physical act of riding the property in the early morning — it's what preserves our dedication to the land and the whole culture of ranching."

A warmth spread throughout Carly that had nothing to do with the rising sun. She needed to break the spell. "Sounds amazing, I love the dedication. I can't think of anything comparable." Her Gram would have picked his brain for stories. "Well, since we don't have a horse for you to ride, I suppose we need to work out some kind of schedule for the car." She shoved her hands into the pockets of her cutoffs and looked over at him through the windblown pieces of hair that hid her eyes.

"I was also hoping to get to the beach today. You can help with recommendations?" He suddenly looked lonely to Carly and she felt a pang of something.

"Absolutely. Burke and Murphy were talking about hitting the beach today too — something about surfing — not sure about their women but..."

"So you're pawning me off?" One side of his face lifted in a small smile. "You must need the car — which is totally fine, I —"

"No, it's not that. I just thought, if everyone's going to the same place, it made sense to maybe carpool? But yeah, now that I'm picturing it, the Jeep Burke and Remi rented won't fit everyone. Not sure they'd be down for that anyway. The car is yours if you want it — we'll figure it out."

"Let's head back," Gus said, "maybe some of the gang is up and we can get more intel."

She felt a longing to be a part of the gang.

Chapter Twenty-Six

URPHY AND HAZEL WERE sitting in the Adirondacks on the grass in the sunshine with mugs of coffee when Gus and Carly reached the top of the steps from the beach.

"Well, look at you early birds," Murphy said, with a smile that took up his whole face. "Did you catch the sunrise?" His hair was tousled in an endearing I-just-woke-up way and he seemed relaxed.

"It sure looks different rising up out of the ocean than it does breaking over the mountains," Gus said.

"I bet," Murphy said, "I'll have to catch it one of these mornings, what do you say, honey?"

"I'm sorry, what?" Hazel said, putting her phone face down on the wide arm of the chair. "I'm sorry, I was checking in on the kids — not that they're even awake yet but I was just getting an update from my mother."

Carly couldn't imagine what a nine- and eleven-year-old could be up to that required such constant updates — but maybe that was the point. She had *no idea*. And there was something awe-inspiring about Hazel, who seemed so dialed into her kids' comfort and happiness that she was willing to put her own on hold.

Of course, you couldn't parent perfectly every second, but Hazel seemed like the kind of mom who stayed in tune, even when she was supposed to be off the clock. Were moms ever *off the clock*? Carly thought how wonderful for those kids to be on the receiving end of that kind of unwavering attention.

"It's just that Liam says he's bored and Sofia's missing her friends and I—"

"It's *two weeks*, Haze, they're *fine*. You've been looking forward to this trip for so long, honey, this will be good for them too," Murphy said, slipping his hand into his wife's and giving it a gentle squeeze.

"You're right, I know you are. Dad's going to take Liam fishing and then for ice-cream and Mom said she and Sofia have a shopping and lunch day planned."

"See? Awesome," Murphy said, "lucky them. Now, what do we want to do with this gorgeous day?"

"Did I hear you say something last night about Burke teaching you to surf?" Hazel said, wrapping her hands around her warm mug and turning her full attention on her husband. "I'd love a beach day."

"Yikes — did I really say that?" Murphy laughed.

"Did you decide on a beach?" Gus asked, "and would you mind company?"

"For surfing you'd either want Cisco Beach or Nobadeer," Carly added, "but I think you can only rent boards at Nobadeer. There aren't decent waves every day though, maybe check a surf app for that?"

"Hey, a beach day is a beach day, right?" Murphy said, "are there food trucks or anything?"

"Not at Nobadeer — you pack your own stuff and you can drive right on the beach." Carly was glad she'd anticipated some of their interests and questions.

"Hell yeah," Burke said, walking out from the porch, "that's why we rented the Jeep. Who's in?"

"Have you checked with Remi?" Hazel asked, "We don't want to intrude on your day."

Valid question, Carly thought, grateful Hazel had thought to ask it.

As if conjured, Remi jogged over from the front of the house. A sheen of sweat coating her perfectly taut and tanned body as she clicked a few selfies.

"There she is," Burke said with a smile, "what do you think, Rem, beach today?"

"The beach?" she asked, as if he'd suggested bowling.

"Yeah, where the ocean meets the sand, baby. There are about eighty miles of it wrapped around this island and we've got the oversand permits for all of it. Let's do some off-roading, woman." Burke tried to put his arm around Remi but she shrank away from his touch listing her needs before hitting the shower.

"You need to find an umbrella, chairs, I need to pack my food, hat, sunblock, and, like, at least a gallon of water. And, oh, we can get some videos of me running at the water's edge, promise?"

"No worries, babe," Burke said with the patience of a saint, "I got you. There's an umbrella around here right, Carly? And we'll pack a cooler and be good to go. Who else is in?"

Six of them would be too much for the Jeep — plus Carly wasn't even sure she was included. Maybe she should just see what Antonia was up to and let the guests figure out their day. Or maybe she could offer to join them with the Land Cruiser. That way they'd have two vehicles in case anyone wanted to leave the beach before the rest of the group. Should she invite Antonia? Was that weird?

By ten o'clock that morning they had a plan, bought food for lunch, and made a beverage run. They would take the Jeep and the Land Cruiser to Nobadeer for the day — the surf was one to three feet which would be good for Murphy to try and get up on a board. And maybe Carly would try too.

Antonia passed on the beach trip and somehow it ended up being just Carly and Gus in the Land Cruiser while the other four piled into the Jeep. Gus asked if he could drive and Carly handed over the keys hiding her relief — riding shotgun suited her fine. They rumbled onto the sand road leading to the beach and Carly prayed Nessie would be okay, and that they'd have no problem letting the right amount of air out of the tires to drive on the soft sand.

She crossed her fingers that Burke wouldn't try to be a tough guy thinking he didn't need to take the tires down to 18 psi. Instagram was full of the *Chads* who dug themselves into a hole in the sand every single time.

She hoped the waves were decent and that they packed enough beer. She was glad that cell service was notoriously nonexistent out there and that Hazel would have to be present and in the moment.

"She was made for this," Gus said, navigating old Nessie up and over the dunes in low gear as it chewed up the soft sand like it was born to. Carly was relieved the vintage rig was handling the off-road conditions like the tank it was. She hadn't been entirely convinced — her original thought was that having been so painstakingly restored, it might only be meant for trips to town and sporting a flower wreath on its front grill for the Daffodil Festival.

They saw Burke's dusty-blue Jeep up ahead swinging around and backing into a choice spot with lots of beach before the tideline. Gus followed suit, doubling the group's real estate beside a family piling out of a Gladiator

"Guess it pays to be an early bird," Gus said, shutting the engine off and double-checking the emergency break, "what happens if you get here after noon?"

"No clue," Carly said, trying not to stare too long at his strong capable hands, "but I imagine you'd be screwed unless you had friends saving you a spot. Like those boogie boards over there stabbed into the sand."

"This is pretty cool," he said, looking in every direction, "I've never driven on the beach before. It's really beautiful out here." He looked like a kid checking out all the gifts under the Christmas tree.

She studied him. Until it could totally be considered staring. "Is this your first time to the ocean?" He looked at her like she'd said something hysterical and she felt foolish. Like she saw him as some small-town country boy who'd never left the farm.

"No," he said, smiling at her, not quite patronizing, but close. "I've been to the west coast. But this is my first time in the presence of the Atlantic."

"Cool," she said, getting out of the car, eager to get her beach chair out of the back and set up near Hazel. She didn't like how self-conscious she felt around Gus. Like she had to filter her thoughts and as though every word needed vetting.

Why couldn't he do something dorky like wear his cowboy hat to the beach or have a cargo-shorts-dad-energy bathing suit? But nope. He fit in so hard. Striped O'Neil board shorts, a vintage Pearl Jam t-shirt, and a pair of OG Ray-Ban Wayfarers.

"Dude — did you see that?" Burke said to Murphy, pointing out at a surfer who'd just got slammed by a wave.

"Hon, you sure you want to try that?" Hazel said, coming to stand by them at that the water's edge. Carly could almost see Murphy's ego pause but stand taller to meet the moment.

"No worries, mate," Burke said, patting Murphy on the back, "they come in sets — trust me, they'll settle down."

"Can you really tell that?" Gus asked, coming to stand with them.

"Took the question right out of my mouth," said Murphy.

"Sure, yeah, totally. It's cyclical. Each set comes in similar-sized waves pretty much, and you'll be able to see when the smaller waves are rolling in. We got a nice offshore wind which will keep them cleaner, no worries."

"*You'll* be able to see that. I sure as hell won't know what's what out there," Murphy said, with a nervous laugh.

"Don't sweat it, Murph, we can sit right here and watch for a bit, okay?" Burke said.

"I need the umbrella, Burke!" Remi shouted from where she stood.

Burke came jogging up from the water to dig the umbrella out of the back of the Jeep and start screwing it into the sand by Remi's chair. And Carly wondered again if her perfectly shaped muscles were all show and no go.

The rest of them set up their chairs in an arc facing the ocean. The sun shined down and the breeze was perfect. The ladies were taking off their t-shirts and shorts and lathering on the sunblock.

"Would you mind getting my back?" Hazel asked Carly, handing her the tube of Neutrogena Beach Defense SPF 70. She was feeling a little awkward and relieved to have a purpose.

"How's that?" Carly asked, rubbing it in as well as she could on Hazel's shoulders and the oval section of her back that showed in the red one-piece suit she wore. "Should I try to spread it out more? It's thicker than I thought, sorry."

"Oh, no, I should have warned you it's like paste — it's fine, thanks so much," Hazel said, "My aunt died of melanoma, it freaks me out so I probably overdo it. And it was her hairdresser who found the mole on her scalp, can you believe that? But it was too late — she was gone in six months."

"That's so sad!" Carly said, "I'm so sorry."

"That is fucking awful," Remi said from her shady cave, "See? Umbrellas ladies..."

Chapter Twenty-Seven

SUMMER WAS IN FULL swing out there on the south shore of the island. SUVs bursting with families, dogs, coolers, and toys. The sky was a flawless blue and there was a prevailing sense of joy — the uninhibited kind that summer inspired.

Gus had joined Burke and Murphy at the surf school rental truck and, Carly had to admit, the three of them looked adorable walking down the beach — each with a longboard under his arm. Why hadn't Burke brought his own? He seemed to be more than a weekend warrior. And didn't he say he retired from ski racing because of a spinal injury? Surfing must not bother it.

She sat back in her chair with her camera to her eye, the waves were firing and the coolest color green before they broke into white water. She was pumped to get some good shots.

Hazel let out a long whistle, "Woohoo, looking good!" she shouted down to her husband and the guys. Poor Murphy, surfing probably looked a lot easier than it actually was. Carly decided she'd stay on the spectator side of things. And she was more than a little curious if the cowboy had it in him. Whatever happened out on the water, they got points for going for it.

Hazel, Remi, and Carly watched from their chairs as Burke had Murphy and Gus practice down on the hard sand jumping to a squat on the board from a prone paddling position.

"Your man is in fine shape," Hazel said to Remi, "not sure how mine's gonna make out with this."

"Aw come on," Carly said, "Murphy is the bomb for giving this a try, he's so cute."

"He's all about trying new things, I love that about him," Hazel said, "and, honestly, is no one gonna comment on the cowboy? I know I'm a married woman, but that man is a dime."

Carly almost spit out her water — it was as though Hazel was in her head reading her guilty mind. She got up out of her chair and walked over to the cooler in the back of the Jeep. "Breakfast beer anyone?"

Remi shot her a look, but Hazel clapped her hands like a little kid on the fourth of July. "Ooh, I like the way you think girlfriend, yes please! But make mine a spiked seltzer."

Sitting back down they tapped their cans then turned their attention to the water. The guys were paddling out — losing as much ground in the white water as they gained. When they finally made it past the breaking waves, Burke straddled his board and took his place in the lineup. It was hard to tell how much coaching had been accomplished but both Gus and Murphy stayed lying down on their boards facing the shore looking over their shoulders for next wave. And the next and the next. How, Carly wondered, did you know which one to go for?

"There goes Burke!" shouted an excited Hazel as he rode a wave all the way in, "damn, he just popped right up like it was nothing. Does he surf a lot?" she asked Remi. Who'd been scrolling photos on her phone and had barely seen his ride.

Tipping her sunglasses down on her nose before pushing them back up, Remi said, "Not really. There's almost nothing he can't do though — it's actually a little annoying."

Neither Hazel nor Carly seemed to know how to respond to that. It wasn't so much that it was an unkind thing to say as much as it was not exactly a ringing endorsement of love, admiration, and the desire to be engaged to the guy. Carly busied herself with her camera, putting it in sport-mode to shoot multiple frames per second — even the wipeouts were epic.

"And of course now he's chatting it up with probably the only girl surfer out there," Remi said, her voice tight with irritation.

"Ah," Hazel said, "life with a hot man, what are you gonna do?"

Carly wasn't sure if Hazel was implying that Murphy was more of a solid, dependable minivan than a shiny Lamborghini. But he seemed like such a good guy and not unattractive by any measure. His gentle nature gave him a unique appeal. Carly wanted to believe that love and attraction lasted. That once you found your person, they would always be beautiful to you.

"He's such a good sport — look at him out there." The mechanical staccato of her camera kept her focused. They watched as Murphy took a wave in on his knees, "he caught one!" Carly hoped she'd get a photo of him riding one in up on his feet — he'd love that.

"Now *that* is hot," Remi said, surprising them both, as they watched Gus pop up to a stand and ride a wave in like it was *not* his first rodeo. "Holy shit..." Remi had taken her sunglasses all the way off and stared as Gus paddled back to the lineup then swung his legs to straddle the board to sit and wait for the next one.

Carly reserved comment, hiding behind the lens hoping the quick ka-shhk, ka-shhk, ka-shhk of her shutter didn't give her away.

"What's his story anyway, Carly, what do we know about him?" Hazel asked, "is that man single?"

"He is very *not* single," Carly said, "as in, he's an engaged man, as far as I know, ladies, so keep your panties on."

"OUR panties?" Hazel said, "I was thinking more about *yours*... And what is your story anyway — gorgeous girl, are *you* single? You cannot be single..."

Carly was on the fence about spilling her guts. In the spirit of *in vino veritas* and all that. But who would care about her boring, painful, cliché relationship past?

"So single it hurts. For one year and seven months. But who's counting?"

"Someone needs another round," Remi said, surprising them a second time, slipping a koozie on a fresh Cisco Summer Rays beer for Carly.

Then Remi actually made herself a drink. Carly didn't recognize the bottle at all but it was as clear as water. "Don't tell me you have some kind of premium protein-infused vodka over there," she said.

"Not quite," Remi said, as she mixed plain seltzer in it with a lime, "but it's the world's cleanest vodka. It's called VING and it's made from organic/non-GMO American corn. Zero sugar or additives, one-hundred-percent transparency that's silky smooth and with a flawless finish."

"And do you have this special concoction shipped to you straight from Russia?" Hazel said, shielding her eyes looking up at Remi from her low chair.

"Nope, It's made in California in small batches, gluten free, by a women-owned company."

"Well, alright then, bottoms up!" Carly was glad Remi had joined the party. And a little ashamed of herself for all the judging. Supporting small women-owned businesses was a flex.

"So how long have you and Burke been together," Hazel said, "he seems like a total catch."

When Remi didn't respond right away, Carly was afraid that her cool exterior hadn't thawed enough yet. The three of them sat staring out at the water. It looked like the waves were getting bigger instead of smaller and the guys were getting wrecked. Except Burke, who was putting on a show.

"We met about a year and a half ago," Remi finally said, "at the company Christmas party. It doesn't get any more basic than that, does it? We worked for the same pharmaceutical company."

Was there more? Carly didn't want to interrupt, but she wanted the deets. "Cool," she said, "was it like some big catered affair with like a band? Or more your garden-variety after-hours office party with cheap wine, making out with the boss in your dark cubicle and scanning body parts at the copy machine?"

"Girl," Hazel said, "you've been watching too much Hulu. Do parties like that even exist in real life?"

"Oh, they do," Remi said, swirling the ice in her cup, "it's not pretty. Takeda is a big company so our party was at a hotel — no band but a DJ — and yeah, a lot of drunk dancing. The same shady booze-infused behavior as any company holiday party — plus a ballroom full of drug reps. Burke was hot and I wasn't taking no for an answer."

What did that even mean, Carly wondered.

"I'd booked a room at the hotel, like most of my coworkers, and I knew I wasn't the only one after Burke. He was seriously the most eligible bachelor in the company, if not the city of West Hartford. No matter what, that guy was going to be in my bed that night."

Carly and Hazel exchanged covert looks at that point. Did Remi go so far as to slip something into his drink that night? What did they really know about her? There had to have been no shortage of pharmaceuticals. Alas, it was a question that would remain unasked. All three guys were walking up the beach toward them, the sea having spit them out.

Chapter Twenty-Eight

CARLY'S GAZE WAS FIXED on Gus, his cut physique, even more chiseled than ex-professional athlete, Burke. She wondered if it was all from the physical demands of the work he did, the life he lived. His wet hair hit below his jaw in long spikes setting off his golden-brown eyes. The three of them were laughing at something Murphy said, his smile bigger than anyone's — until it fell, noting Hazel's empty chair. Carly hadn't even noticed she'd gotten up, but she turned to see Hazel holding her phone up in the air in the dunes trying for a cell signal. Ouch.

"Nice job guys," Carly said, coaxing Murphy's smile back, "very impressive!"

"Did you see me out there?" Murphy said, "I finally caught one standing up!"

"Of course I did, we all did! Hazel was *right* here a second ago, I swear. Plus, I caught every frame," she said, waggling the camera she still held, "Now what can I get you to drink, Murph? You've earned it." Carly had the sense she was overcompensating for Hazel's absence with her own cheer. "We haven't done too much damage in the cooler, yet."

Burke leaned his dripping body over Remi's and kissed her on the head. Naturally she pretended to be annoyed. Or maybe she really was. Carly couldn't figure her out. How could she be so certain Burke was hers? Her indifference was puzzling. Weren't you supposed to keep trying at *least* until you were married? A guy like Burke surely had plenty of options.

It occurred to Carly that she was paying attention to everyone and everything but Gus, though she could feel his eyes on her as she moved from the cooler in the Jeep to the back of the Land Cruiser in search of a trash bag.

"You missed a spot," he said, his thumb brushing across her upper back, nearly causing her feet to leave the ground, "it's a little red, let me rub some more suntan cream in." He was so friggin cute — *suntan cream*. And before she could either allow or disallow, his calloused fingers were working a small pool of Coppertone into that spot on her back that was just beyond her reach.

Beads of sweat prickled her armpits and heat gathered in her core, dropping south. She had no business reacting to this man's touch — not that an engaged man had any business touching her at all — except that it was *sunblock*. Which didn't count at all. She felt silly and stupid, he of course meant nothing at all by it and her traitorous body pissed her off.

"Thanks," she said, ducking away from his touch, "I think I'm good. Hey, can you go tie this to the back of the Jeep? I'll get another one for recyclables." She heard the stumbling clutter of her words and squinted past him.

Murphy drank his beer and ate a sandwich standing up with one eye on his wife up in the dunes on her phone. Did it ever cross his mind if his wife was texting anyone other than their kids or her parents? Carly would bet money that Hazel absolutely was not, but she also knew that anything was possible. And maybe it almost felt the same way for Murphy — to simply not be the object of her love and devotion.

But maybe, on some level, Hazel felt his neediness — especially there on the island where it was just the two of them and no kids. Maybe subconsciously this was a turnoff for Hazel and she was gravitating away from it. Was their time alone together backfiring?

What was her preoccupation with their relationship anyway? All she could come up with was that she wanted to believe that love matches worked and could stand the test of time.

And there was Burke, having dragged his chair out from under the umbrella next to Remi to sit in the sun. With all the beautiful, scantily clad, hot young people walking by it was like watching a parade. She figured most of those people were strutting up and down the beach in a rainbow of bikinis just to strut. Young, old, and everything in between — everyone in basically their underwear. Summer.

"You're pretty badass on a surfboard," Carly said, "surfing doesn't bother your back?"

"Thank you! Right?" Remi said smugly. As if she'd be happier if he never surfed again. "He's no good to anyone if he ends up in a wheel chair."

He definitely seemed to dig being out there on display, Carly mused, in one kind of spotlight or another. Or maybe it was the sport of it — he must miss that, not being able to ski race anymore — going hard, balls to the wall. That had to be a blow to his identity. Carly's brother had never been a professional skier, but being an avid one didn't begin to describe it. Grayson would rather be skiing than doing almost anything else. She couldn't imagine the toll it would take if he never could again.

"Nah, it's all good," Burke said, taking a deep drink of his beer, looking out at the water. "We gonna get you up on a board, Carly?" She knew he was deflecting and that was totally okay. God, even someone like Burke, who appeared to have it all going on, probably had scars you couldn't see.

"Maybe," she said, "definitely not a hard pass."

"*Yes*, I love it! You let me know when you're ready," Burke said with a disarming grin. Gus looked over at them from his seat with something in his expression that Carly couldn't read. "I can't get Remi to give it a go," Burke said, pulling a face, "I love a girl who accepts a challenge."

"You love a girl who what?" Remi chimed in from behind them under the umbrella. But the question went unanswered when a couple of guys walked over to where they were sitting.

"Hey! How've you been?" Carly might not have recognized Brett if not for his being six foot, four, and his brother Evan. "How's Nessie running, no problems I hope?"

"Oh, hi!" she said, "nope, no problems at all, thanks. Hey — come meet everyone."

"Wow," Evan said, "you make friends fast."

"No, I mean, yeah, but these are the people staying at the house," Carly said, wondering if that made her more or less lame, to be hanging out with the guests of the house she was technically hired to manage.

"Ah, gotcha," Evan said, while Brett then introduced himself, shaking everyone's hands.

"How's the surf," Evan asked, noticing the boards lying in the sand, "feels like the wind is shifting — waves don't look as clean as they did this morning."

"Agreed," Burke said, "we caught a few good ones a bit ago. Have you been out today?"

Gus had slipped on his sunglasses, but she wished she could see his eyes — see if he was sizing them up, wondering if she was interested in either of them. Oh God, she was insane. Of course he couldn't have cared less.

"Brett and I hit the dawn session— water was glass and the waves were stacked to the horizon," Evan said.

"Sweet," Burke said without hesitation or judgement, smiling like he could picture it and wished he were there.

Carly offered them drinks and they got to talking, just the three of them, down by the water. Carly was relieved for the company — sometimes it felt awkward hanging out with the *guests*. Was it weird? Did they really want her around or were they just being polite?

Standing there ankle-deep in the ocean with the sun shining down catching up with the Kinsman brothers gave her an unexpected jolt of happiness. She barely knew them but there was something about summer vibes that seemed to fast-track relationships and bond people in their joy. Brett was telling her about a party at a friend's place out in Madaket saying she should come.

"West end of the island, California sunsets — amazing — and you'd meet a bunch more people. You know, so you don't have to hang out with the house guests," Brett said. Evan laughed in agreement.

"Aw, come on, they're super nice," she said, kicking at some seaweed that had wrapped around her ankle.

"But it's not, like, weird?" Evan asked, looking over her shoulder at the little group.

"Hey, they're good people. *And*, it turns out I'm sharing the Land Cruiser with *that* guy," Carly said, gesturing to Gus, who was suddenly out of his chair and walking away from them down the beach.

"What?" Brett said, "sharing the car with one of the guests? Why? How'd that happen?"

"The owner of the house is a friend of his. He's here alone from Colorado. It shouldn't be that big a deal. I hope." But as soon as Carly said the words, she imagined taking the car to Madaket to this party they'd invited her to, which was on the opposite end of the island, and would leave Gus stranded.

"Is the dude single? He's not a kid," Evan said, as the three of them seemed to study Gus as he walked away.

Yeah, Carly thought, he definitely had the body of a man, not a kid, the build of someone who put in regular physical work. She thought how his strength was not for show. But earned, each muscle a testament to hours of labor and experience. Her mouth went dry and a heat spread through her.

"Nope, not single, engaged," Carly said, "he seems lonely though, right?"

"Bring him to the party — more the merrier," Brett said.

"Dude, no — what?" Evan chimed in, "No. We're trying to get Carly out and away from *work*. Besides, he seems...I don't know like he wouldn't want to hang out with a bunch of people so much younger than him."

"How old do you think he is bro? He's like thirty-six," Carly said, "but yeah, I can't picture it either." Gus seemed worlds more mature than these guys. She really should go the party. She wasn't going to make connections or find her Prince Charming hanging out with people in relationships or walking conservation trails alone taking photos.

Chapter Twenty-Nine

G US WAS QUIET ON the drive home from the beach and Carly reached to turn the radio on. She loved that Nantucket had its own country station. Parker McCollum's "Handle on You" came on and she cranked it and sang along, *"after all this back and forth, a fifth won't do — I finally got a handle on you... I* just love that line — see what he did there? Back and *forth,* a *fifth* won't do...he had to get a *handle?* Oh my God, I just love it." Gus had his sunglasses on and she didn't have access to his eyes. But she was almost positive she saw the corners of his mouth turn up like he was trying not to smile. "Oh, and this line too — wait for it — *I tell myself that I should quit but I don't listen to drunks* — Ha! Don't you love that?" Still, no rise out of him. "Hey, what's with you anyway? Don't like country music?"

"Is that really how you picture us? Drowning in booze and heartbreak like some country song cliché? Whiskey-soaked and heartbroken? Believe me when I tell you that real-life cowboys are too busy handling the daily grind of the ranch, managing livestock, and keeping up with technology running a business to be fitting into those stereotypes. So, you can just get that image of the lonely guy strumming a guitar by a campfire with his bottle of bourbon right out of your head."

"So, not a big country music fan, huh?"

"How do you know those guys from the beach — I thought you just got here yourself?"

Ah. So he'd totally flipped the script — what was it to him? She wished he were jealous. Not that she'd be taking that out for examination. She turned in her seat to face him as they took Milestone Road off the rotary, which meant she had about six miles to figure out where his head was at.

"Well, if you must know, Brett, the tall one, was the guy who worked on this car to get it ready for the summer. He stopped by the house one of my first days here, and well, made me take it out for a spin with him — you know — to make sure I could handle it, drive a stick-shift and all that. And the other guy, Evan, is his brother."

She was met with silence again and the same inability to read his expression. But since the silence always made her feel like she had to fill it in, she continued, "They picked me up the next day and we all went to the brewery. Very cool spot by the way, you should check it out while you're here." Still nothing. He wore silence easily, never rushing to speak. He got under her skin — her blood seemed to vibrate being near him.

"So, how do you like Nantucket so far?" she asked, not wearing the silence as well, "has to feel way different than Colorado I imagine. You must miss—"

"Very different," he said, cutting her off, "not sure what all the fuss is about. It's pretty small and so flat — not sure I could get used to that."

She wasn't sure if he was missing the fiancée or just feeling like a fish out of water, but he definitely seemed more down than up. "Well, you don't have to, right? Your home is in the Rockies, if I'm not mistaken, so maybe just try to enjoy this while you're here — y'know? The smell of the ocean, awesome beaches, the historic places downtown — have you read about the island's whaling history at all? I mean it's not your Lewis-and-Clark-gold-rush-mining history, but it's pretty interesting. Can you even imagine this little island actually being the whaling hub of the world at one time?" More rambling to fill the space.

"Lewis and Clark didn't go through Colorado."

"Okaayyy…"

"They mostly traveled long the Missouri River. But you're right about the mining history — Colorado was *the* place during the Pike's Peak Gold Rush and then later it was the silver mining boom."

"And you know what? The Gold Rush was part of what killed Nantucket back then."

"And how's that?" Gus said, with a hint of a smile, "I wasn't aware Nantucket had died."

She felt a rush of victory at having gotten him to laugh a little. "Well, whaling died down because of overhunting, also the discovery of petroleum which was replacing whale oil, then the Great Fire really decimated downtown. And then the Gold Rush was right around that same time, the mid 1800's, right? Boom — people couldn't make a living — Nantucket as it was known was over, a ghost town. Until tourism took hold and voila!"

"And you know all this how?" he said, holding onto that grin.

"Um, duh, Mr. Google and me are tight," she said, waving her phone in front of her, "plus it's in every guide book — there are several in your room you know, crack one open, educate yourself." They were at the end of Milestone Road and into Sconset. It was almost five o'clock and she hadn't given thought to the rest of the evening.

"Did you want to get out before I pull into the garage?" he asked, "I know it's tight in there. Or — sorry, I'm being presumptuous — are you going out again tonight? Should I just park it outside for now?"

"You know what — I have no idea. Let's just leave it here. Do you have plans for dinner? Not prying, just, if you want the car, it's all yours." Carly needed to get out of the car before she kept rambling or asked Gus if he wanted to go downtown to the Gazebo for mudslides.

"I hadn't thought about it either but maybe I'll go downtown — thoughts?"

"Let me think on it… I know Rose & Crown is decent, low-key."

The late summer sun was still high enough in the sky and in some unspoken agreement, instead of walking into the house through the front door, they went around to the back to sit on the porch. "Hey, that looks like the perfect idea," Gus said to Murphy, who was sitting there alone with a beer. "Where's your better half?"

"She can't get enough of that outside shower," Murphy said, with his unfailing smile, "I'm gonna check it out when she's done. What are you guys up to for dinner?"

You guys? Oh God, Gus probably did not want to be seen as a pair, she really needed to separate herself — maybe see what Antonia was up to.

"I was thinking of heading into town — haven't done that yet," Gus said, running a hand through his salt-stiff hair, "What about you?"

"Exactly that — we were thinking Brotherhood of Thieves, have you heard of that place? Seems like a cool pub vibe — craft burgers, huge beer list. Hazel said something about craving chowder and a lobster roll."

Carly literally felt her mouth water — that sounded so good. She wondered if they were going to Uber or get a cab or the shuttle maybe? It would be so easy to say, *hey let's all jump in the Land Cruiser and head down town!* But she really needed to give them their space — they were trying to have a romantic vacation.

"You guys need a lift?" Gus offered, "I could check out...what was that place you mentioned, Carly? Rose & Thorn or something?"

"Ha! Close — Rose & Crown, it's right around the corner from Brotherhood," Carly said.

"Not to intrude — just thought if you guys need a lift we could easily head down together and go our separate ways, right?" Gus said, looking from Murphy to her. Why was he looking at her? Was he asking for use of the car or inviting her along? Was she part of the *we*?

"Um — sure," Murphy said, leaning forward in his chair, "Thanks. I'd better check with the boss first, you know, make sure it's okay with her?"

"I hear ya, man, you got it," Gus said, "I need to make a couple calls — just let me know."

Gus went into the house and Murphy followed, leaving Carly alone on the long empty porch. She sank into the wicker loveseat and let out a happy sigh — the view stole her breath and she was suddenly glad for a little solitude to bask in her contentment.

Chapter Thirty

SHE FINALLY HAD A moment to respond to texts that had come in over the day from her mother. Carly was proud of herself for not dwelling on the fact that her parents had just up and moved a thousand miles away. Leaving her basically homeless. She understood it wasn't their responsibility to house their adult daughter.

Her mother's tone was upbeat — the move had been uneventful and North Carolina wasn't as crazy-hot as they'd expected. That was all good. But Carly couldn't help feeling torn, equally glad for them and abandoned by them.

Until she looked up from her phone at where she was. And tasted the salt in the air and breathed in the perfume of the beach roses riding on the breeze, and heard the waves rolling over themselves to break on the sand. It was temporary, but it was sublime.

"There you are," Antonia's lilting voice broke into her reverie, "look at you all sun-kissed and gorgeous, how was the beach?"

"The beach was fun but you're the one who's gorgeous — that dress is flames — got a hot date?" Carly took in Antonia's blown-out do with its artfully, careless, cornsilk-blonde layers framing her face, and the fuchsia linen sheath that hugged her curves. Would she ever look as put together as that?

"How'd ya guess? It was really just the craziest thing — I was at the Marine Home Center looking for a garlic press of all things when this handsome man asked me if he could help me with anything. He didn't even work there! Can you believe that?"

Carly could believe that. "Give me the deets, woman, does he live here year-round? Or is he some silver-fox with a stacked portfolio? Is he picking you up? Where's he taking you? Name? Age?" Jeeze, talk about role reversal.

"Slow down, girl, slow down. His name is David, he could be younger than me — he could be older. I didn't get his life story but I know he spends his summers here and he's picking me up in twenty minutes."

"So, you're comfortable with that? You sure you don't want to meet him somewhere instead so you have your own getaway car? I mean what do you really know about this guy? Besides the fact that he must be loaded. I mean if he lives here for the summer, must own a place — obvi a second home — in is fifties and doesn't have to work all summer?"

Carly was making a lot of assumptions but still. She almost envied Antonia for her age — the guys Antonia would be dating were already established and past all the immature bullshit of not knowing what they want or how to communicate. She totally admired a dude who saw what he liked and went for it just like that.

"Are you finished?" Antonia said, good naturedly, "He lives in Tom Nevers so it just makes sense to drive together, and you get a feeling about someone, you know? About whether or not you can trust them, and well, I'm not worried about David. He lost his wife to cancer a few years back, the kids are grown and spread out, and well, a guy gets lonely. He's taking me to Straight Wharf Restaurant. Are you going to make me bring him over here to meet you? Or give me a curfew?"

"No and no," Carly chuckled, "but how about a glass of wine? Or whiskey — we should pregame — you must be nervous..." She didn't look nervous at all. She looked like a teenager waiting for the hottest boy in school to pick her up for the prom.

"No, darlin, I'm so excited," her southern lilt powered up to ten. "I just hope I don't wind up breakin' his heart," she said, smoothing the front of her dress then double-checking her small diamond-hoop earrings.

Of course she'd be worried about that and not the other way around. Antonia was definitely more of a heart-breaker than a heart-breakee. What was *that* like? "So, is that a yes to a drink or no?"

"Oh, maybe just a quick glass of wine. I'm a lightweight you know and I gotta keep my head on straight."

∞

Carly and Antonia sipped their wine on the porch in the purpling dusk before Antonia went to wait for her date. Carly was ready for a shower under the beautiful sky to watch the early stars poke through, but first she wanted to fold the load of towels in the dryer. It was always a challenge to drag herself out of the postcard view but she made it into the laundry room to find the towels already folded and in a neat stack. She decided to put them in the linen closet at the top of the stairs next to Gus's room where everyone had access.

She heard the muffled sound of "Mr. Brightside" playing in Murphy and Hazel's room and then Gus's low voice on the phone with someone behind his closed door. His voice became clearer when she opened the closet to shelve the towels.

Honey —sshh, listen to me, it's gonna be alright, I promise. Take a deep breath for me...that's it...I'll be home before you know it... Yes it is beautiful here, though I haven't seen very much of the island yet. I surfed today if you can believe that. No, I do not have photos...Okay... yes, yes, we'll talk tomorrow, okay, love you too.

Carly froze place. And she couldn't accurately define what she was feeling. But she was feeling way too much. Guilt for listening, searing jealousy for whoever was on the receiving end of that kind of adoration, and confusion for feeling any type of way at all. And she *did* have photos.

Had he been speaking to the love of his life? Or possibly a *child* he might have? She didn't know Augst Wilder at all. Why on earth was she feeling so deflated? So disappointed? It made no sense — she hadn't let herself *like him* — like him, had she?

She nearly dropped the stack of towels she'd been arranging when she heard Gus's door open. "Oh, hey, just replenishing your towels — did you need some for your bathroom? Here, take a couple," she said, pushing a small pile in his direction, the words coming too fast and in some weird high voice she barely recognized.

"Um, thanks, I think I'm all set but, well, sure I'll just put—"

"Sorry, sorry — what you don't need can stay right here in this closet," Carly said, hurrying back down the stairs making everything way more awkward than it had to be.

"Wait," he called after her, "I was coming to look for you — do you feel like going downtown for dinner? Whether or not Murph and Hazel take me up on my offer I'd still like to go — it'd be nice to have some company," he stood staring at her, halfway down the stairs unmoving, "unless you have other plans?"

He was so fucking hot.

"You know, I might, sorry. But also I might not — I'm actually waiting for a text — and I was just headed outside to shower." She was a blathering lunatic, "can I get back to you?" Jesus. What she wanted to say was, *hell YES, you gorgeous sexy man.* She needed a minute to get a towel and her shit together.

Chapter Thirty-One

W ISPS OF STEAM CURLED from her skin in the evening air as hot water sluiced down over her body. It was the most luxurious thing. Carly breathed in the sunbaked cedar walls mingling with the salty-sweet summer air and tried to clear her head.

Any attempts to reconcile her misplaced feelings for Gus evaporated like mist in the enchantment of the setting. *Enchantment,* maybe that was exactly it. What she was feeling defied logic, of course, the guy was taken and she barely knew him. But there was no doubt that she felt irrationally captivated and charmed by this man. It went beyond simple attraction. Carly felt some unholy mix of admiration and awe, like she was under some spell that was making it hard to pay attention to the reality of it all. Had she projected her *Yellowstone* crush so thoroughly that she was losing her mind?

Ugh, whatever, she said, titling her head back under the pulsing stream of water. She needed to just enjoy this last summer of being a nomad, a rolling stone with no direction home. She was feeling ready for more. She would name her options, consider her choices, and make decisions — it would be her birthday present to herself.

Her posts were landing—people were engaging, sharing, asking for more. It felt like she was getting real traction— even some reposts. She felt inspired. One of her favorites had been Gibbs Pond, with the shot of mist hanging low over the still surface of the pond, reeds in the foreground, moody blues and greens. Her caption seemed to resonate:

This one doesn't show up on many top ten lists, which is probably why it feels like a secret. Nothing curated, nothing glossy—just a pocket of quiet that doesn't care whether you showed up with answers.

Also: pro tip—bring a layer, fog rolls in fast and has no sympathy for your cute top.

#GibbsPondMood #HiddenNantucket #PhotoDiaries #NantucketNotJustBeaches #InternalWeatherReport

Seeing people connect with her content sparked something, like maybe she was stepping into something that mattered. Every message, every *like*, was a little nudge forward — a real appreciation for her eye, her voice, her work. It wasn't just about capturing the moment — she was telling a story, one that spanned both the outward journey and her own inner evolution. Each photographic capture had more meaning now, a way to show not just what was in front of her, but how it was changing her too.

Had she just been posting pics before now? This felt different, the blend of heart and horizon was hitting home for people. She hadn't considered that sharing both the places she explored and the feelings she was working through would strike a chord with so many, that layering emotion into her landscapes would create a kind of echo in others.

Her skin was pruning up as options rushed in of where this might take her, like doing freelance for brands and publications — shooting lifestyle or product photos for small brands with a story. Maybe contributing visual essays to online mags or indie print publications.

She was practically crackling with the possibilities. And so what if she had an unreasonable crush on an engaged man she'd known for five minutes who lived 2000 miles away. She needed to lean into opportunity wherever it showed up. And she'd had no better offers for dinner.

"Knock, knock," the words came with a soft rapping on the cedar door.

"What the hell, dude? Boundaries!" Recognizing Gus's voice, she scrambled for her towel, feeling exposed in all ways. Like her thoughts were floating above her in the cloud of steam.

"Apologies — just checking to see if it was occupied," Gus said.

"Um, the locked door wasn't a clue?" She scrambled to dry her body and wring the water from her hair. "Hold your horses." With no choice but to step out wrapped only in a towel, she pushed open the door and gestured grandly. "All yours," she said, dodging his amber gaze as she brushed past him.

"Have you decided on dinner yet?" he called after her. She could hear the smile in his voice — she was annoyed and undone at the same time.

"I'm in," she said, thinking *I'm in trouble with you, that's what I'm in.*

"Excellent," he said.

"I'll be ready in twenty. I hope you are too, I'm starving."

"Yes, Ma'am," was all he said before he latched the door and slipped under the steaming flow of the rainforest showerhead.

Having finally decided what to wear, Carly emerged from her room to find Murphy and Hazel sitting at the island having a drink together. They'd brought their JBL speaker down and a Coldplay song was on. "Well, don't you guys look nice," Carly said, noting the comb marks in Murphy's hair, his very on-point Nantucket Red shorts, and the blue oxford shirt cuffed at his wrists. Hazel looked adorable in a pale mint sundress and Murphy could barely take his eyes off the way it shelved her ample breasts.

"Aw, thanks Carly," Hazel said, "and thanks so much for letting us tag along down town tonight. If we're killing your vibe, please tell me."

"What? *No.* Jeeze. We're not—"

"Ah, a little pregaming I see, perfect," Gus interrupted, coming into the kitchen, "what's everybody drinking?"

Carly tried not to stare. At the way his jeans sat low on his narrow hips and hugged his perfect ass. Or his white linen shirt rolled to the elbows exposing tanned, muscled forearms as he poured himself two fingers of Bulleit bourbon.

She'd chosen white jeans for herself and a terracotta sleeveless top. Her hair was down and bending into beachy waves just past her shoulders. She felt pretty. And she felt his eyes on her. He held up the bottle to ask if she wanted one, she nodded slowly. A song from Pearl Jam's latest album came on, "Wreckage", that she recognized and she was psyched they weren't playing Taylor Swift of Beyoncé.

"Pearl Jam fans, excellent," Carly said, "what do you think of the latest album?"

She was looking from Murphy to Hazel because it was their playlist and she was surprised when Gus answered.

"It's definitely a return to their grunge roots," Gus said, "Y'know, with those high-octane rock tracks like their early work, But also with some slower songs — more introspective stuff — I think it's a pretty decent mix of their old and new style."

"I totally agree — these guys are timeless," Murphy said, "I mean every song hits. What's Vedder now, late fifties? They get nostalgic on a few tracks — remembering friends they've lost and sort of passing the torch to the next generation. 'Something Special' is slower and softer — definitely a tribute to Vedder's daughters, *Do it yourself/You're not the type to need a man* — with the true dad-rock realization that matters are out of his hands, you know?"

"Spoken like a dad," Gus said, raising his glass to his lips, "Not sure I'd have picked up on that."

"It goes fast!" Hazel said, "Can't believe ours our nine and eleven already..."

It made Carly take silent stock of her own life, kissing her twenties goodbye but so far removed from parenthood.

"Jeeze, I can remember being eleven years old so clearly — that *is* scary," Carly said, "camping out in a tent in the backyard with my friends, pizza and s'mores, Dad keeping the firepit going...and just like that, it's almost twenty years later — *how is that possible?*"

"Goes by even faster when you have kids, trust me," Murphy said.

"Are people still bringing kids into this fucked-up world?" Remi said, walking into the kitchen with Burke, "I mean, no offense but..." She marched over to the freezer for her vodka and ice as though she hadn't just been completely offensive. "Just let me make a roadie, B, then we can go."

Men really seemed so much less complicated, Carly decided, watching as Gus poured Burke some bourbon. She took a moment to appreciate his generosity and the comradery blooming among them. The booze trickled into her brain untying her thoughts, spreading a reckless burn through her veins. "So, where's everybody headed tonight? Hazel, did you guys decide on Brotherhood?"

"We did," Hazel said, in between taps on her phone. "Sorry, just telling the kids that their dad and I are going out and that I will *not* be returning texts."

"Damn straight," said Murphy, "or I might make you leave your phone here, young lady. Now let's go find you that lobster roll." He was a good sport about it but Carly could tell he wished he had more of her undivided attention. He took the last slug of his drink and asked Gus if we were leaving soon. "No problem at all if you're not, I just don't want to lose our reservation."

"Hey, we're heading out now — want to ride with us?" Burke said.

Murphy looked from Burke to Carly, "is that okay, do you mind if we go with Burke and Remi?"

"Of course!" Carly said, "Go, go, go, I totally get it. Maybe we'll see you downtown at some point? There's a place called Gaslight that has live music some nights — not sure about tonight but..."

"Awesome," Murphy said, as the four of them headed to the front door out to the Jeep, leaving Carly and Gus alone with the remnants of their drinks.

The door had barely closed behind the four of them when Murphy stormed back in with Hazel's phone in his hand. "Could you do me a favor," he said to Carly, "would you please put this up in our room? I'm sorry to ask—"

"Got it. Go, no worries. Have FUN!"

Carly jogged up the steps in her bare feet to the New Dawn Rose room. And as she was setting Hazel's phone on top of the bureau it vibrated with the name Steven.

> Hi there, just confirming Thursday evening at five o'clock. I've got the wine and cheese — going to be a beautiful night. Your secret is safe with me.

Chapter Thirty-Two

WHY DID SHE HAVE to just see that? *Who in the world was Steven?* He could be family, a friend — it was none of her business. She didn't want to think about Hazel cheating on Murphy, but it popped into her head anyway. She'd been on the receiving end of that game with her college boyfriend before Jake and it was the worst feeling there was.

Nah, no way, she said under her breath exiting the room and heading for the stairs.

"No way what?" Gus asked, coming out of his room at the same time. "Everything alright?"

"Yup. Let's go cowboy, I'm hungry." She hustled down the stairs putting Hazel's phone out of her mind. "Did you pick a place? Not Brotherhood."

"I didn't know I was picking, but okay. Let's do Rose & Thorn."

She turned her head around to face him with her eyebrows arching halfway up her forehead. He could barely contain his laugh — of course he was kidding.

"Rose & Crown it is," he said, "maybe you need a roadie..."

Maybe she did. Something to blot out noticing how good he smelled. Like leather and sunshine. But then she thought that booze wouldn't stand a chance against that distraction. "I'm good, let's go." She made sure her phone and wallet were tucked into her purse as they walked out the front door to the car. She tried the passenger side door but it was locked. He was coming up behind her, keys jingling in his hand to open her door. Then it was she who was holding back a smile. "Ah…chivalry lives."

"So, what's good at this place — what's your favorite?" She felt him look in her direction as they cruised down the only road into town. It was too late for sunglasses — having access to those eyes felt dangerous.

"I don't know — it's a tavern with, you know, pub food. I mean they literally have everything: burgers, wings, fish tacos, lobster mac and cheese. I imagine you're a beef guy?"

"More stereotypes? We do eat other things you know. In fact I love fried calamari. Not a huge oyster guy but maybe I just need convincing…"

"Don't look at me. Oysters are not my thing either. I mean I kind of wish they were — they always look so cool — a million different kinds with their condiments and saucy things. I don't know, I just don't get the swallowing whole part — what can you taste swallowing something whole? And then aren't you just tasting whatever you've dumped on in?" Who knew she had so much to say about oysters? Her voice seemed to reverberate in the old car.

"Not that you've given it much thought," he said, with that damn smile again, and even a low growl of a laugh, "how about next time, we to go a place that's known for its oysters — gotta be one on-island, right? We really should know, definitively, if we're oyster people or not."

Next time? We? Was this a good precedent to be setting? "Do we know where Burke and Remi were headed?" she asked to skirt the topic of dinner with him *next time*. "And do you see those two as a couple? I'm not so sure… They just seem….she seems…. I mean he's so nice and—" She hated being so gossipy. Maybe whiskey was her truth serum — maybe she should *not* be drinking it. "I apologize, it is absolutely none of my business. That was—"

"A spot-on observation," he said, "but who are we to say? Love and logic hardly go together."

They hit the cobblestones of Main Street. The car lurched and Carly bumped the side of her head against her window. "I suppose I deserved that," she said, rubbing her head, telling herself to quit layering other people's relationship drama onto the hypothetical wreckage of her own romantic future.

"Should I park here? It says two hours," he said, as he expertly parallel parked Nessie in between an old Defender with surfboards stacked to the sky and an old Wagoneer with bikes and beach chairs strapped to the back.

"Looks good to me," Carly said, "do you want to walk around a little before we eat? Check out some of the historic homes on upper Main?"

"Weren't you starving a minute ago?" Gus said, removing his sunglasses from the top of his head and leaving them on the dash. "It's your call."

She was leading him up Main Street before she could give into her hunger, wanting to see the famous Three Bricks she'd read about. When they stood in front of the three identical brick federal-style mansions, she looked at Gus to see if he was impressed at all or just bored. He gave a low whistle of appreciation and took in the view.

"Is this what you mean by whaling wealth? *Ooowee.* Definitely not fishing shacks."

"Right? Very different feel from Sconset. So, Joseph Starbuck, one of the richest whale-oil merchants of his time, built these three brick mansions in the mid 1800's for his three sons when Nantucket was at the top of its whaling game. Cool, huh?"

"Crazy. You can't tour these, can you?"

"No," Carly said, "they're all privately owned now, but you can go online and see photos of the full historical restoration of the East

Brick — and we're talking like thirty rooms! The amount of work and attention to historical detail is insane — just beautiful." She noticed that Gus was staring longer at her than at the imposing brick mansions. It stirred a conflicting blend of self-consciousness and satisfaction in her. "You can go in that one," she said, pointing to the towering Greek Revival mansion across the street. "That's the Hadwen House — built around the same time by another rich whaling merchant, William Hadwen, who was married to the daughter of Daddy Starbuck who built the three bricks. It's now owned by the Nantucket Historical Association and they do tours."

"I'm making a mental note," he said, trying but failing to hold back a grin, "Were you always this interested in history? Or more since your work with the travel accounts?"

"My work has definitely influenced my curiosity, but there's just something about this island, I mean walking along these cobblestones that were once ballast on eighteenth century whaling ships — that's pretty cool, right? I mean I've lived in Boston! We've got the American Revolution! The Tea Party and Paul Revere! But I'm embarrassed to say that I've never even done the Freedom Trail. We have way more history there than your wild west, that's for sure. I can't really explain why I've been so sucked in by this little island's history..."

"History's good, I get it. I can see the charm of it having been so well preserved here. Maybe it's the feeling of going back in time that you like, or maybe it's the whole maritime thing — living and dying at the hands of the sea," he said dramatically, as Carly led him further up Main Street, away from the direction of dinner.

"Just one more, before it gets totally dark, I promise, then we eat." They walked along the ancient cobblestoned road to 141 Main Street. "I've been wanting to check this one out too, it's the George Gardner house, it looks nothing like those others. And it used to be on the ghost tour once upon a time."

"The what now?"

"Yeah, there are these ghost walks or haunted hikes — whatever they're called — at dusk. This is it — oh my God it's beautiful," Carly said, from the sidewalk looking out at the gorgeous white clapboard house. "It's hard to believe this was almost completely dilapidated in the late 1990's. I mean look at it now — that roofwalk looks so fancy with the decorative railings in between those stately chimneys. And those columns — what do you call those, Corinthian?"

"I really don't know, Carly, but yes it is a beautiful property, simple but elegant I guess you'd say. Very distinctive. Was it a gift from someone's rich daddy too?"

"I can't remember, let me pull it up here," she said, googling it, "Okay, it was built in 1834 for sea captain, George Gardner, who was a descendant of Richard Gardner, an early white settler on the island. Yada, yada, yada — ooh, here's the ghost story part — so apparently there was a bitter divorce between the owners and the place was pretty much left to rot. So, as the story goes, there was a Chinese servant who fell in love with one of the Gardner daughters and he was hanged! And his body is rumored to be buried on the grounds of the house. Someone bought it in the early 2000's and restored it — then sold it for ten mil! So crazy."

"Ten million dollars?"

"Oh you have no idea. Two mil will get you a *fixer-upper* on this island. I don't get it either, I'm just sayin."

"*There's* your scary story." Gus laughed at his own joke.

"Right? Ah, but look at it...those hydrangeas in full lavender bloom, those perfectly rounded boxwoods, the fieldstone path set into the lawn, the white picket gate... can't you just picture a summer party here with roaring twenties energy? A Gatsby-level summer bash with men in straw boater hats, women in long bright dresses, everyone drinking spiked lemonade and sloe gin fizzes?"

"I can now," Gus said, looking out at the property as if he were seeing those very guests, "you do have vision — no wonder you're a professional content creator. Now, I don't know about you, but all that talk about spiked lemonade and gin fizzes is making me thirsty."

Chapter Thirty-Three

ROSE & CROWN WAS buzzing with a good crowd; couples, families, outside and in — it was the perfect choice. Carly loved the rustic feel, the old wooden signs on the walls and along the rafters. It was one of the places that stayed open for lunch and dinner all year round, easy to see why it was a favorite for locals as well as tourists. They were seated in a booth under a giant carved mermaid near the wall of windows open to the sidewalk.

"I'm so hungry, everything looks good," Gus said.

"I second that. Ooh, do you want to start with the nachos? Never mind — there's the calamari you said you were in the mood for."

"Did I say that?"

His eyes were always a little twinkly, as if he was going to tell her a secret that would make her laugh.

"Actually I'd get too full anyway and I really want to try the smokehouse burger. Smoked gouda, bacon, and onion straws? Yes, please."

"Quite the appetite. Where do you put it all?" he said, as the server came to take their drink order. She was cute with her pixie cut of chocolate-brown hair, petite features and milky skin. She had an infinity symbol tattooed on the inside of her wrist and a tiny diamond stud in her nose. She directed her ice-blue eyes at Gus as she ran down the draft beer list. Her name was Isabelle and she would be taking care of them.

Carly studied this Isabelle, it was impossible to tell how old or young she was. But it was easy to see by the way she angled her lithe body toward Gus that she was caught in the pull of his charisma. Who would blame her? Did Gus even noticed his effect on women? What was that like — to walk through the world with that look, that aura — where people couldn't help but orbit you, drawn in like they didn't have a choice?

The unexpected collapse of her relationship with Jake had done little to inspire future confidence. He hadn't possessed half of Gus's qualities — but still got plenty of attention from female species. Only he wasn't cool about it, he ate it up, leaving Carly feeling so much less-than.

There'd been signs that he wasn't *the one*. But she'd shoved them aside. Until the pile was too high. Like how he accused her of being afraid to commit and not wanting to move to where he was, while he was still splitting rent with two college buddies and using his oven for sneaker storage. How she'd walk away from their texts, her mind spinning, wondering why she always felt like the villain. Jake would say she was gaslighting him, that she wasn't validating his feelings — but somehow, it was always her emotions up for debate, her needs on the chopping block.

Gus was not Jake.

Once they'd ordered, Carly couldn't pretend to look at her menu anymore. She either had to look at him or the giant mermaid over their booth. He had the view that looked out over the rest of the place and beyond to the street where happy people were strolling by.

She wanted to know so much more about him — like did he have a hot *single* brother? She wanted and didn't want to know about his fiancée. It was none of her business, for starters, and she wasn't certain how much she was supposed to know. Had Keith told her things about Gus's situation in confidence? Why had he done that?

"So..." they both said at the same time.

"After you," he said. Their drinks arrived pausing the moment, his Cisco Whale's Tale Ale and her tequila with grapefruit and lime juice, salted rim, rocks.

"Cheers," she said, "and don't give me that look. I like a good Paloma, what can I say." He put his hands up in surrender then tapped her drink with his. "So, does your whole family live on the ranch, brothers, sisters?" Subtle.

"Yes, actually," he said, stretching out his legs under the table bumping hers, for which he apologized, then rearranged them. They still leaned against hers and their body heat mingled in the tight space. "I have a brother and a sister. I'm the younger son and poised to take over for my father — which, as you can probably imagine, has been a source of tension."

"Ah, so a sibling power struggle *is* part of the plot," she said, sipping her drink, "family drama after all. Who wants to take over — your sister?"

"No. Celia has her own business. She and her best friend, Ruby, run tourist trail rides that include campouts and canyons and a little bit of treasure hunting. You wouldn't believe the amount of money some high-powered city types are willing to throw down for a genuine cowboy experience."

"That sounds so cool! You mostly hear of the fake dude-ranch stuff. Is cattle driving involved? Is there like a big barbeque party the last day with Lainey Wilson performing?"

Gus dropped the calamari loop he held and put his head in his hands laughing, "Life is *not* a *Yellowstone* episode, woman! How many times do I have to tell you that?" He took a long pull of his beer, his eyes pinning hers with amusement and something she couldn't name. "Anyway, Celia is not the problem. It's my older brother, Jesse, who for obvious reasons — being the oldest son — believes he should be the one to replace my father when the time comes, that it's his birthright."

"Understandable," she said, before taking the first big bite of her burger. "Oh my *God* this is delicious," she said with a mouthful, "*sorry*. So what did Jesse do to lose the reins?" When Gus didn't answer right away, she feared she'd overstepped. "You don't have to answer! I'm just curious. And nosey. I'll just fill my face and shut up."

"Jesse has a substance abuse problem. It's a long sordid story. He's sober for now, but he'll always be in recovery. Our father is a conservative, old-school guy who doesn't trust it and won't risk it."

"Yikes, poor Jesse. Do you think that will affect his long-term sobriety? I mean that's gotta be a tough pill to swallow — oops, terrible metaphor, sorry! I just mean that if your own dad doesn't trust you, have that steadfast faith in your recovery, what does that say? How do you overcome that? And this must be terrible for your relationship with your brother."

"All valid points, and a good part of the reason I'm here. Our father sees through all of it and needs to know if I can handle the responsibility, if I am the man for the job. On the one hand, I know I am. I know every inch of our land like my own reflection, can see the future of it like I'm staring into a crystal ball. But on the other, I can't stand to see what it's doing to my brother. How can I usurp his birthright like that and possibly send him spiraling out of control?" A pair of lines furrowed between his eyebrows, etched there, giving away his troubled thoughts.

Carly found herself wanting to reach over and smooth away the lines, the worry. He was a good man to put his brother's happiness in front of his own. "Of course I know nothing about any of it, but isn't there a way you two could work together?"

"But someone has to be the number one, standing at the forefront calling the shots," he said.

"Holding the reins, keeping everything on track," she said.

"Captain of the ship, responsible for the entire vessel, its crew, and the success of the voyage. The navigating, maintaining discipline, and overseeing the hunt," he said, draining the last of his beer.

"Look at you with your whaling metaphors, Captain. And let me guess, Jesse is no one's second-in-command." What she really wanted to know was *what does the fiancée think about everything? Who was she, what did she do? How long had they known each other, when was the wedding? Was she GORGEOUS?* "What does your mother think of all this?"

Gus looked at her, into one eye then the other, lines furrowing his brow gain. He rested his elbows gently on the table and steepled his hands. "My mother died seventeen years ago, when I was a freshman in college."

"Oh my God, I'm so sorry, I didn't know." Saying you're sorry was the stupidest thing. But what else was there to say?

"Thank you. She was sick, it all happened so fast once they found the cancer. She told me not to come home, that she was doing okay. But she was wrong and I got there too late and I—"

Carly reached across the table to put her hand over his. It was automatic. He squeezed her hand lightly before putting his hands in his lap. "I was at the University of California, Berkeley, majoring in Fish and Wildlife and Environmental Biology — my course load was huge. I should have stayed local — should have gone to Colorado State, but Mom wanted more for me. So when I got the scholarship to CAL, she made me promise her I'd go. Known for its College of Natural Resources, Berkeley offered the best programs in environmental science, policy, and ecosystem sciences. I couldn't pass it up."

Carly couldn't say she was sorry again but she felt so, so sorry. Her own mother may not have been the most attentive parent on the planet but she was there. Loosely anyway. And it was easy to take that for granted. "I'm sure you made her so happy, Gus, so proud."

"My father's never been the same. And Jesse, obviously, has struggled. Celia is so much like my mom — loves her horses and the ranch and adventure. Mom lives on in her. We're very close, she's feeling a little anxious with me so far away. In fact I had a phone conversation with her earlier — she wants pics of me surfing or it didn't happen, ha!"

"That's pretty funny — I in fact can help you with that — I got pics!"

Carly was too busy being glad the conversation she'd overheard was with his *sister* to get sucked into remembering the pain of her own losses — first her brother and then her Gram.

Her throat tightened and her thoughts shifted back to Gus. He was insightful and compassionate. Carly's curiosity was waking up alongside her caution...who was this man?

Chapter Thirty-Four

C ARLY AND GUS DECIDED to check out The Gaslight around the corner on North Union for another drink and to see if they had live music. They needed to shake up the mood. There was a line at the door which meant it was a place to be. "I wonder if we'll run into Burke and Remi? Or maybe Murphy and Hazel?" she said.

"Maybe," he said, "have you heard of this band? Crooked Coast?"

"I have not," she said as they got up to the door, "live music is always a vibe though, right? Let's get drinks and head back to check them out."

"Hey!" It was Burke standing next to them at the bar, "Thought we might run into you guys — how was dinner?" His eyes were a glassy blue and his sandy hair was sticking up in places as though the sun and surf were still trapped there. Without waiting for Carly to respond he said, "Cru was super cool, wall-to-wall beautiful people, just mobbed — place to see and be seen for sure. And, man, their oyster bar..."

"Food good?" Gus asked, as if he could not care less about the scene of people with more money than class. "I, we, were just talking about where the best place was to get oysters."

"Oh, the food was phenomenal — I had the sea bass, Remi stuck with the oysters — they have a decent NY strip steak too if you don't go for seafood. Super pricey but nice view of the yachts and a real party vibe."

Carly couldn't speak for Gus but Cru sounded like *a lot*. In all ways. The see-and-be-seen thing wasn't her style, she liked cozier spots. But she could totally picture Burke and Remi there.

"It was THE place to be, let me tell you," Remi said, slurring just a little, "our waiter was this *gorgeous* dude, just *so* nice — yeah he was probably like twenty two or something but *whatever*, so cute, know what I mean?" She leaned into Carly and giggled like a teenager. She didn't get Remi — how was some twenty-something kid appealing to her even a little when she had a man like Burke?

"Okay — let's go check out the band," Carly said, steering the group away from the bar. Crooked Coast had such a fun sound. She couldn't decide if they were more reggae, hip-hop, rock, or some crazy combination of all three. They were belting out *do you feel it*, and Carly was definitely feeling it. The warm summer night buzzed with the energy of happy people, good music, and living exactly in the moment.

She watched Remi doing a kind of drunk sway with her drink raised up in the air baring her carved abs to anyone interested. The abundant cleavage further drew attention from the younger guys who didn't know any better than to stare and smile and sway with her, as if she danced for them. Burke either didn't notice or was too used to it to care. His attention was similarly diverted to the female version of inebriated twenty-somethings moving and grooving.

Then there was Gus, standing back from the crowd, taking it all in. He nodded his head with the beat and seemed to be enjoying the sound, but Carly really couldn't tell what was going on in his head. She saw him reach for his phone in the back pocket of his jeans and read a text. He looked up to find her and came over to where she stood.

"Just got a text from Murph," he said, shouting to be heard over the music, "they're in some long line at the Juice Bar for ice-cream wondering where we are and if they can bum a ride back."

"The Juice Bar, ha! That line is legend apparently," Carly said, leaning in close to Gus so he could hear her, "what do you want to do?" Warmth from the small crowd rose up, intensifying his scent in the pocket of space they stood. She breathed in the heady mix of leather, whisky, and summer nights before taking a step back.

"We could stay for another couple songs then go meet them?" he suggested, leaning in, his mouth a whisper away from her ear. She stepped back, giving him a thumbs up with an exaggerated casualness, masking her confused longing.

They slipped out with barely a wave to Burke and Remi who were working on another round of drinks and flirting wildly — just not with each other.

A thin veil of fog was swirling in the amber light of the antique lampposts adding a chill to the night. Everywhere Carly looked, couples seemed to be drawn close—fingers interlaced, or simply drifting in step close enough that they'd occasionally bump and lean into each other. People of every age had found their person, or at least a summer love.

She couldn't believe she was about to be thirty and still single! She may as well have been wearing a sash that, instead of saying *Bride to Be* or *Last Fling Before the Ring*, screamed *Hot Mess* or *Maid of Dishonor*. She hated that she couldn't be happy as a self-sufficient woman, satisfied with her own company — that she wanted/needed a man, a partner, to feel complete. But despite her independence, she couldn't help but ache for the companionship she had convinced herself she didn't need. She was tired of the emotional rollercoaster. Was she undesirable, unlovable? She'd lost perspective.

The toe of her sandal caught a raised corner of brick on the sidewalk and she grabbed Gus's arm. "Easy — I got you, everything okay?" Gus asked, steadying her with his warm calloused hand on her low back. Great, now she felt like a basic drunk chic. "Whoa, is that the line for the ice-cream?" he said, once they reached the bottom of Broad

Street and saw people wrapped around Sunken Ship souvenir shop and up South Water.

"Yup." She was torn between dissing such a waste-of-time thing OR telling him that it was a must-do, that just the smell of the batter cooking on a hot waffle cone iron would be worth the wait. She was a child when it came to ice-cream.

"That's all you got, *yup*? I feel like there's more," he said, with the sweetest, sexiest sideways grin.

"Okay, you got me. I'm an ice-cream slut. I've walked miles for the best, waited an hour for the worst, could replace every meal with it — it's a problem. It was my first love. It'll probably be my last. *Hi, my name is Carly Hill and I'm addicted to Chunky Monkey and New York Super Fudge Chunk.*" She looked over at him to gauge his reaction. "Too much?"

"What, no Cherry Garcia?" he asked, "And as an addict you can't possibly restrict yourself to Ben & Jerry's. Come on, be honest, you've tried every flavor east of the Mississippi haven't you..."

Carly let out a one-syllable laugh and shoved him with her shoulder. "You got me. Love it all. But cherry ice-cream? Ew, just *no.*" Damn, it was easy being with Gus. He looked at her the same way whether she was wearing a towel or a sexy top and tight jeans. She bit back a memory of Jake asking her, before they went out to meet his friends, *is that what you're wearing?* God, she really needed to stop holding every man up to such an asshole.

"Hey you guys!" Hazel said, out of the misty darkness, "Over here!" She was simultaneously trying to get her dripping waffle cone under control and pulling Murphy toward her and Gus. Her smile took up her whole face and her pretty hair was springing into curls before Carly's eyes in the wisps of fog circling them. Murphy's smile mirrored his wife's — it always did. Carly felt a quick stab wondering at the source of Hazel's joy as she remembered the incoming text on her phone that she'd entrusted to Carly.

Chapter Thirty-Five

THE DRIVE BACK TO Sconset was slow. Fog had rolled in thick and low and it felt like a living thing. It wrapped the landscape in a damp, heavy silence, moving with a sentient slowness, as if it had its own intentions. It didn't dampen Hazel's spirit as she spoke animatedly about their dinner at Brotherhood and the cool souvenir ideas for the kids they'd seen at Sunken Ship and Nantucket Bookworks.

Murphy was quiet but seemed content to Carly, as Hazel rambled on about whether to get Liam a stuffed whale and a Nantucket hoodie or would he rather have a baseball hat?

"I know he's getting older," Hazel said, in defense of her choice, "but he still loves his stuffies and why would we want him in a rush to grow up, right? Or maybe you're thinking something like a mask and a snorkel, honey?" Without giving her husband a chance to respond, she continued, "And Sofia would just die for that lightship basket charm bracelet, don't you think? Also a hoodie. Or maybe one of those cropped ones we saw?"

"Slow down, woman," Murphy said with a chuckle, "all good choices — except the crop top. She's eleven years old, hon, I'm afraid to go there yet. You know what, I was also thinking how Liam would love that mini remote-control speedboat we saw...anyway, we have time. Let's just enjoy tonight, okay? Maybe a nightcap on the back porch when we get back. We won't be able to see the ocean but I bet we can hear it."

The fog turned the headlights of oncoming cars into hazy dizzying orbs in the black night. Without warning, Gus slammed on the brakes, sending the Land Cruiser skidding on the slick road. The tires squealed as they veered to the side and spun one hundred and eighty degrees before coming to a stop, facing the opposite direction on the bike path.

A thick silence hung in the vehicle for long seconds.

"Is everybody okay?" Gus's voice pierced the quiet.

"That was the biggest buck I have ever seen," Murphy said, softly from the back seat, "that could have ended very differently — good job, man."

Hazel's muffled sobs landed heavily from behind Carly's seat as she pressed herself into her husband. "It's okay, we're okay, right? We're okay..."

"Sshh," Murphy whispered, stroking his wife's hair.

Carly registered these things peripherally as she touched the spot on her head that had slammed against the window in the spinout. It hurt. Her fingers ran over the egg that was forming there before tracing the old scar on her temple.

"Carly," Gus said, "are you hurt? Look at me, are you bleeding? Carly? *Carly—*"

There's so much blood! Mom! Mommy! He's bleeding, MOM, MOM, help him, there's so much blood!

Carly was eight years old again and back in her mother's luxury BMW on that horrible night. The night her mother lost control of the fancy car she bought instead of the Volvo her dad wanted her to buy. It was dark, raining so hard, and her mother lost control of the car, spinning out into a tree on her little brother's side of the car in the back seat beside her. So much blood. The white light of the street lamp had glared off the shattered glass all over them and painted her brother in an unearthly scarlet shimmer. Carly had screamed and screamed until her throat burned. But her mother didn't answer. She was slumped over the steering wheel.

All Carly would remember later was the quiet inside that car, how completely alone she was, until sirens pierced the night. She never saw her brother again. He was four years old and he was dead.

"Carly," Gus said, shaking her shoulder gently, "talk to me, are you hurt?"

Carly nodded slowly. "I'm fine," it came out as a whisper, "how's the car? Can we drive it? I want to go home." She sat staring at the strip of grass that separated the bike path from the woods, rubbing the side of her head that hit the window. She put the window down and took in gulps of the damp air as Gus maneuvered the car back onto Milestone Road.

They drove in silence the rest of the way until Gus saw Carly shaking and asked Murphy if there was a beach towel or blanket in the back. Murphy found an old quilt and did his best to reach up front and drape it around Carly's shoulders.

"Do you think she's in shock or something?" Hazel said, once her own sobs had settled, "should she see a doctor?"

As soon as they'd pulled into the driveway of the house Carly unbuckled her seatbelt, opened her door and vomited on the shell driveway.

"Water would be good," Carly said, softly, straightening in her seat, "I'm fine."

"Could you get a cup of water while I sit with her a minute?" Gus said to Hazel. "Maybe it was the tequila? I got this, go ahead in you guys."

"Thanks," Carly said to Gus when they were alone, "nobody wants an audience when you're puking your guts out. How about we sit out back for a bit?"

"How about I get you set up out on the porch with your water and this blanket while I hose this little protein spill down and join you in a minute — how does that sound?"

"I owe you one," she said, opening the glove box in search of a napkin, "can't take me anywhere. And I completely understand if you do not want to join me out back, really dude, above and beyond the call of duty."

"Not at all," he said, settling Carly in one of the deep wicker chairs, putting her cup of water on the side table and settling the quilt over her. "BRB, as the kids say."

"You did not just say that, oh Jesus."

He grinned, tossing her a finger-gun over his shoulder as he walked around to the front of the house. Carly watched as he disappeared behind a hedge of hydrangeas, struggling to untangle the whirlwind of emotions he left in his wake.

She pulled the blanket tighter around her as her body gave an involuntary shiver. Arbitrary thoughts pinged inside her brain, steering her in any direction but the one that threatened to take her down.

Was Antonia still on her date? Where did they end up — did she and David have chemistry? Would they go out again, become a thing, would Carly lose the company of the first friend she'd made? How about Hazel and Murphy? Were they having wild sex upstairs or was Hazel back on her phone while Murphy channel surfed? Was Remi blackout drunk yet? Flirting with men, *boys*, she wouldn't remember but that Burke would?

Her thoughts ricocheted — fading before taking root, failing to land on the most important one. The accident that stole her little brother away from her forever. And in many ways, her mother too. She'd been repressing it for twenty-one years, her entire adulthood. Her parents had gotten her therapy but it had always seemed to Carly that it was happening to someone else. How did an eight-year-old truly grieve the loss of a sibling? A horrific, bloody loss that she'd actually seen happen?

She'd pushed it down and away, telling her parents, her teachers, anyone who asked, that she was fine. It was all she could do. Should it have been her to die instead of Dillon? Had her mother wished it had been her? *Why had she survived?*

Her grandmother had been the one to hold her while she cried, never rushing her grief, never trying to hush it away with empty words. She just stroked Carly's hair, let her tears soak into her sweatshirt and told her it would all be alright. Her own mother was inconsolable, unreachable.

In the months that followed, when the house felt hollow and her heart was a stone, it was Gram who sat with her on the porch swing, their hands wrapped around warm mugs of tea. She'd listened, never asking Carly to move on, only reminding her that she wasn't alone. Gram's love was steady, a safe space in a world that suddenly felt cruel and unpredictable.

Losing her Gram years later felt like a brutal reminder that the world didn't care, that everything could be ripped away in an instant. It was as if the universe had shown her the worst of its cruelty, and she'd obsessed for years about unforgiving twists of fate befalling the people in her life.

Was there anyone or anything that could help her rise above her fear and the weight of her unworthiness? What great enough thing could Carly possibly do in the world to compensate for being the one to live?

Chapter Thirty-Six

CARLY JUMPED IN HER seat when Gus put a mug of hot tea on the table beside her. "Oh my God, you scared me," she said, sitting up, "this is so nice, you didn't have to do that." She brought the hot tea to her lips then wrapped her hands around the mug. He took the seat beside her, and tapped her drink with his.

"Mmm, this is delicious — what flavor is this?" she said.

"Orange Grove vanilla herbal tea. Decaf. It was my mom's favorite and her remedy for all things."

"And is that *your* remedy for all things?" she asked, nodding toward his tumbler of whiskey. Or do I just have that I-need-a-drink effect on you?"

"No. I do enjoy a good glass of bourbon or two, but I don't abuse it as a fix-all — if that's what you're asking. And there isn't anyone or anything that could make me feel like I need to get drunk."

"A self-possessed man. I can see that about you," she said, leaning back in the chair and staring out at the fog that danced in a ghostly swirl around the porch lights. She shivered again.

Gus was quiet for a beat. "It wasn't the tequila, was it," he said, turning to face her silhouette, "that upset you like that. You seemed almost traumatized — like you'd seen a ghost or something. I could be totally overstepping, but if you want to talk about it, I just want you to know that I'm here."

There was a long silence. They could hear revelers a few doors down, a happy summer party somewhere near — laughing and animated strains of conversation drifted over to them on the wind. "And perceptive too," she finally said, "No. It wasn't the tequila."

"Does that mean you want a splash of bourbon in your tea?" he said.

"I mean, I wouldn't say no..."

Gus tipped a dash into her Orange Grove and turned out the porch lamps to see what they could see. Which wasn't very much and only heightened their other senses. The smell of the salty, piney, ocean air swirling around them and the hypnotic sound of the muffled surf rolling in and then back out.

"I watched my little brother, Dillon, die," she said into the darkness, "he was four and I was eight. We were both in the back seat of my mother's 7 Series BMW — notoriously terrible in weather — I would later learn. It was a stormy night on a winding back road, sideways rain. We spun around — it felt like ten times — before the car careened to a crashing stop after bouncing off a huge tree. It was on my brother's side, and my mother's. The night was black but for the eerie light of the lamppost on my brother — covered in dark shining blood and sparkling broken glass. It was the last time I saw Dillon. If you don't count my dreams."

Gus reached for her hand across their chairs in the dark, his fingers brushing lightly over hers. She responded by turning her palm up to settle comfortably in his, a silent understanding passing between them. The moment was over as soon as it had started as she slid her hand out of his and wrapped it back around her mug. She couldn't, wouldn't let herself get carried away by sentiment, sorrow, or any other damn thing with this man.

"I never think about it," she said, "that probably sounds so cold. And I can't say that I remember very much of who I was before. There is only after. *After Dillon.* It was Grayson's loss too, my big brother, but I guess I always carried some level of guilt about it — about being there, about not being able to prevent it. About being the one to live. *Survivor's guilt*, therapists call it. But having a name for it doesn't help."

"I can't imagine it would," Gus said, staying mostly quiet.

"I was in second grade. I was a guest reader that very day in Dill's preschool class down the hall from mine at our elementary school. He'd been so excited. We chose *Cloudy With a Chance of Meatballs*. And he got to sit next to me in front of the class while I read. Dillon loved my voices —I always did the best voices. He would giggle like a little maniac. Which got everyone else laughing." Carly swiped at the tears before they could fall and struggled to get the cry out of her voice.

"That kid was pure light. Such an excellent human, you know? Always including everyone, especially if they were sad — asking them why, sharing his stuff — running to hug me at school every time our paths crossed in the hall and on the playground. Mom used to tell me to keep an eye on him. Grayson was already in the upper school across town, so Dill felt like my responsibility. And I loved it! I loved him so much. He was the coolest kid — it was like I was proud he was mine, you know?"

Carly dropped her head in her hands and her shoulders shook. Her whole body quaked with the loss as though it were fresh. "I never wanted to love anything or anyone that much again, ever. I think that's why I skirt around connection," she said quietly. "I can pretend all I want that I'm not looking for it, like I'm too independent, too busy, or too picky. But the truth is, I'm scared. Losing someone like that — so suddenly, so young — it teaches you how fragile everything is. But even with all that... I can't help but still want it. I still hope for it."

Gus didn't rush to fill the silence. He let it sit between them for a moment, like something sacred. Then he reached over, not grabbing, just resting his hand over hers. "Isn't that the most human thing? To crave connection and be terrified of it at the same time? I totally get it," he said, his voice low. "You don't come back from something like that the same. But maybe that's not a bad thing. Maybe it just means you love deep."

She looked down at their hands, the warmth of his touch anchoring her.

"I'm not here to push," he added. "But if you ever do decide to let someone in... they'd be lucky as hell to be the one. You have your whole big, beautiful life ahead of you, you know that, right?"

"Oh, I want to believe that on some level, but it's hard to see sometimes, transient life that I lead. Never in one place very long," she said.

"By design, it sounds like? And what's wrong with trying out lots of things and places? That's how you'll find the right fit."

"Yeah, well, seeing everyone else start to put down roots, get married, and talk about babies just makes me feel behind the eight ball, you know? Like there is no right place or person for me. And like I've done that to myself. After this summer gig, I have no actual idea where I'll be living."

"You're mostly remote with work, right?"

"Yeah..."

"Well, that's the interesting dynamic about remote work. The freedom to live anywhere with an internet connection is both a gift and a challenge. On one hand, it liberates you from geographical constraints, allowing you to choose a home based on personal preference rather than proximity to an office. This flexibility can boost your quality of life, allow you to prioritize lifestyle, family needs, cost of living — all that good stuff, right?" Gus leaned forward in his chair, resting his elbows on his knees, his body language earnest, relaxed. The edges of his hair curled slightly where they brushed the collar of his shirt, and as he spoke, his gaze shifted intermittently to meet hers, a mix of thoughtfulness and vulnerability threading through his words.

"But on the flip side," he continued, "that freedom can also complicate decision-making. With so many options, it must feel hard for you to commit to one place. But I can see that the lack of any sort of anchor location is making you feel rudderless — understandable. Add to that the burden of balancing work-life boundaries and staying productive all falls on you — your self-management skills." She wondered where all this insight was coming from — his work was the farthest thing from being remote.

"Do you charge by the hour, Dr. Wilder?"

He chuckled again. "Let me finish my thought here, Carly. For those who embrace it, remote work's flexibility can open doors to incredible opportunities—living in dream locations, traveling more, sort of custom-building the lifestyle that you want! Sure, it requires a strong sense of self-discipline and clarity about what 'home' means to you — but it also means that *home* doesn't have to be a static place."

"I can get behind that. Lately, I've been spending more time thinking about my photography — how it inspires me to pair the landscapes I capture with the emotional path I'm navigating, creating something that feels real, raw, and connected."

"Sounds like you're onto something. You have the whole world outside your door — and you can choose to live anywhere your heart desires, bound only by the reach of a good internet connection and your imagination."

"You do make it sound dreamy." She was powerless to help the warm crawl of awareness that this compassionate, beautiful man and she would be sleeping under the same roof of this very romantic place.

Chapter Thirty-Seven

THE FOGGY UNREST OF last night had vanished entirely, peeling back a day bathed in sparkling blue clarity. Carly got up with the sun and with purpose. She had that all-over happy feeling you get from a lingering good dream. Nothing she could put her finger on, but rather than overthinking it, she chose to embrace the lightness it brought. She decided to take a bike to Wicked Island Bakery for a loaf of their famous Portuguese bread, *The Islander* breakfast sandwich for herself, and a dozen of their amazing Morning Buns. She was feeling generous and wanted enough to share.

With the salty wind teasing her hair on the bike ride back from the bakery on Bayberry Court, she made up her mind to track down Antonia and get the scoop on her date. She tried not to let herself feel weird about that — about her fifty-five-year-old, gorgeous friend who was out living large while she seemed content to enjoy it vicariously.

Carly pulled the bike beside the shed and was removing her goodies from the basket when Brett's brother, Evan, rolled into the driveway. It was early for visitors and she wondered what he was doing there instead of his parents' place in Tom Nevers where he was staying.

"Hey, morning," Evan said, climbing out from behind the wheel of the Jeep, "glad I caught you."

"It's early — what's up?" Carly said, putting her hand up to shield her eyes from the sun. "Is this your morning outfit or walk-of-shame?"

she said, gesturing to his Nantucket Red pants, Gucci loafers and a wrinkled Brooks Brothers button-down. He kept his sunglasses on so she could neither confirm nor deny evidence of a hangover.

"Ha," he barked, putting his hands in his pockets, "guilty. Crashed at my buddy's in Sconset. Rehearsal dinner last night — turned out to be quite the rager. Had zero clue how much of a party crew his new in-laws are."

"Still a little drunk maybe?" Carly said.

"Nah. Anway, so, we still on for that party out in Madaket?" He stood leaning back against his car, legs casually crossed at the ankles. As though he liked the pose too much to undo it. He radiated that effortless blend of rich-kid privilege and bad-boy charm — straight out of *Pretty in Pink*. His eyes took in the big old house in front of them and paused at an upstairs window. He moved closer with his hands on his hips, "What's the rancher doing up there in the window — spying on you? Not too creepy..."

"What are you talking about," Carly started to say, squinting up into the bright morning sun at Gus's empty window. She didn't know what to think — about Evan or Gus. Was Evan putting the moves on her? What would Gus think seeing them out there? Did it matter? Any misplaced feelings she had for him were just that — *misplaced*. All she knew was that her breakfast sandwich was getting cold and she wanted to be eating it out on her back porch with the sound of the sea serenading her. "Hey, I gotta go, I'll let you know about Madaket."

"Let me put my number in your phone," Evan said, "I know you have Brett's but let's do it this way — he'll space out about getting in touch." Carly gave him her phone to wrap up the conversation and caught the alcohol fumes rising off him.

"Thanks, now go get some sleep maybe?" she said, "or go for a run — that works too, ha!"

"Wise guy," he said, leaning in and kissing her on the cheek, "talk soon."

What? What the absolute hell was going on with this guy? Still drunk, she decided, turning to walk in the front door as Evan backed out of the driveway. She hoped Gus didn't catch *that* — he'd have the completely wrong idea.

Finally, she sank into a chair on the back porch looking out at the aquamarine sea, small cresting swells shimmering in the light. Their easy rocking sway a contrast to the churn of her thoughts.

The egg sandwich was better than she could have hoped; local farm eggs, house-cured bacon, and Vermont cheddar oozing into it all on their special 21-grain bread. The only thing missing was a strong mug of French Roast. She'd been so excited to dive into her sandwich that she forgot to make coffee. Closing her eyes against the sun, she let its warmth seep into her skin, its delicate heat unfurling through her body and quieting her mind.

The slap of the porch screen door broke her from her swimming thoughts, the smell of fresh brewed coffee had her sitting up. The rich steaming roast felt like a hug.

"Morning," Gus said, offering Carly a cup, black, the way she liked it. He paid attention. Jake brought her coffee with milk for three years.

"This is exactly what I needed, thank you so much," she said, "you read my mind. Oh! Go grab a bun from the kitchen — I bought a bunch."

"Now you're reading my mind — my mouth started to water just at the sight of them in that glass dome thing — wasn't sure they were up for grabs."

"I should have put a sticky note on it that says *eat me*! They're amazing, all super buttery and vanilla-y and cinnamon-y and whatever sorcery they're using over at Wicked Island Bakery. Grab me one too! I need to dip it in this coffee." She couldn't quite account for her bouncy mood but stopped herself from questioning it.

No sooner had Gus settled into the chair beside her, placing their goodies on the little table with napkins then Antonia came around the privet hedge from her place, cup of coffee in hand.

"Howdy neighbors," she said, in her sunny Georgia lilt, "well, isn't this adorable!"

"Mor-ning!" Carly sang, "pull up a chair — you want a bakery-fresh treat? We'll split mine — I mean do I really need this on top of my breakfast sammy? No."

"Ooh, I might just have a tiny taste if that's alright," Antonia said, folding her petite form into the seat beside Gus. "Isn't this the most gorgeous morning? What are y'all up to today?"

"Oh, no — no you don't. Not so fast — we're gonna need date details. And how do you look this put together already?" Carly asked, taking in Antonia's perfectly applied but barely-there eye makeup, her white top and cream shorts, and impeccable mani-pedi. Flawless.

"Well, let's just say it's not exactly effortless, darlin," Antonia said, with a grin, "it takes more time than you think to make it look like I've spent no time at all. Don't you be fooled. And don't take your beautiful, supple, young skin for granted for a single minute, you hear me?"

"I do hear you. But how are we supposed to appreciate our youthful complexion when we're so consumed with losing it to the wrong moisturizer, the collapse of the ozone, and sunscreen that causes cancer instead of protecting against it? It's like we've been brainwashed into believing we're already falling apart. That the voo-doo chemicals and processed crap in *everything* today will age us twice as fast. I mean there are people *my* age getting Botox and fillers and plumpers — I don't even know what to do with that."

"Remember this, *today is as young as you'll ever be...*"

"Great." Carly sighed and leaned back in her chair. She knew you weren't supposed to compare yourself to everyone else. But how you do it anyway. Antonia seemed effortlessly youthful and glamorous— had the best that money could buy — but at what expense in the grand scheme of things?

They sat quietly, lost in their own thoughts. Carly considered Hazel and Murphy, who'd carefully mapped out their lives together

— relationship, marriage, kids — the whole plan. But life doesn't always follow a script. What happens when your children become your entire world, and somewhere in the chaos, you forget to nurture your marriage?

And what about Remi and Burke — where were they headed? Carly didn't think it was the altar. Or maybe they would make the perfect couple, their mutual self-interest creating some unlikely but workable balance.

And then there was August Wilder, Colorado cowboy... Carly couldn't help but allow glimpses of a life with someone like him in a place like that — with big skies, majestic peaks, and endless land and horses and adventure. A house tucked in the foothills, a husband she'd be wildly attracted to forever, and curious, compassionate children.

Not that she'd given it *any* thought at all. Was she afraid of wanting that for herself? Had she become so fixated on other people's relationships, scanning for cracks and failures, because she was worried those same things might befall her? Then she remembered something her father had told her: the only guarantee in life was that there were no guarantees.

"What are you thinkin about?" Gus asked Carly, "pretty quiet over there."

Yikes. He wasn't getting any of that out of her. Good thing her thoughts weren't dancing over her head in a glossy bubble. "Enough about me," she diverted, "Antonia still hasn't filled us in on her date with Dave."

Chapter Thirty-Eight

GUS FINISHED HIS COFFEE and pastry leaving the ladies to their date talk. Carly felt a tug of disappointment at his departure.

"Okay, spill the tea, woman, was there chemistry? Kissing? There def wasn't a sleepover because you look like this," Carly teased, gesturing with a game show hostess flourish toward Antonia.

"Actually....."

"Wait, *what*? You spent the *night*?" Carly asked, leaning forward in her seat, swatting at Antonia's smooth tanned leg, "you did *not*!"

"Oh don't you look at me like that, we're not kids! He was lovely and, yes, we definitely had chemistry. And his spot over in Tom Nevers, ooh-wee, let me tell you! On a little rise with his infinity pool looking like it might just might spill down onto the rolling moors, with the ocean in the distance...it was really something."

"Infinity pool? Hot tub too, I imagine? Wow, how the other half lives... What am I talking about, you *are* the other half." Carly sat back, picturing the property, *just a little summer place*, trying to imagine that life.

"Yup, sold his tech company a few years back after he lost his wife to breast cancer and bought this place to hide from the world. His words. Two grown kids who visit in the summer, but nowhere near as much as he thought they would. Isn't it always the way?"

As if Carly would have any idea about that. Nope. Carly's parents weren't buying island summer retreats or indulging their children with big family vacations. They'd been busy working. And as soon as she and Grayson were old enough, they worked all summer too. Work had filled the hours, the days, the years for her family — she'd always figured that was by design. They'd been irreparably fractured the night Dillon died. The silent, invisible hemorrhaging of that loss had never truly stopped. And Carly never questioned it, and she'd been afraid to want more.

"So, are you and David going to see each other again?" Carly said, shaking off the lingering shadow of grief that always seemed to loom just beneath the surface. "You seem happy, I'm glad you guys had fun."

"Oh, sweetheart, don't look so sad — I'm not abandoning you," Antonia said, putting her perfectly manicured, bejeweled hand over Carly's.

It was silly, Carly decided, she and Antonia barely knew each other. Why shouldn't she go out on dates every night? More power to her. Even as fresh instincts and tentative plans were starting to poke through the surface, Carly couldn't shake the feeling that she should be further ahead by now.

"Don't be crazy, Antonia, that's why you're *here* — in a beach house on Nantucket — to have so much fun for yourself. You deserve it, you've earned it. Please. Do not worry about me. I have a party to go to and everything — you remember those guys I told you about? The brothers, Brett and Evan? Well, Brett was one of the guys who helped restore the Land Cruiser and they grew up here and they know people. They're super nice, took me to the brewery one day — and then we ran into them on the beach. They invited me to a house party out in Madaket and *boom,* we're like besties. *And* they're good-looking guys so hopefully have some hot friends, you know?" she said with a weird little laugh she barely recognized as her own. The caffeine was hitting.

"Well then, I am glad to hear all that," Antonia said.

If Carly could have seen the look on Gus's face at the screen door, she'd have known that he was *not* so glad to hear all that.

"Maybe we can have a double date or something, if, you know, things work out with you and Brett. Or was it Evan?"

"Oh, no, no, no, it's not like that at all. Brett has a girlfriend and Evan — well he has *player vibes* coming out of every pore of his body, so, yeah, *no*—"

Before Carly could finish her thought, she heard the sound of the Land Cruiser roaring to life and seashells spinning under its wheels as it left the driveway. Which was odd — Gus hadn't asked if she needed the car or mentioned that he did. She wondered if everything was alright. Come to think of it, she hadn't heard from Keith in a couple days since she'd double-checked on the status of the hot water heater — maybe she should check in.

If she were being honest with herself, what she wanted to do was low-key pick Keith's brain about August Wilder. Specifically details on the fiancée. Carly thought Gus would have brought her up by now and that she'd have learned more about her, about *them*, organically. But that didn't seem to be happening.

"Penny for your thoughts?" Antonia asked, the concern in her eyes clear, despite the smooth, Botoxed forehead that refused to betray even a hint of a furrow.

"Not worth even that. I was just wondering about Gus's personal life and why he hasn't mentioned his fiancée at all, I mean it's not like we haven't spent time together and talked about a ton of other stuff, you know? I mean, I know it's none of my business or anything but..."

Antonia did a little gasp, covering her open mouth with her hand, "Wait a minute — you *like* him, like him don't you? How did I not see that?"

"Okay, we are not *twelve,* and no, no, I do not. How stupid would that be anyway? He lives two thousand miles away and, oh yeah, he's getting *married!*"

"Oh my dear lord, I should have seen this right away," Antonia said, "Oh, sugar, what are we going to do with you?" Antonia seemed to look at her through a new lens and Carly felt ten kinds of stupid. "David must know some single eligible men here—"

"Stop. Please do not do that. What you can do is maybe help me come up with something cute to wear to this party? And I don't mean shopping in the bougie boutiques downtown — can't afford that — but help me pick from what I already have, okay?"

"I can do that," Antonia said, "and of course you're welcome to anything of mine."

Carly spit out a short laugh, "Ha! As if anything of yours would fit me."

Just then, Remi walked out onto the porch with a glass of water in one hand and a giant cup of coffee in the other. She took a seat next to Carly, lowering herself gingerly down into the chair. Even her hair looked hungover.

"Never again," she said, "it always feels like such a good idea at the time."

"Looked like you guys were having a good time," Carly said.

"Wait, you were at the Chicken Box last night? I don't remember seeing you at all," Remi said, "that band was sick though, right?"

"You went to the Box?" Carly asked, "um, no, I wasn't there. I was talking about Gaslight. You and Burke were partying pretty hard and telling us about Cru."

Remi sat quietly, leaning back in her chair, her mouth slightly open. Carly couldn't tell if she'd drifted off or was just lost in trying to piece together the night.

"There you are!" Burke said, letting the screen door slap behind him.

"Sshh," Remi said, leaning slowly forward, resting her elbows on her knees, cradling her head in her hands, "Jesus, not so loud. And where were you?" she asked, craning her neck to face Burke standing there in running clothes, dripping with sweat, and drinking a tall glass of something green.

"What — is it opposite day?" Murphy said, coming around from the front of the house with Hazel after parking their bikes beside the shed. "Isn't Remi usually the one drinking something green?"

"Instead of *looking* green?" Hazel added. "Girl, you do not look so good."

"I feel *great*," Burke said, taking a long swig of his kale concoction.

"Nobody asked," Remi said, "and it must have been all the dancing with that redhead — you were such a tool out there." There was a collective eyebrow raise among the group.

"Well, babe, you looked pretty busy at the pool table. Or was it that the pool table was busy holding you up—"

They were interrupted by Murphy's pants ringing with Hazel's phone. He caught the name *Steven* on the screen as he was handing it over to his wife.

"Who is Steven?" Murphy said, as Hazel fumbled to deny the call, "Help me out here, Haze..."

"It's not what you think, Murph, I promise you," Hazel said, shifting her small bag from the Sconset Market to the other arm.

Everyone turned in unison at the sound of Remi scrambling off the porch and retching into the bushes. A flurry of hasty exits followed, leaving Carly and Antonia behind, exchanging a glance before looking out at the ocean in shared silence.

Chapter Thirty-Nine

T HE SWEET, RICH MORNING Buns mocked Carly from inside the crystal dome. Everyone had scattered to their own corners leaving Carly alone in the big kitchen contemplating life. How had the clear blue day collapsed already?

Carly had assumed that happy would be the prevailing mood for people on vacation. But was human nature so fraught that you, on some unconscious level, couldn't help but sabotage your own joy? Why was it so hard to be content? Why didn't it last? She had friends who used ChatGPT as their own personal AI therapist, their Magic 8-Ball — maybe there was something to it.

"Well, look at that," she said to herself, staring at the screen of her phone, my robot counselor is giving me a whole list of reasons why we kill our own joy. *Fear of vulnerability* made sense. Then there's how we sort of *dress-rehearse tragedy* to guard against disappointment. If you imagine the worst, you won't be blindsided if it happens. Totally reasonable.

Then there was *unresolved trauma*, where loss or failure create the narrative that good things don't last. Of course! You'd crush a good thing before anything else can destroy it.

Everyone in that house had their own stuff.

Her thoughts drifted back to Gus—why had he peeled out like that? Was it bad news from home, or something to do with the girlfriend? *Was there even a girlfriend?* She had no way of knowing, and it really shouldn't matter to her... but it did. She felt like she had glimpses of his world, pieces of his story, yet so much remained a mystery—pages of his life that were blank. Or just out of reach.

She took her phone out to a chair on the lawn and pulled up Keith's contact in her email.

Hey Keith, It's been a minute. Just checking in. Things are fine here at the house, we've been pretty lucky weatherwise. I can totally see why your grandmother loved it here so much. I was just wondering about your buddy, Gus. Has he reached out at all — said anything about how things are going? I know you shared some of his personal stuff with me because he's your friend and you want him to enjoy his time here — but I'm afraid of overstepping.

You mentioned a fiancée — why isn't she here? Is he supposed to be taking a break from her too? He hasn't said a thing about her. God, this is all probably none of my business — but any insight you could pass along would be great.

Thanks, Carly

She reread what she'd written, squinting in the bright sun, and decided it was all wrong — not professional at all. On her way to delete the draft, she hit *send* instead.

Her stomach dropped, what had she done? How the hell would all that sound to Keith? She could picture it now — Keith sharing it with Gus — subject line: WTF? Her stomach rolled.

By the time she'd googled *unsending an email*, the thirty-second window she would have had to do so had expired. All she could do was wait for a reply and hope Keith was too busy to read too much into it. And she sure as shit wasn't going to sit there and wait for it.

"Are you busy?" Hazel said, startling Carly as she materialized beside her. Her eyes were red and watery as she flopped back into the chair beside Carly.

"Hi, not busy, what's up?" Murphy and Hazel's cell phone drama was fresh in Carly's mind as she considered her desired level of involvement. Of course she was curious, but how much of their chaos did she want to absorb into her own day. She really did not want Hazel to be cheating on Murphy with some dude named Steve. She couldn't believe it, wouldn't believe it, and certainly wouldn't be complicit. Her heart clenched like a fist hoping Hazel wouldn't confide the unthinkable.

Did love ever last?

"Everything is backfiring," Hazel began, "I wanted this week to be so special, you know? Kind of like a second honeymoon. Which seems like forever ago. Why is everything falling apart?"

Carly was hoping Hazel would continue, be more specific, so she kept quiet and waited a beat.

"I mean, I tried," Hazel said, "I tried not to text so much — but once you have kids, all bets are off, nothing is the same. You don't just stop thinking about them and worrying about them because you're not with them. It just doesn't work that way! I guess this can't really be a second honeymoon — it has to be something different."

Carly could get behind that, it made some sort of sense. "And Murphy doesn't share this sentiment exactly?"

"Not exactly. I mean he is great, don't get me wrong, he's the best! A thoughtful husband, a hands-on dad...but he's just way better at the *out of sight, out of mind*, you know? Like he doesn't get the damage control necessary for a tween daughter who's beside herself because she thinks she's missing *everything* back home. The absolute crushing

FOMO of the Instagram posts of the pool parties she's not there for, or the photo of the boy she's been fantasizing about for the last six months sitting next to her best friend on a blanket at the beach. Her world is reeling and I'm here on fantasy island."

"Whew," Carly said, "sorry you're going through all this. I can't imagine balancing it all." *Was Hazel getting to the Steven guy?*

"Right? So there I was, trying to come up with something super fun and special for Murph — but something that both of us would enjoy. Enter Steven, boat captain. Did I want to charter a fishing excursion for Murphy? He loves to fish, but me, not so much. So then I thought of the sunset cruise — perfect, right?"

"Yes, sounds good," Carly said, "I'm with you so far..."

"SO many choices: cocktail cruise with a larger group, cheaper but, meh... Or a private charter? Sail boat or a less romantic fishing boat charter situation? That's why I've been in contact with this Steven — only I wanted it to be a *surprise*, of course, which looks a whole lot like I'm keeping some secret. Which, duh, I am!"

"Aahh. Now I get it. This is such a sweet idea, Hazel, *ugh,* I'm so sorry this is happening. So what did you tell your husband? I mean, I'm just trying to see this from his perspective, like if you saw some strange girl's name come up on his phone, what would you be thinking?"

"I would trust him! Like I want him to trust me. No, I'm keeping the surprise, dammit."

"Okay, okay...we can work around this. Let's think. I mean, you guys are such awesome people — I'm aware I barely know you, but anyone can see what a devoted mom and wife you are and how Murphy worships the ground you walk on. Maybe you're both kind of struggling with how to just be a couple without the kids around 24/7... Maybe Murphy's feeling a little lost without them, just like you, but doesn't know how to express that? A little identity crisis maybe? I mean, I have those all the time."

"You might be onto something, Carly — why didn't I see that? And he probably thinks I'm spending more time on the phone with the kids than paying attention to him, oh my God..."

"You're just trying to be all things to all people! You're amazing, Hazel, a natural caregiver! And that's such a good thing. We can fix this."

Hazel sat hunched over, elbows on her knees, head cradled in her hands. Walkers passed along the bluff walk, their glances flitting between the grand old houses and the unintentional intimacy of Carly and Hazel's moment.

What about all those people just strolling by—what was their story, who did they love, were they celebrating something, hiding from something?

What was the secret to making the delicate threads that tied relationships together endure? Against time's relentless wear....

Carly could imagine people in love staring out at the homes on the bluff overlooking the big blue sea — searching for some great beauty to match the enormity of their own emotions. The grandeur of it all becoming a canvas on which to project the largesse of their own desires, disappointments, dreams.

When you were in love, did you see everything as some reflection of your own story? And when you were feeling lost, did you see everything as a reminder of what you didn't have?

"How about telling Murph that the texts with this Steven guy have to do with a surprise for him — but you don't have to tell him what the surprise is — will that work?" Carly said.

"I guess," Hazel said, "but now he'll try to guess and he'll ruin it, I *know* it — he'll guess it's something to do with a boat. *Dammit.* I had this whole vision in mind — we'd be down town, walking along the wharf like we were just going out to dinner, and then we'd step aboard some gorgeous yacht — the look on his face!"

"He'll still have that look! It will still be awesome, Hazel. And you know what I think? That part of the fun is in the looking *forward* to something, that huge anticipation. Right? Like when you're a kid — thinking about Christmas morning was the biggest, best thing in the entire world. Seeing that pile of presents under the tree, wondering which were for you and what they might be. It was never about what was inside the wrapping — can we even remember the gifts? It was the anticipation..."

"You're right, Carly, thanks for the perspective. And we're grownups for crissakes — we make adjustments."

"Exactly. Now go find your husband and do something fun."

Chapter Forty

Once she was alone again, Carly found her thoughts circling back to Gus. Where had he gone, and when would he be back? Not that she needed the car or felt necessarily marooned—it wasn't about logistics. It was just some unsettled, peculiar sense of being left behind. It gave her pause. And it shouldn't. The fact that it did meant she'd crossed a line, letting herself spend too much time in his orbit.

Her phone pinged with an email notification. It was Keith. A queasiness shoved in. She was terrified to open Keith's reply to her accidental email. Sweat beaded on her forehead as her fingers hovered over her phone.

Good Morning Carly,

I'm glad to hear all is well on the *far away island* — I bet you didn't know that's what the word Nantucket means! So you think Gus is the shit, huh? I should have predicted that — most women do. I guess rugged handsome cowboys are in these days. Well then you'll be interested to know that he is, in fact, not engaged. That ended a bit ago apparently. (Not that I'm encouraging you to hook up with the guests!) Evidently Gus and Emelia had some sort of falling out which was part of the reason behind this east coast sabbatical. I haven't heard much from him — I assumed that meant he was living it up, getting lucky, and whatever jackassery goes on out there, before returning to reality.

I was glad to hear the water heater is functioning properly with sufficient hot water for all the showers — and can I assume no issues with the washer and dryer? Both are new after having plumbing issues — corrosion and that sort of thing.

Let me know if you need anything.

Best,
Keith

Gus was *single*? A tumble of emotions knocked around inside her. Confusion, relief, doubt, jealousy. A spark of possibility. Thoughts collided, shifting and rearranging like the bright shards of a kaleidoscope. *Living it up? Getting lucky?* Is that what he was there to do? Sweet Jesus. This information was as intoxicating as it was complicated. Carly couldn't decide which feeling to land on or how to proceed.

What did she even want? That was a question Carly needed to answer before doing anything at all with Gus. And what *didn't* she want? Was she clear on any of it? Her insides were a Ping-Pong ball game, she couldn't sit still one more minute. She wanted to think about anything else besides Gus being single. But it was also the only thing she wanted to think about.

She put her bikini on under her t-shirt and shorts, made a quick turkey and cheddar sandwich on thick slices of the fresh Portuguese loaf she'd bought, grabbed sunscreen, a towel, and a book, putting it all in the basket of her bike and took off for Sconset Beach.

On Sankaty Road, she crossed to head east to the beach and nearly skidded out in the sand when she saw the very distinct green and white Land Cruiser headed her way. Gus. Her legs turned to goo. She didn't trust herself to muster a casual wave and panicked — choosing the most awkward strategy of pretending not to see him.

Had he seen her? With her new Cisco trucker hat jammed over a messy ponytail it was possible he didn't. Bikes were everywhere, possibly outnumbering cars in the village of Sconset. She pushed on until she reached the bike rack on the beach then grabbed her things to find a quiet spot. She was suddenly desperate to be lying in the sun, limbs molten in the perfect seventy-four degrees, with the breeze off the water lifting the hair from her forehead. The low surf rolled in and rushed out in a rhythmic hush.

In that foyer of sleep, Carly's mind broke free, detaching itself from the constraints of reality. Loose scenarios unspooled like flickering stories on a movie screen rendering her weightless, untethered, and brimming with the possibility of everything and nothing all at once.

A distant squeal broke into her semiconscious...a seagull wheeling overhead? A little kid being chased by his big brother? It rose and fell before breaking apart then startled her awake. *Dillon!* her heart shouted the way it sometimes did and the memory unlocked.

Shallow breathing replaced her peace of mind as her heart raced with the jittery memory. Carly sat up and hugged her knees, staring out at the blue water. Her little brother had been gone so much longer than he'd been alive, but sometimes the weight of his absence hit her as though no time had passed. People assumed that four short years with him couldn't leave a lasting wound, that being just a kid herself when it happened — she'd surely have moved on. Wasn't that what she'd told herself over the years?

It didn't haunt her every day; she'd learned to navigate life around the void. But every so often, something would crack the seal — an unexpected reminder or fleeting memory — and the pain would resurface. In those moments, she faced a choice: allow herself to sit with the grief and feel its full weight, or carefully box it back up and return it to the quiet corner of her heart where it lived.

Had it shaped her? How she approached life and love — always with a cautious hand, as if she were bracing herself for more inevitable loss? How she knew that everything precious could slip away in a single cruel instant? In the time it took a heart to beat. Or to stop.

After the accident, Carly poured all the love she had into her parents and big brother, as if by loving them enough, she could make up for the hollow Dillon's death had left behind. But her family seemed fractured beyond repair, each of them trapped in their own cocoon of grief. Carly started to realize that no matter how much love she gave, she was pouring herself into a hole that wouldn't fill.

Eventually, her family reshaped itself around the absence, a quiet recalibration of daily life. Four place settings at the dinner table instead of five, four stockings hung by the fire on Christmas morning. The new normal — a patch in their family's tapestry. They didn't speak of it, but the missing fifth presence was always there, woven into the fabric of their lives.

Carly stood, brushing off the sand and the weight of those memories, and walked into the water. It was cool and it grounded her back to the present. The pull of the past loosened as she went deeper, each cool step rooting her in the present.

She reflected on how nature and life seemed to renew itself every day in subtle yet profound ways. After fires and floods, land and its wildlife instinctively healed—trees sprouted, rivers cleared, animals returned.

Every single thing in nature, like the daily rise of the sun and the rhythms of the seasons, echoed a quiet reminder of life's ability to rebuild and persist, reminding her to focus on the here and now. The music of the waves lapping at her legs whispered a quiet promise to carry her forward, one moment at a time.

"Thought I might find you here," Gus's voice was carried on the wind as he walked up behind her in the low waves.

"How—"

"I passed you on the road. Figured with your beach towel hanging out of the bike basket you probably weren't headed to the market. And I felt bad about taking the car."

He stood there, hands tucked into the pockets of his shorts. The wind played with his hair, brushing it across his eyes. His pale feet, magnified by the clear, shallow water, caught her eye and made her smile. There was something vulnerable and endearing seeing him like that, the contrast of the wardrobe he was more used to of jeans, boots, and a cowboy hat. It was as though he had stepped out of one world and into hers, there was a softness to it.

"Don't feel bad about that — Keith said it was yours to use." Just saying Keith's name made her pulse pick up speed, his email looming, daring her to confront it.

"I know, but it was rude to just take off without asking if you'd had plans to use it."

"Yeah — and what was that taking off like a bat outta hell? Can't do that around here, bro, you could take out old Mrs. DuPont on her vintage Schwinn from a couple doors down."

"Of *the* DuPonts?"

"How should I know, probably, ha!" It felt good to laugh, "this island is stupid with billionaires you know. You got your old money, your new money, and then there's your stolen money — like how many Ponzi schemes are we gonna read about, right?" Then Carly's eyes lit with a recent memory, "Wait a minute — and what about the latest — that guy actually from Colorado — what was his name? He was arrested right here on Nantucket, *fugitive Aspen investor* or something like that — he had some twelve-million-dollar place here somewhere that sold at a foreclosure auction."

"Oh yeah, Burrell, I remember reading something about that guy — wanted in Colorado *and* Nevada. Bad dude. He actually owned a ranch in Taos Valley Ranch, saying he planned to turn it into a therapy retreat center for screen-addicted teens, never happened. Big surprise. He was being tagged across several states for defaulting on big-money loans that he took out against luxury properties. Nantucket got lucky in catching him."

"Like, how much is enough anyway," Carly pondered, making small circles in the water with her foot. "Some of the ridiculously huge estates tucked away here, it's nuts. But it's also a small island, lots of wealthy, politically and financially connected people — it's not like you can hide if you're screwing people over."

She was totally dodging the only thing she wanted to talk to Gus about.

"Is it true that the next body of land out there is Portugal?" he asked, as they stood side by side, looking out over the the vast expanse of the Atlantic.

"Yup, the Azores."

"Hey, what do you say we grab some lunch somewhere? That bun and coffee seem like a long time ago."

Could she leave her turkey sandwich behind for the sea gulls without him seeing?

Chapter Forty-One

THEY MANAGED TO SECURE her bike in the back of the Land Cruiser with the window popped open, handlebars sticking out. The whole effort felt ridiculous in hindsight, considering they were mere steps from the Beachside Bistro, right across the street from the main Summer House restaurant, down by the pool. Tiered flower and herb gardens lined the walkway to the Bistro's bluestone patio overlooking the ocean, where cozy outdoor seating was nestled in the dunes on the beach. A quintessential summer vibe.

Once they were seated with drinks, Carly felt the coil of tension unwind. The sweet perfume of the wild Rugosa roses in bloom all around them and the briny sea beyond.

"This couldn't be more different from Colorado," Gus said, "but I can see the appeal."

Carly thought he'd never looked more handsome than in that moment, in that light with a smile that lit his eyes. She was sure he would see her heart beating against her white tank top.

"Hey gorgeous!" It was like a needle scratching a record in the middle of your favorite song. Evan. "We really have to stop meeting like this," he said, looking way too cocky in a linen shirt and shorts, those Gucci Horsebit loafers again, and grinning from behind his Ray-Bans.

Carly wondered if her expression had betrayed the sweeping shift from dreamy contentment to thinly veiled annoyance. "Evan," she said, nodding to Gus across the table, "you remember Gus from the beach the other day, right?"

"Sure, the ranch hand, right?" Evan delivered the words with a casual smirk that did nothing to mask their sting.

Gus's expression barely changed but the flash in his eyes said everything. Evan had just unmasked himself as an entitled jerk, the kind who saw the world in tiers with himself at the top. The arrogance, the casual dig, the unmistakable air of a narcissist.

Without giving Gus an opportunity to respond, Evan turned back to Carly to say that a bunch of people were going on a pub crawl later downtown ending up at the Box — did she want to join them? Carly definitely did not want to join them. Before he walked away Evan further excluded Gus by reminding her about the party out in Madaket, that Brett and Marin were looking forward to seeing her.

"What a gem that guy is," Gus said, taking a long drink of his water, seeming to gauge Carly's relationship with Evan, "all shiny on the outside but..."

"He's not a bad guy — maybe a little high on himself but not mean-spirited I wouldn't say," Ugh. Was she actually defending the guy who just called Gus a ranch hand? "Maybe he feels threatened, I don't know, no excuses for acting like a douche though. I met him through his brother Brett — who's super nice by the way — before all you guys arrived. It was nice to meet people to hang out with, you know?" She was rambling. Luckily their server appeared at their table to take their order.

"Hmm, I really want to try the chowder but I'll be too full to eat anything else," Carly said, more to herself than anyone else. Looking up at the waiter, she ordered, "I think I'll go with the Baja fish tacos, please. Oh! And that blueberry vodka drink also." She caught the grin on Gus's face as he waited, watching her with an amused expression — as though he found her entertaining. "What?" she asked playfully, "you laughing at me?"

"Never," he said looking into her eyes, before adjusting his focus to order. "Could I please have the bacon cheeseburger, cheddar, fries, medium rare please. And another Grey Lady when you get a chance."

Carly looked out over the dunes to the ocean thinking about how perfect their table was. This was actually the second restaurant meal she and Gus had shared — which was weird, but also...not. What did he think of her? As just a buddy to hang out with? Or worse, like a sister?

"Very cool spot," he said, reading her mind, "So, you like chowder, huh? How about we get all the ingredients to make chowder sometime? We'll go to a fish market, maybe find a farm stand, it'll be fun."

"Sounds like a plan. Should we make it like, I don't know, maybe a family meal with everyone? The six of us?"

He was smiling again, almost laughing. Then he put up a hand to stop her from saying whatever she was going to say, "I'm not laughing at you — it's just that you're so adorable — the way your eyes light up...whether it's for a cheeseburger, fish tacos, or blueberry vodka, or making a big pot of chowder."

The sun shifted, angling his way, and he slipped on his sunglasses. Instantly she felt robbed of the depth of those whiskey eyes.

"And yes, I think that's a great idea including everyone," he said, "and we can eat outside at that long teak table out on the porch."

She clapped her hands at that idea like a little kid. "Oh I love that, perfect! We have those hurricane lanterns we can light and we can do like a cool tablescape with shells and sea glass, I can picture it! Oh and Antonia too, maybe we can get her to make a dessert."

"What's wrong? Your smile just tilted," Gus said.

"Is this all crazy? God, we don't even know if any of them would want this — wouldn't they have plans? Dinner reservations? Cocktail cruise, whale watching? Antonia with her new *David*? I mean, we all just met — maybe this is too much. And it's not like we have to do it tomorrow, we have plenty of time." Carly hadn't anticipated this merging of the limits of her role.

"Exactly. Don't overthink it. We'll figure it out. And even if there's no firm commitment, no worries. We'll make a big pot of chowder anyway, whoever can join will join, it'll be fine. Better than fine."

Carly let go of the breath she was holding, he was right. She couldn't stop herself from imagining the fun she and Gus would have finding the perfect recipe, shopping for all the ingredients, and creating this delicious thing together. She hoped her new knowledge of his single status wouldn't change how she was around him — turn her into some gushing starry-eyed weirdo with a crush.

Their meals came and they dived in hungrily. "Best. Bite. Ever." Carly declared, forming the words around the flaky fish and chipotle aioli perfection.

Feeling buzzed and just the right amount of full after lunch Carly decided nothing could wreck her mood. She would have ridden her bike back to the house but decided it was pretty possible she'd end up tipping over into a hedge. It was less than a two-minute drive to the house, and once she parked her bike in the shed, she grabbed her camera from her room and headed out on foot.

Climbing roses blanketed the cottages of Sconset in June and into July, and Carly was determined to capture their full splendor, knowing those images would be the pièce de résistance of her project. Her first stop was the famous cottage on the corner of Mitchell Street and Broadway, where deep pink roses cascaded over the entire cedar-shingled exterior of the antique home. She paused, ogling at the sheer abundance of blooms, wondering how old the vines were that embraced the little house.

Next stop was Eagle Cottage, a whaling captain's home built in the late 1700's. Possibly the most photographed and painted image on the island, it was an absolute fairytale image with its flowing blush-pink New Dawn roses set against its iconic pink door of the same shade. Carly couldn't take enough photos, switching between wide shots that captured the storybook backdrop and tight closeups of the intricate unfolding blossoms. No wonder Sconset was a paradise for photographers and painters, it hardly seemed real.

Color and antiquity exploded from every corner, every pocket garden and abundant window box, Carly could fill a coffee table book with her photos, a website, a gallery. And she'd barely begun to uncover the charm and magic that was Nantucket Island.

Inside that moment everything in the world seemed possible: finding a love that would stand the test of time, making her home any gorgeous wonderful place she decided, and having the job of her dreams — capturing the breathtaking beauty of the smallest and grandest things — and sharing her view with the world. It would never feel like work.

The vibrating ring of her phone in her pocket jolted her back to the present moment. It was her father. Her mother had been rushed to the hospital, something about chest pains, heart attack or panic attack — they were running tests.

Chapter Forty-Two

WORRY ABOUT HER MOTHER consumed her, along with the haunting feeling of always being in the wrong place at the wrong time. Would she have to leave the island? The responsibility would fall to her — as the single one, the unattached one, with work she could do anywhere. *None of that mattered*, she scolded herself. Her poor mom — Carly only wanted peace and an exciting new life for her mother and her father. Why was this happening? They deserved only wonderful things.

Then her dad specifically told her *not* to come. That her mother was going to be fine — that they were almost 100% sure it had been a panic attack — which can mimic a heart attack, and something about tweaking her meds, blood pressure, or something, she was only fifty-nine. Carly took deep breaths as she walked back along the narrow road to the house. Relief flooded her.

Behind the closed door of her room she flopped back on the bed. She should call Grayson — find out if their dad was being completely honest with her or just trying to spare her the trip south. She hated how far away her parents felt. She hoped she didn't have to leave the island — knowing it would be two or three flights to Asheville, North Carolina.

Carly was at that post-buzz place where things felt dingy when Grayson called. They talked for less than fifteen minutes. Their mother would be fine. Relief and exhaustion gripped her like an undertow. She crawled under her covers and fell asleep until all the light was gone from the sky.

∞

Muffled conversation and laughter pulled her from fractured dreams. Remnants of the afternoon drifted into her foggy brain. She followed their trail, piecing them together before landing on a calm gratitude that her mom was going to be totally fine. The conversation with her brother Grayson had put her heart and mind at an ease that sent her into the sleep of the dead.

She wandered out to the porch where Hazel, Antonia, and Gus were sitting in the late evening sun.

"Hey there, "Antonia said, "we were worried about you, darlin, the captain of our little ship.

"I thought I was the cruise director?" Carly said sleepily, "Captain?"

"Sorry girl," Hazel said, "you have that leader quality about you."

Carly looked from one of them to the other. She was remembering her heart-to-heart with Hazel earlier — wondering how Hazel had decided to handle the mysterious texts from Steven. And the last she'd seen of Remi was her puking in the bushes — had Burke gone about his day solo?

"Status update?" Carly asked, "Is the ship sinking?"

Gus's phone was ringing in his pocket and he excused himself to answer it. "Shoot, does that boy get more handsome every time I see him?" Antonia said, patting the seat next to her for Carly to join them.

"Right?" Hazel said, "he is completely dreamy, but so serious."

"Not that serious," Carly offered, "I mean he can be pretty chill. Like at lunch today we made a bet about the couple beside us — how long it would take before one or both of them looked at their phones

— the winner got to pick the next drink for the other person. I won and he was such a good sport about the Pink Squirrel I ordered him."

"Wait, back that lunch truck up," Hazel said, "at lunch today? Like you were on a date?"

"Shh, NO, Jesus," Carly said, "Summer House Bistro is like steps away from the beach and we were starving."

"The beach?" Antonia said, "you lost me. You two do a lot of hanging out."

"It's not like that," Carly sighed, explaining it to them, about how he'd gone looking for her at the beach after feeling bad about storming off in the car.

"Um, *hello*? Can you hear yourself?" Hazel said, "Stalking you at the beach because he was worried? Taking you to lunch at one of the most romantic spots on the island?"

"Thank you Hazel," Antonia said, "I thought it was just me, but you see it too, right?"

"Ladies, ladies," Carly said, "until this morning I was under the impression that August Wilder was an engaged man, every moment in his company has been purely platonic, he's the quintessential gentleman."

"Until *this morning*?" Antonia said, her voice rising, "well what in the blue blazes are you getting at then? Carly Hill? Are you telling us that Gus is a free agent?"

"I don't know what I'm telling you," Carly said, her eyes dancing. "Do I think that guy is a total catch? Yes. But he lives a couple thousand miles away for one thing, and he apparently, only fairly recently, broke off an engagement for another thing — or worse, *she* did, I don't know. And if we need a third thing, I'm pretty sure he doesn't see me that way."

"You're pretty sure? Are you also pretty blind?" Antonia said, reaching out to squeeze Carly's leg. "We need an intervention," she continued, turning to Hazel, "don't you think?"

"Stop," Carly said, leaning back in the chair, "there will be no intervention, no matchmaking, no nothing. You all have your own stuff going on, seriously, do not worry about me. I have a million photos I want to take of this island just for pure pleasure, and honestly, I need to figure out where I'm going to be living once this gig is over. A lot on my plate — my parents' health notwithstanding."

Hazel and Antonia exchanged a look. They were ten and twenty-five years older than Carly, respectively. Suddenly, Carly felt like an infant — lacking experience, perspective and with exactly zero wisdom about matters of the heart or life in general. She wasn't a carefree college kid anymore, or a twenty-five-year-old who could still get away with flying by the seat of her pants. Still, she'd been holding onto those old rhythms, as if staying in motion could keep her from facing what was really holding her back.

Chapter Forty-Three

A FEW DAYS ARRIVED wrapped in fog and soaked by rain, and everyone scattered to do their own thing. Some curled up with books, others dove into the board games stashed in the old coffee table chest. There were naps, endless rounds of Crazy Eights and Solitaire, and day drinking on the porch, watching the rain run off the roof. The pace slowed and no one seemed to mind the lazy respite from being on the go.

The skies cleared just in time for the day of the sunset sail for Hazel and Murphy, as well as the party out in Madaket that Carly had decided to go to. Gus had explored the whaling museum and Maria Mitchell's birth place on his own and Carly reluctantly admitted that she missed their easy camaraderie. Then scolded herself for being naïve. Madaket would be perfect and she had yet to experience the west coast of the island — to witness the *California sunset* everyone talked about.

She decided on the coral Tommy Bahama sundress she'd scored at TJ Maxx with her jean jacket —a look that struck the perfect balance between effortlessly cute and *I did not overthink this outfit.* Brett and Evan would pick her up which checked three boxes: one, she wouldn't have to haggle with Gus for the car; two, Brett and Marin would be there to dilute Evan; and three, she wouldn't have to be super conservative about her drinking since she wouldn't be driving. The only drawback she could see was being at their mercy for a ride home. Did Ubers or taxis even go all the way out to Madaket—and then back across the entire island to Sconset? A problem for later.

She had about forty minutes before they would be there to pick her up and the late afternoon light shimmered like champagne in a crystal glass. Instead of trying to capture more images with her camera or check work emails, Carly decided to just sit outside on the porch and be in the moment. The sky was a smooth denim blue reigning over her 180-degree view of the Atlantic Ocean.

"Taste these!" Antonia said, holding two drinks, practically running over from her house next door, "David will be here in less than an hour and I'm trying something new with an Aperol Spritz. I can't decide between adding a splash of gin to deepen the flavor and add complexity? Or maybe swapping out the Prosecco with sparkling rosé for a pinker, fruitier take? Then I was thinking maybe I could add a sprig of fresh rosemary for more of an earthy vibe." Antonia took a seat next to Carly, frantic for her opinion.

"Putting a lot of thought into this, no?" Carly said, taking one of the glasses from Antonia for a deep sip, "Ew, NO, no — is this the gin one? And with the rosemary, oh my God, I may as well be drinking a pine tree. I need a palette cleanser, ick. Why are you trying to masculinize this girly drink?" Carly took a bigger slug of the other one, "Ooh, yes, the rosé is perfect in this one, this is the winner. If he doesn't mind pink and sugar!"

Antonia sat back in the chair seeming to have more on her mind than the drink. "Well, bottoms up then," she said, taking the gin version from Carly and throwing back a healthy slug."

"Um, this is more of a sipping beverage, don't you think?" Carly said, studying her friend, everything a little less put together than usual, "you alright?"

"Kaitlyn's coming." Antonia said.

"Wait, *what*? Kaitlyn, your daughter? Isn't that what you *want*?"

"Yes, YES! I just...she said she might bring her father and—"

"As in your ex? This is crazy — you were so sure she wouldn't come and now she's bringing your ex-husband? Is this a new version of the Parent Trap? What gives?"

"I don't know! I used to think that's what I wanted, you know, for the both of them to give me a second chance," Antonia said, her usual careful composure crumpling, "but dating a man like David has reaffirmed that no, no, I do not want to go back to a guy like Beau."

"Dating? You just met him!"

"I know, it's not like that, I mean I'm not saying I'm head over heels for David, it's just that I like the ease of it, the way he appreciates who I am. You know, that I have my own opinions, that I'm an independent woman — instead of holding those things against me the way I feel Beau did."

"I hear all that. Absolutely, you don't want to go backwards. But what makes you think that's what's going on? I mean, there they are, landlocked out there in the wild west — it's summer — why wouldn't they jump at the chance to come to Nantucket? Maybe you're overthinking everything — your emotions are on the surface."

"How'd you get so wise," Antonia said, giving Carly's leg a little squeeze, and as if really looking at her for the first time said, "and why are you looking so adorable, what did I miss?"

"Party. Madaket — we talked about this."

"Oh yeah, but I thought you were on the fence about it...with Brett's brother really leaning into his condescending, holier-than-thou act."

"Meh — it crossed my mind to blow it off. But I should get to know more people here, you know? And Evan's harmless — you know how guys get their peacock feathers all twisted in the presence of another dude. Besides, I feel like I'm cramping the cowboy's style — he doesn't want to waste all his time with me."

"Well, now how would you know that?" Antonia said, taking another deep sip of her drink, "strikes me as the type of man who knows what he wants, who wouldn't spend one drop of his time doing anything other than that."

"Yeah, well, what's the point exactly? We've been over this. Anyway — good luck with your spritz, I should wait out front for my ride."

"Have a blast, Carly. Maybe your rich, handsome, knight in shining armor is there waiting to meet you."

"Oh brother," Carly said, standing and smoothing the front of her dress, "did you read a lot of Danielle Steele back in the day?"

"Of course I did! And Judith Krantz and Nora Roberts, you betcha. Now, go have some fun."

The ride out to Madaket with the Jeep's top off was a windy one. Carly was glad she didn't spend much time on her hair — she'd learned to embrace the Nantucket version of it. She didn't hate the wavy look compared to the way it normally hung straight and without flair. Evan was in the passenger's seat with a Yeti tumbler of God knew what and she was glad she had a little buzz from Antonia's drink experiment.

"Everyone in the house getting along?" Brett shouted over the wind from the front seat, "it seemed pretty quiet."

"Well, it's not like it's a frat house — they are mature adults, you know," Carly said, rolling her eyes to Marin next to her and leaning forward in her seat.

"Snore," Evan said, "doesn't sound like much fun." He was looking as slick as ever, with that smooth smile, eyes hidden behind his shades. "We'll make up for that tonight, you're gonna love Jeff's place — the beach is basically his back yard."

Sometimes, the six miles of Milestone Road felt endless, but it was the only road in and out of Sconset. And Madaket was another seven miles beyond that—clear across the island. Carly pushed aside her thin reservations about being stranded so far out if she decided she wanted to leave. The wind made it a challenge to have a conversation so she took her phone out to pass the time. She saw a missed text from Gus and couldn't help how her pulse sprinted.

> Just checking to see if you need the car — I'm heading
> into town in a bit. Where are you — beach? Let me
> know.

Pretty straightforward — not a trace of emotion attached to the message. Why did disappointment trickle in? She decided to reply right away instead of agonizing over some witty, perfectly crafted response.

> No worries — I'm on my way to Madaket with Brett
> and Evan. Enjoy.

She hit send and put her phone away. She tried not to wonder where Gus was going or with whom, if there was a *whom*. "Are we there yet?" she whined theatrically from the back seat, "I'm ready for a cocktail."

"Almost," Evan said looking back at her, "shoulda brought a road soda." He clinked the ice in his tumbler with a grin for good measure before draining its contents.

Chapter Forty-Four

BRETT SLOWED THE JEEP as they got into the rugged western tip of the island. It wasn't at all like entering the fairytale village of Sconset but stunning in its remote natural simplicity. Right away Carly could feel its laid-back, rustic charm, with its quiet streets and fewer scattered cottages and homes that feel like they belonged to another era. It was a different kind of escape and a more raw beauty.

They rumbled up the sand driveway of Jeff's house where Jeeps, cars, and trucks were launched haphazardly on the sand along the property. The house sat southwest, high enough to offer sweeping views of the Atlantic and swaths of untouched stretches of beach bordered by swaying beach grass and pathways through the dunes. It felt tucked away and windswept. Carly could already hear the rhythmic sound of waves just beyond and could imagine the constant lull of the ocean.

The wraparound porch of weather-beaten cedar planks was dotted with mismatched wooden chairs and already thick with party people whose laughter and chatter blended with the summer wind. She could imagine reclining there for morning coffee and sunset cocktails .

A driftwood bench sat at one end of the porch next to a pot overflowing with blue and white lobelia. The yard was a mix of wild beach grasses and pockets of blooming hydrangeas in shades of blue and pink. A crooked wooden gate opened to a sandy path that meandered through the dunes where tufts of sea oats swayed and spilled out onto Madaket's wide, golden beach. A fire pit encircled by weathered chairs sat off to the side of the yard where Carly could picture the party moving toward it as it got cooler and darker.

The house had a casual vibe — nothing fancy or overdone where she'd feel like she didn't belong. The stretch of beach and the wide open sea did the heavy lifting. Brett introduced her to a few people before steering her inside for drinks and a bite to eat. She was told Jeff would be grilling the fresh striper he'd caught that morning and also some gourmet sliders with caramelized onions, sharp cheddar, and arugula, with giant portobello mushrooms as a vegetarian option. Her mouth watered just thinking about it.

The kitchen was just what she'd expected in a quintessential summer cottage, with painted wooden cabinets and open shelves that set the mismatched pottery and hand-thrown mugs on display and glass jars filled with beach treasures. The wide cherry island held a plethora of delicious looking things artfully prepared. Had Jeff done it all or was there a girlfriend behind it? There was an enormous charcuterie board with ten kinds of cheese and cured meats, a platter of mini-lobster rolls with lemon aioli served on buttered brioche buns, caprese skewers with fresh mozzarella, cherry tomatoes, and basil, drizzled with olive oil and a balsamic glaze, and a watermelon, feta, and mint salad.

"This is impressive," Carly said to the gorgeous woman arranging napkins and small plates around the platters. Carly marveled at her confidence in white jeans and diaphanous white top.

"Most of the credit goes to Jeff," she said, meeting Carly with her honey-brown gaze, "he has the vision — I just help him spin it into a reality."

"The one with the magic wand — well, you seem like a great team then. I'm Carly by the way, I came with Brett, Marin, and Evan."

"Well hi, Carly, welcome. I'm Hannah. And Jeff and I have been together a while — he loves to entertain so I either had to be his first mate or jump ship, you know?"

"Well, good for you. And everything looks amazing." It occurred to Carly that she should be mingling instead of bothering the hostess, but she was feeling intimidated. Everyone seemed so self-possessed and put together — she wasn't feeling either of those things.

"What can I get you to drink, you look like you could use a little something? We have beers in the galvanized tub out back, we have rosé and sauvignon blanc on ice over here, and *this* is my famous sangria."

"You read my mind, this is a work of art," Carly said, dipping the ladle into the crystal punch bowl of sangria. Round slices of orange and lemon floated lazily on the surface alongside jewel-like berries, the colors shimmering in the early evening sun, "thank you so much."

Paige would die — she absolutely loved sangria. Carly snapped some pics of it and the view to text her friend, who felt so far away at this moment.

"And Shawn out there will make you his famous whiskey lemonade if you're in the mood for that — it's a pretty refreshing cocktail he does with fresh squeezed lemonade and mint from the garden. Hey, I gotta see if Jeff needs anything — grab a bite then come on out, okay?"

Carly put a lobster roll and caprese skewer on a plate and took in the rest of the space — a cozy dining nook with a built-in banquette, its cushions covered in faded ticking-striped fabric.

The heart of the house was the open living room with deep sofas, a stone fireplace, and wide-plank pine floors that creaked when she moved. Every window offered a view of either hilly dunes or sparkling ocean in the distance.

"What are you doing inside?" Evan's loud voice startled her.

"Oh, hi, I was just on my way out — this place is perfect, isn't it?"

"Sure — if you don't mind more shabby than chic." God, he was arrogant. "An incredible spread though, I must say. And Jeff is the balls when it comes to food."

"Everything is amazing," she said, "the view from every window is crazy. Very cool to see this part of the island, you were right, it's so unspoiled out here."

"Right? And you haven't even seen the sunset yet."

The party was in full swing, spilling from the deck down to the beach below. Laughter and animated conversation mingled with the faint crash of waves, and drinks flowed as easily as the tide. Carly looked around, curious about the crowd. How many of these people were locals, or bona fide summer people with their fancy cottage mansions and trust funds? Or like her—some hybrid of tourist and temporary worker, trying to find her place in the rhythm of the island.

Soundbites of conversations drifted on the wind to where she stood, drink in hand, beside Evan who she'd tuned out.

I swear, she only brought him to show off...

Seriously? Grad school? At this point in your life? WHY?

Nah, dude, Nicaragua has better surf breaks than Costa Rica...

Yeah, tech companies are going off now — maybe head to Boston at the end of the summer...

Friggin tourists got stuck the other night right at the entrance to Smith Point — nobody could get on or off...

No, seriously the Box is such a dive — what is the obsession? It's filled with children with fake IDs, trust me...

So many different perspectives, Carly thought, but at the end of the day, people were still just people—trading barbs, one-upping each other, and caught up in the confusion of feeling both superior and inferior.

Carly enjoyed Brett and Marin's company and it was good to sit with them around the fire pit eating Jeff's incredible grilled fare. She wasn't sure she'd like the Striped Bass but wanted to try something local. The first bite surprised her—it was somehow both delicate and rich, with a faint hint of sweetness. All Jeff had done was brush it with olive oil, a sprinkle of sea salt and a squeeze of fresh lemon — it felt like a mouthful of a seaside summer.

It made her wonder if Gus would like to try surfcasting — maybe out at Great Point? But why the hell was she thinking about August Wilder when she was at a fun party on the beach with so many cool people.

The sun was sinking and the light was almost purple. Further down the beach couples and families had brought picnic suppers in order to watch the sunset like a movie.

"People drive out here every night for this," Evan said, with awe in his voice, "each one is a masterpiece." He'd reappeared by her side after playing some Spikeball drinking game down on the beach.

Carly was curious about this unexpected softer side — he seemed mesmerized by the sun's descent into the sea, how it changed the sky and the water. The sun seemed to hover on the thin blue seam, lingering as if reluctant to leave, casting long shadows across the dunes. The sky was changing by the second, a melting canvas of blue to purple to red. The ocean a mirror reflecting and shifting the colors forever.

Everyone stood to witness as it finally dipped into the sea, erupting into a deep red that dissolved into a dusky violet. Evan slipped his hand into hers, and she let him, the gesture easy, comfortable. As the sun disappeared the crowd broke into spontaneous applause, as though the stunning display had been orchestrated just for them.

She'd lost track of the number of signature cocktails she'd experimented with but she was feeling good — a kind of content she hadn't let herself feel for a while. Like she could lay back in the dunes right there and stare at the sky until the first stars began to wink into view.

"Did you know that Sirius, aka the Dog Star, is the brightest star in the night sky?" Evan said, reclining in the sand beside her, their bent knees knocking gently together.

"I did not," Carly said, "tell me more. I only know Cassiopeia because it's shaped like a W and I can find it easily."

"Okay, so one of the brightest and first stars to appear in the Northern Hemisphere is Vega — part of the Summer Triangle."

"The what? There's a summer triangle?" Her mind was swimmy and she was enjoying this version of Evan.

"Sshh," Evan said, rolling onto his side to face Carly. He kissed the corner of her mouth so softly it was like a whisper. "Altair is another point in the Summer Triangle, with Deneb completing the triangle — which is in the constellation Cygnus, the Swan."

The kiss had barely happened, Carly wondered if she'd imagined it. "How do you know all that?" She was surprised and had to admit she was a little impressed. As he pointed out Vega and Deneb, tracing invisible lines in the sky to form the Summer Triangle, she found herself picturing him as an inquisitive little boy growing up on the island—studying the stars and the ways of the sea with his grandfather. It was a sweet image, one that softened the edges of the cocky dude she'd come to know.

Carly felt decidedly more buzzed lying down, her limbs heavy and her thoughts freefalling without direction. The world around her seemed to tilt and sway, the gentle hum of voices and the distant crash of waves blended into a dreamlike haze.

The stars seemed impossibly close as Carly lay on the sand, without the heat of the sun it was satiny cool beneath her palms. Evan leaned over her, his face was shadowed but she could see the smile playing on his lips. He brushed a strand of hair from her cheek, his fingers lingering a moment too long.

"I've been wanting to do this all night," he murmured, his breath warm against her skin. Before she could respond, his lips found hers— tentative at first, then more insistent. It wasn't unpleasant and she leaned into the moment. His weight shifted, and suddenly he was on top of her deepening the kiss. She felt his hips push against hers, his arousal impossible to ignore.

Her body tensed, a surge of panic flaring like a warning signal in her mind. She moved her hands to his chest, gently at first. "Evan," she said, her voice muffled against his kiss. He didn't seem to hear her. She pushed harder, her tone firm now. "Evan, *stop.*"

He froze, pulling back just enough to look at her, his expression a mix of confusion and embarrassment. "What's wrong?" he asked, his voice low.

"I just—" she struggled for the right words, her heart pounding. "I don't want this. Not like this."

He didn't move, his weight pinning her to the sand like an anchor. Her pulse quickened as she shifted beneath him, trying to slide out from under his body, but her limbs were lead weights, her strength diminished by drinks and the sinking realization that he wasn't letting up.

"*Evan,*" she said sharply, her voice cutting through the haze. But he didn't respond, instead he lowered his head to her breasts. What started as a trickle of discomfort now spiked into fear. She pushed harder against him, twisting to free herself, her breath coming faster. "Evan, get off!" Her voice was hard with rising panic.

That seemed to jar him. He paused, his movements halting as he looked down at her, confused. "What?" he muttered, as though he didn't understand what was happening.

"Get. *Off,*" she repeated, her voice cold and unwavering. She planted her hands against his shoulders and shoved with all the force she could manage.

"Come on, you know you want this as much as I do," Evan said in a low whisper, "Oh, what — you want to be on top? Like a cowgirl and ride me, that's how you like it, isn't it…"

Scenarios reeled about how this could end. The crash of the waves was deafening now, the once-cozy darkness of the beach suddenly vast and cold.

Chapter Forty-Five

CARLY'S PANIC SPIKED AS Evan's hand moved lower, his fingers fumbling to push up her dress. Her breath caught and instinct took over. She wedged her hands desperately between their bodies trying to create enough space to free herself, but his weight bore down on her. Her pulse pounded in her ears as her knee found its way between them, and with every ounce of force she could manage, drove it upward. The contact was solid, and his groan of pain immediate. He rolled off her, clutching himself as he collapsed onto the sand.

Carly scrambled backward, her breaths ragged and her limbs trembling. The reality of what had just happened roared like thunder, mingling fear with relief as she put space between them, reaching to find her phone in the pocket of her jean jacket.

Evan lay curled on his side, his face twisted in agony. "What the hell, Carly?" he wheezed, his voice strained.

She didn't answer. She couldn't. Her throat felt tight, and all she wanted was to get away. Rising to her feet, she brushed the sand from her legs and dress with shaking hands, her vision blurring as her eyes filled with tears.

"*Don't*," she finally managed, her voice wobbling with anger and disbelief. "Don't you *ever* come near me again."

She turned and walked away, her legs unsteady in the sand but driven by the need to put as much distance as possible between them.

She wished Paige were there, her wing-woman — she felt so completely alone. And the last person she wanted to call was also the only shot she had of getting home. Gus. There was no way she was returning to the house of partying people — she'd walk home if she had to.

Where were her flip-flops? It was getting so dark. Her heart was still racing as she crouched down, frantically patting the sand around her. The bonfire's glow felt miles away now. Her fingers fumbled as she scrolled through her contacts for Gus's name. The thought of calling felt like too much — too raw, exposed. But texting felt impossible too; she could hardly see the screen through her blurry vision, let alone string together coherent words.

Her thumb hovered over his name. A single thought pulsed through her mind — *I need someone I can trust.* She hit *call* before she could change her mind as she found her way out of the dunes barefoot. He answered on the third ring. She tried to arrange her voice so that it sounded normal, but the tight bar of fear across her throat was still there.

"Hey," she said, in a voice higher than she'd intended, "you wouldn't by any chance be able to come out to Madaket to give me a ride home, would you?" The line was so quiet she thought she'd lost him — cell service was not a sure thing and she tried to slow the roll of panic.

"Sure," he said, without the twenty questions, "can you text the address?"

Relief flooded through her at the sound of his voice, steady and concerned, present. Without an exact address she explained generally where she was, stumbling over her words but managing to convey the urgency.

"Stay put," he said firmly. "I'll come get you. Just drop me a pin."

∞

She nodded, even though he couldn't see her, her shoulders easing as she hung up. I'll be fine, she told herself. Home safe soon, instead of wandering barefoot to the other end of the island in a rumpled dress.

But as she followed the sandy path leading away from the beach, doubt crept in. The dunes all looked the same in the dark and paths reached out like arms. By the time got to the road, her stomach sank. No street sign. No landmarks. Just a stretch of sand disappearing into the shadows in both directions. She put her phone in the top pocket of her jean jacket and jogged a little way back up the dune for a better vantage point.

But her only point of reference was the distant hum of the ocean and the glow of the party somewhere behind her. She was glad she'd decided against bringing a purse and had everything she needed in her PopSocket phone wallet — ID, debit card and twenty bucks. She swallowed hard, her breath hitching as she typed:

No street signs — sand roads — I'll send location and wait, THX!

She decided to get out of the dunes and back to the road before dropping a pin for Gus. The chill of the night air and the reality of her situation began to sober her up, but her legs still felt unsteady as she trudged through the soft sand. She stumbled on an uneven patch just before she got to the road, catching herself before falling completely. Once she steadied herself, she instinctively patted her pocket to check for her phone. Empty.

She stopped dead, spinning in the dark, her pulse a beating drum in her ears. She scanned the ground around her but saw nothing. Panic built in her chest as she retraced her steps feeling around with her feet, then crouching low to move the sand around with her hands. *Where is it?* she whispered out loud, her voice barely audible over the sound of the surf. The comforting rectangle glow of her phone was nowhere.

She crouched down again, frantically combing the sand, her knees getting caught in the hem of her dress nearly toppling her over. She sat back hard on the cold sand and choked out a sob, she was so frustrated and angry with herself. She wiped roughly at the hot tears spilling down her face, it scratched and stung. Without even a shard of moonlight the darkness pressed in on all sides. For a moment, she closed her eyes and listened to the waves, trying to calm herself. But every shift of the wind, every distant sound, only reminded her how alone she was.

Drowning in self-pity won't teach you to swim, her grandfather used to tell her, *feeling sorry for yourself won't change the story*. She got herself up, literally dusted herself off, and headed for the road. With any luck, she'd end up on Madaket Road — the only way into and out of this part of the island.

Gus — what was he thinking now that she'd gone radio silent? Shit, he'd probably be worried, thinking the absolute worst. This was awful, she felt like such a fool. And *dammit!* Her phone, her wallet, everything — *fuck*!

What must she look like traipsing barefoot on the side of the road? She had sand in her hair, mascara smudged under her eyes — a wrecking ball in a storm of bad decisions. When she saw headlights coming toward her she was paralyzed by indecision. Wave? Hide? It could be anyone. Her breath caught as the vehicle drew closer, and she hovered at the edge of the road, frozen between hope and dread.

And there she was. Nessie. That trusty two-toned antique, headlights cutting through the night like a beacon. The universe had thrown her a rope. And Gus.

He pulled over, and as Carly folded herself into the front seat, her mind raced with a barrage of reactions he might have: *I knew that guy was no good. I knew this party would be trouble. Why didn't you ask me for the car? Where the hell are your shoes? And why didn't you text me your location?*

She deserved every bit of it, but was interested in none of it.

"So at some point my phone fell out of my jacket in the sand. Before we take off, do you think we could try to find it with yours?"

"You think a flashlight is all you'll need to find a slim electronic device in a mountain of sand in the pitch black?"

Sarcasm. That was better than pity.

"No, doofus, I'm pretty sure we can sign into the Find My app on your phone and find mine." He shot her a look that was some potent mix of skepticism and amusement before indulging her. "May I?" she said, gesturing for his phone. "Let's see....first we open your Find My app, then choose the Me tab. Then, see how it says *Help a Friend*?" she said, showing Gus, "so, I'm just gonna select that and sign into iCloud with my Apple ID, okay?"

"This is nuts," he said, "have at it, I'll believe it when I see it."

They parked as close to the beach as the terrain allowed, stepping out into the damp night air. Carly barely noticed the cold, her focus entirely on recovering her phone. It was absurd to think about, but that tiny device felt like her entire life — ID, contacts, bank accounts, all of it.

"I'm not sure how well this app works out here," she said, tapping on her phone's icon from Gus's screen. The app opened Apple Maps, and a blinking dot appeared. "Okay..." she said, tilting her head, "looks like we've got something. It's saying to head west — toward the water. Which, by the way, totally fries my east-coast brain."

Gus chuckled beside her, the sound grounding her as she continued, "Oh look! I can make it play a sound when we get close. High-tech treasure hunting at its finest."

"How do you know how to do all this? Are you a serial phone loser?"

"Ha-ha, no," she said, "but my roommate had her purse stolen out of her boyfriend's truck last summer in Texas and this is how they found her phone — in the dirt and brush on the side of the road where the assholes had thrown it out the window. I mean, can you imagine thinking you're getting away with that but the phone is tracking your every move in real time? Would have led the cops right to them if they hadn't wised up to that."

"Wait," Gus said, holding up a hand. "Stop. Do you hear that?"

Carly froze, her blood pounding. She strained to hear as Gus took a few steps forward, tilting his head. The wind played tricks, teasing the sound into fragments — faint, then gone, then suddenly clear again.

"It's coming from this way," he said, his voice low but urgent. He picked up his pace, the soft sand muffling his strides. Carly stumbled after him, her legs unsteady in the deep dunes, every step an effort.

Carly stilled, her breath catching as she strained to listen. "It's getting closer...is that—?"

Gus turned his head, focusing like a bloodhound catching a scent. "Yeah, that's it." He took a few steps forward, the wind teasing the sound away and then back again. "It's clearer now — this way."

She followed, her legs burning with the exertion, feet sinking in the sand with every step. The ping grew louder, more distinct, her chest tightened with anticipation.

"It's getting louder," Gus said, over his shoulder. Suddenly he stopped, crouching low to the ground. Carly stumbled to a halt behind him, panting. He started moving the sand aside with careful swipes of his hand, and the faint glow of a screen peeked through the grains. "Here it is!" he said, lifting it over his head triumphantly like it was the Dead Sea Scrolls.

Carly let out a breathless laugh, relief flooding in. "I can't believe it actually worked!" She took the phone from him, brushing and blowing off as much of the sand as she could see. The screen flashed with missed notifications. She stared at it like a lost love.

"Here, let me see it for a sec," he said, taking the phone with careful hands. Turning it, squinting at the charging port, then tightening his lips to blow quick, sharp breaths into the headphone jack and speaker grill.

The air shot through with a faint whistle, and he grinned sheepishly. "A little old-school, but you don't want sand stuck in there."

Carly caught herself staring at his mouth as he blew into the phone, the focused set of his lips heating her up inside. His dark hair blended with the shadows of the night and she was suddenly anchored by his eyes as he handed the phone back.

Their hands brushed in the exchange, the warmth of his skin lingering a beat longer than necessary. Sparks set off inside her and she quickly looked away, grateful for the cover of night that disguised her burning cheeks.

Chapter Forty-Six

THE RIDE BACK TO the house was awkward silence after their enforced collaboration and collective effort. Carly wasn't sure if Gus sat in judgement of her — he must have at least ten questions he wasn't asking. She felt stupid and not yet clear-headed.

"Thanks for coming to get me," she said, after a few minutes, "how'd you get out to Madaket so fast anyway?"

He seemed to pause a beat before responding, his eyes never leaving the long dark road. "I, um, I thought maybe I'd try one of Millie's famous fish tacos..."

"Wait, you *what*? You were already in Madaket? So, what are you like, a stage-five stalker?"

"Whoa, whoa, whoa, I didn't say I was actually *at* Millie's. Yet. I was on my way there..."

"And what was your plan exactly?" Carly couldn't tell if she should feel protected or patronized. Gus had made his opinion of Evan known — and who could blame him — but Carly shuddered to think he felt the need to drive all the way out there because he didn't think she could take care of herself. Even though she'd done a shit job of that. "And you really had to drive to the opposite end of the island for fish tacos?"

"You told me to do my research — Millie's has the best! Okay, look, call it a sixth sense, but I had a feeling you might need a ride home.

I didn't entirely trust the Kinsman brothers to get you home when you wanted to leave — or to necessarily be sober enough to do so. And, yeah, I felt a little guilty about having the car — you'd never originally planned on having to share it and so it only seemed right to make sure you got home safely." His voice had a rich comforting depth, it was a fortress of calm.

He took his eyes off the road to meet hers and she looked to see if there was more. He wasn't addressing the elephant in the room — her panicked call, the missing shoes, the lost phone.

She tilted her head, trying to read his expression in the faint glow of the dashboard lights. Was there more? She crossed her arms, leaning into the corner of her seat, still barefoot and sandy from their trek through the dunes.

"Well, thanks," she said, softly, but the gratitude felt hollow. It wasn't just the ride she wanted to thank him for — it was the quiet assurance he brought when she'd been unraveling. That, and maybe for not asking the obvious. But the silence hung in the air, taut as a guitar string. She shifted uncomfortably. "You're not going to say it, are you?"

He glanced at her, his brow furrowing in genuine confusion. "Say what?"

"You know. The part where you grill me about why I was out there by myself, a hot mess — why I didn't go back to the party — why I had to call you?" She whipped the visor down to examine the state of her face in the small mirror — smudging away the makeup under her eyes. "About why I look like a dumpster fire..."

He let out a low laugh, and shook his head. "I figured you'd tell me if you wanted to."

His response softened her. She was used to people assuming the worst, prying, trying to connect dots she hadn't even drawn yet. His cool restraint was... unexpected.

"Well," she ventured, her voice quieter, "let's just say I found myself in a less than desirable situation and I just wanted to get out of there."

Gus didn't press, but the silence that followed felt alive, like he was turning over her words, looking for the gaps. She held her breath, unsure if she wanted him to leave it alone or to know the gory details.

"Well," he finally said, voice steady, "sounds like you made the right call then."

Her gaze flicked to him, caught off guard. "Yeah?"

He shrugged, his hands loose on the wheel. "Sometimes your gut tells you everything you need to know. You don't need to stick around and justify yourself to anyone."

Carly let that sink in, her shoulders relaxing a little. Maybe it was the way he said it — with a certainty she hadn't realized she'd needed to hear — but it felt like permission to let go of the mess she'd left behind at the beach.

"Thanks," she murmured, almost to herself.

He glanced at her briefly, a faint smile playing on his lips. "Of course. You good? If you're good, I'm good and we'll leave it at that." He looked like he wanted to say more. "Unless," he added, "there's someone who needs a beat down — then you just let me know—"

Carly couldn't help but smile at that, her lips curving upward despite herself. "A beat down, huh? What are you, my security detail now?"

Gus grinned, his eyes flicking to hers for a moment before returning to the road. "Hey, everyone needs backup sometimes."

She laughed softly, shaking her head. "I think I'm good for now. But I'll keep you on speed dial, just in case."

"Deal." His voice was light, but there was something steady underneath it — like he meant it, no matter how casual he sounded.

Carly hadn't realized how deeply she craved that kind of steady, uncomplicated support. The way he said *deal* wasn't just a throwaway line — it was a quiet assurance that someone had her back. It carried a comforting heft. Like finding an anchor in a storm you didn't realize you were caught in.

For so long she'd been navigating life on her own terms — guarding her independence, shielding herself from too much vulnerability, unwilling to lean on anyone who might leave her standing alone. Her parents had had their own cross to bear — she'd grown up hyperaware of adding to their plate. She'd built the proverbial walls to avoid disappointment. But now, here was this unassuming man, offering a simple solid thing, without conditions or expectations. It was like a window cracked open, letting in air she hadn't known she'd been deprived of.

The tension that had knotted her chest was finally unspooling. She turned her attention to the passing landscape, the shadowed moors with quick peeks of the dark ocean beyond, their conversation weaving a delicate thread between them.

Carly wasn't ready to fully revisit where things went sideways with Evan that night, but thoughts rushed in. The way things had spiraled, her lack of control, letting her guard so far down. What could she have done differently? Had she gotten caught up in the moment and ignored her gut? She struggled with blaming herself, but she knew that Evan's behavior was entirely on him. His decisions, his actions.

She'd have to be more vigilant in the future — set clearer boundaries, learn to recognize the red flags for what they were. She couldn't afford to let herself be swept up again. But she wouldn't let this moment, this one misstep in judgement, define her.

She'd had enough of that. She'd spent so much of her life carrying the emotional burdens of other people's fault lines — Dillon's death, her parents' grief, and their inattentiveness to how the loss of Dillon affected her whole life. Never mind the emotional minefield that was Jake. And now this. She was over it. Over letting everyone else's burdens weigh so much. The self-blame cycle was getting old.

For the first time that night, Carly felt a flicker of something she couldn't quite name. Not relief, not gratitude — something more charged. She turned to the window, the dark road rolling out ahead of them like a blank slate. The rhythm of the car and the hum of the tires filled the space between them.

There was something fragile in the silence. But there was a connection. She'd sensed it before, she couldn't explain it. She didn't know if it meant anything or if it would lead to something.

Probably not, all things considered. All she knew was that she wanted more of it.

Chapter Forty-Seven

CARLY'S RESTLESS NIGHT WAS fragmented by dreams about Gus. Each time she managed to let sleep claim her, he appeared — sometimes as just a feeling or a fleeting image, other times he appeared with startling clarity as though he had come for her. It wasn't a peaceful sleep, but instead of waking up groggy, it left her pulsing with an energy and awareness of how deeply he'd settled into her mind.

She wanted so badly to give in — to surrender to thoughts of this beautiful man with his pure heart and genuine intentions. She wanted, for a change, to forget about the walls she'd allowed to rise up around her heart and indulge in the idea of being with him, to let herself hope for something real. She also wanted to check out Great Point — and she would love to explore that part of the island with Gus.

Should she text him or sit outside with her coffee and wait for him to surface and speak in person? She decided to have her coffee in the early sunshine and let the morning unfold as it would.

"Morning," Gus said, startling her and claiming the seat beside her on the lawn looking out at the teal water, "you know what today would be perfect for?" Carly held her own thoughts — curious what his idea for the day was. "Rumbling out to Great Point — I've been wanting to check that out — what do you think?"

"I was just thinking that *exact* thing — crazy"

"Great minds..." His two-day stubble caught the sun and she had the urge to see if it felt like velvet.

"We could pack a lunch and drinks," she said, her mind running with the idea, "Oh, and we could bring the fishing rods — would you want to try surfcasting? I hear there are some good spots to catch striped bass and blue fish out there."

He grinned at her enthusiasm. "How cool would it be to grill something we pulled out of the ocean like that?"

"Yikes, I was thinking more catch and release — I could never do the gutting or fileting or any of that, but if you—"

"I suppose it' s pretty cocky to assume we'd even catch something. Let's just see how it goes, enjoy the day no matter what."

Energized with their plan, they finished their coffees and took inventory of their lunch provisions. They decided to make a pitstop at the Sconset Market for some shrimp and their special horseradish cocktail sauce to supplement what they had, sparkling water, beers, and two big chocolate chip cookies.

With the sun shining down on them they drove out of Sconset along Polpis Road, past Sankaty Lighthouse and the golf course, past the flat blue expanse of Sesachacha Pond, to the Wauwinet turnoff. The road turned winding and rural — surrounded by farmhouses and stretches of open land, and a thicket of leafy trees just before they reached the gatehouse of the luxury oceanfront resort, the Wauwinet.

They both got started on letting air out of the tires before the long rumble out on the sand to the point. The eel grass swayed and gulls dipped and swooped unpredictably in the wind as they bounced over the slender arm of sand where the landscape seemed to empty out — houses and trees disappearing — until it was just beach, the sea, and grassy dunes. At one point the ocean was unfolding on one side and Nantucket Sound lapping on the other. It was a dramatic stretch with huge views of water on both sides, like they were being embraced by the sea.

They chose a spot where they could see the Great Point Lighthouse standing sentinel in the distance surrounded by rugged, windswept, natural beauty. The sand was creamy white and the vegetation around them was made up of low-lying bayberry and Rosa rugosa bushes. The ocean was a deep blue, not as rough as the south shore, and crabs scuttled past the seagulls and oystercatchers.

"It feels like we're the only ones in the world," Carly said, getting out of the Land Cruiser to feel the warm sand between her toes. They saw only a couple of anglers in the distance standing at the water's edge casting their lines into the rolling waves with precision. She watched the low waves fold over themselves again and again — it was hypnotic.

Gus busied himself getting their chairs from the back of the car and setting them up facing the sun. "It's so peaceful out here," he said, "should we go for a walk, explore a little?"

"Absolutely. Let me get a bucket to collect treasures."

"You thought of everything," he said, smiling, his eyes crinkling in the bright sun, "what will we find out here?"

"Well, it's my first time out here too so I guess we'll see." They walked along the water's edge where the ruffled tide dropped treasures at their feet. Shimmering slipper shells in soft blush pinks caught the sunlight, and translucent jingle shells glinted in hues of gold and sherbet orange. Scattered among them were smooth sea-polished stones that glowed emerald green when wet, tempting her to collect them — though she knew their luster would fade once dry.

"When we were kids going to the beach in Maine, my brother and I always picked up any shell with a hole in it to make a necklace out of it," she said, with a faraway smile, "it's funny how I'm still tempted! And finding sea glass is always the big prize — green especially — so pay attention."

"Will do. What do you call this?" Gus said, bending to pick up a long serpentine chain of translucent disk-like capsules.

"Ooh, that's a whelk egg case," Carly said, excited to show him what was hidden in each disk. "Let's crack one of these disks open — you won't believe what's inside." She held out her hand, cradling a collection of tiny, perfectly preserved baby whelk shells. "How cool is that?" she said, glancing up to catch his reaction. Her heart lifted seeing her delight mirrored in his expression.

"Who knew?" he said, examining the tiny brittle shells in his calloused hands. "I wonder how big they get."

"Three, maybe four inches, I think. Now *this*," Carly said, bending to retrieve another find, "is what we call a mermaid's purse," she held out the brown leathery oval with stiff horn-like tendrils at the corners. "it's also a kind of egg case from a skate, I believe — you know, in the ray species."

"I'll take your word for it," Gus said, smiling at her, his eyes flecked with gold in the light. "There's so much to know about the natural world, so many miracles of the survival of species — it's mind-blowing."

"I feel that way all the time," she said, depositing a few treasures into her bucket, "Ooh, a sand dollar! Aw, it's only a half. Did you know they're in the sea urchin family?"

"I did not," Gus said, "not many sea urchins in the mid-west."

"Never pick up a brown one though — that means they're still alive," she said, her eyes combing the tideline for a whole one, "If it's grayish or white, then it's just the skeleton and you can keep it. Like this one! Look — and it's whole!" She held the fragile disk out to show him, "Just look at this five-pointed star — so beautiful. And you know what I read somewhere as a kid? That they can live for ten years, can you believe that? And that as they age, they develop rings around their exoskeleton, which show how long a sand dollar has been around."

"Ah, like trees and the rings within their trunks?"

"Yup — crazy, right?"

"So much to know...all the parallels between life on the land and life in the sea," Gus said, his gaze holding a quiet reverence for everything around him.

Carly took his hand and placed the sand dollar carefully in his palm. "To remember me by, back in Colorado." She thought he'd appreciate that — but instead he looked wistful.

But then he smiled at the sand dollar he held, "I'm rich."

They stood ankle-deep in the water, the cool rush swirling around their feet before retreating in a gentle pull, rolling shells and polished stones back along the ocean floor. His expression was unreadable. But suddenly the thought of this new friendship ending as soon as it had begun — of him heading home, 2,000 miles away from where they stood — sent a sharp ache through her chest and her stomach sank with the weight of it.

A gust of wind blew her hair across her face, tangling strands against her lips. Before she could lift a hand to tuck it behind her ear, his thumb was there, brushing it gently away, his touch lingering, sending a ripple straight through her. He eased the bucket from her grasp and put it on the sand behind them without ever taking his eyes from hers. Then he cupped her face in his hands with such tenderness that her knees threatened to buckle.

The second his lips met hers, she had the spiraling sensation of never having been kissed before. They were satin yet deliberate, his tongue softly searching for hers. Heat speared through her. He tasted like the sea and she wanted to drink him in. A chemistry she'd barely allowed herself to consider between them hummed in her like a live wire. She wanted his kiss for hours — adrenaline dumped heat into her bloodstream.

It was powerful, whatever was between them, like the wet air and the smell of every summer day in bloom.

All she could think about was closing the space between them, reaching out to draw him in. Her hands met with the impossibly carved planes of his torso before sliding up to the broad strength of his back. His hands moved slowly down her body, resting on her hips, deepening the kiss. Then with an imperceptible slowness he eased away, taking the breath from her body.

Her eyes searched his, praying he wasn't about to apologize for the kiss, or do anything to diminish what had just passed between them.

"WOOHOOO!" The shout of a fisherman farther down the beach was carried on the wind, drawing Gus and Carly's attention. His rod bent in a deep arc as he wrestled with something big, and without a word, they broke into a jog to see the action up close.

"Dammit! I had a solid blue on the line just now," the fisherman lamented, shaking his head. "But I set the drag too tight, and when it made a run, the line snapped. I should've adjusted the tension to give it some leeway, shit."

"Sorry man," Gus said, "from the bend in your rod, it looked decent-sized — you'll get the next one."

The fisherman either didn't hear Gus or was too angry with himself to respond. Then another dude came walking down the beach with his rod to investigate.

"I've been using mackerel chunks as bait, but that was my only bite," the first guy said, "and I lost him."

The other guy nodded, suggesting, "Maybe try switching to a noisy topwater lure like a popper. I've found that the blues are really attracted to surface commotion."

"Yeah," the fisherman agreed, reaching into his tackle box. "I have a Cotton Cordell pencil popper here; they love the rattle and dance it does out there, thanks man."

"No worries, good luck," the second guy said, as he continued down the beach.

Gus glanced at Carly with a sheepish grin. "Maybe I'm out of my league fishing here today. What do you say we grab a swim then dive into that lunch? I'm starving. Race you back?"

Before Carly could respond, Gus took off, laughing as his feet scattered sand in his wake. He spun around to run backward, flashing a triumphant smile — until Carly blew by him with a burst of speed, leaving him in her dust. She reached their spot first, imitating a touchdown victory dance, holding up the bucket of treasures she'd retrieved along the way.

The day drifted by like the cotton-ball clouds scudding overhead. They took turns talking, laughing, reading, swimming, and napping in the mellow warmth of the afternoon until it was time to pack up.

As they turned and cruised over the sandy tracks, Great Point Light winked behind them like a secret.

Chapter Forty-Eight

CARLY WOKE UP THE next morning with a jolt of anticipation at getting to spend more time with Gus. They'd talked at the beach about making their seafood chowder that evening which included shopping together for everything they'd need. Some new brightness had slid between the careful walls she'd constructed to keep her heart safe.

She'd tucked away the kiss they'd shared at the beach, not wanting to take it apart by examining it too closely. It was its own precious thing, a spray of fire, a Roman candle, that had left sparklers in her veins the rest of the day.

But had he just been caught up in their easy camaraderie? Had he pulled away, or was it the fisherman's shouts that broke them apart? She didn't know for sure, and the uncertainty pricked tiny holes in her reflective haze. She let hope expand inside her until it seemed to push every other feeling aside.

They'd get an idea of who was interested in their chowderfest — but would make a big batch regardless. She remembered seeing a couple of Nantucket cookbooks on the living room bookshelf — now would be a good time to check them out and make a list. Sitting up in bed she reached for her phone to google the island's best fish markets first, then she'd text her mom. No, she should call her mother, and do *that* first. She hated that it gave her pause.

She loved her mother but felt anchored to her by the invisible chains that tethered them. Carly understood that she might never completely shed the guilt of surviving the car crash that took her brother's life. But what haunted her most was the unspoken question that she would never put a voice to: had her mother ever wished, even for a fleeting moment, that Carly's life had been the one lost instead? Dillon was the family favorite, the baby.

Carly couldn't truly know the weight her mother carried — to not only have lost a child, but to have been the one behind the wheel when it happened. Was her mother's guilt responsible for her blood pressure issues? The panic attacks? Carly thought that pain and loss would get easier with time for her mother, if not just more distant. But lately she'd wondered if the stored guilt and trauma was starting to have more physical consequences that were being compounded by age. Her heart resisted all of it. She knew she had to call her mom.

Carly allowed herself a moment of relief that her parents had chosen to make North Carolina their home. Initially, the decision had left her feeling abandoned, on some primal level, a sense of rejection. But if she were being honest, the distance — both emotional and physical — was liberating. Maybe it was exactly the space she'd been needing, even if she hadn't realized it until now. She felt an opening up, a freedom suddenly to explore her own identity without the constant pull of her family's emotional needs.

She scrolled to her mother's contact in favorites and tapped it before she could change her mind.

Things were fine, she was fine, everybody was fine, her mother assured her. They were almost done unpacking and settled into their new home. Cynthia sounded particularly excited about touring the Biltmore Estate — *the largest privately-owned residence in the country,* she said. She couldn't stop raving about the old-world charm of the Gilded Age mansion built in 1895 for the Vanderbilt family, and the eight thousand acres of gardens she couldn't wait to explore. Carly tried to picture the scale of it but couldn't. She was thrilled by her mother's enthusiasm — how it sparked a ripple of joy in her voice. She needed that, her parents deserved to be happy and excited in their new frontier.

Ending the conversation on a high note felt like a small victory. Better than being there, holding her breath, and waiting for something to fall apart. The roller coaster was killer. This new arrangement with her parents carving out a fresh start in North Carolina could be just what Carly needed too.

Sayle's Seafood or Glidden's — both equidistant from Bartlett's Farm — and then maybe downtown to poke around. Her excitement about the day was building and she was determined to stay in the moment.

Slowly the house started waking up and the rich smell of coffee filled the kitchen. It looked like the day-old Morning Buns had been a hit and there was a palpable buzz of energy in the air.

"Carly! Our sunset cruise was amazing," Hazel said, adding a splash of oat milk to her coffee, "grab a cup and I'll tell you about it outside — it's gorgeous out there this morning."

Murphy was whistling as he slathered his cinnamon raisin bagel with cream cheese and Carly caught herself hiding a grin. "Fun night?" she asked him, filling her favorite mug with the steaming brew.

"The best," Murphy said, licking the cream cheese from his thumb, "Hazel said you helped her plan the night — you really go above and beyond, Carly, we can't thank you enough."

"Aw," Carly said, as they both walked onto the sunny porch, "your wife was the mastermind, I just helped with suggestions. I'm so glad it worked out and the weather held for you — were you surprised?"

"Very. Hazel gets a little seasick sometimes so I never thought she'd plan a boat excursion," Murphy said, reaching for Hazel's hand to give it a tender squeeze, "what a selfless gal, huh? I love you, honey," he said, leaning in to give her a kiss that made Carly feel like three was a crowd. She was glad to see they'd worked things out and seemed to be finally enjoying each other without the kids.

"It was this beautiful Chris-Craft with horseshoe seating in the bow and stern," Murphy said, "pretty sleek for its size, and so smooth, what a treat."

"There were two other couples, plenty of room, and that boat just glided over the water," Hazel added, "didn't spill a drop of wine. Our view of the horizon was unbroken as the sky changed from gold to deep pink, then fading to indigo... Oh my God it was like a dream. The air had a salty bite to it but we were never cold. And when the sun dipped below the waterline, the lighting completely changed to this ethereal glow. You'd have gotten great shots with your camera, Carly, my phone pics don't do it justice."

"It sounds amazing and I'm so happy for you two," Carly said. "Hey — so, do you have plans tonight for dinner? No worries at all if you do, but Gus and I want to make a big batch of seafood chowder with all local ingredients. And we can do a goat cheese and arugula salad, warm crusty bread — and we thought how cool would it be to eat outside at the big table! We'll light lots of candles and lay a blanket on the back of every chair in case it gets chilly. Doesn't that sound so cool?"

"Wait, wait, wait a minute — you and Gus? As in—"

"As in nothing! We were both just craving chowder the other day at the Summer House , but decided, why not make the chowder ourselves?"

"Yes! Quintessential Nantucket," Hazel said, "that sounds amazing, we're due for a cozy night at home — count us in! What can we do to help?"

"Nothing at all," Carly said. But then a memory surfaced — something her Gram once told her about how much more meaningful an experience is when people feel like they contributed to it. "Actually, wait! Would you like to handle the tablescape? You could cut some blossoms from the flower beds to put in mason jars for the table, some candles, and how about some cool shells?

Hazel clapped her hand over her mouth like she'd just been named Miss America, "Oh my God, that's perfect, yes, I'd love to do that!"

"Do what? What'd I miss?" Remi said, materializing from inside with her tumbler of green juice.

Carly filled her in about their chowder supper plans — watching Remi's face as she considered the horror of the heavy creamy dish and the buttered warm bread. "I'm sure Burke would be all over that — the more carbs and saturated fat, the better," Remi said, "Don't get me wrong, I'm not judging, it's just that I can't put that stuff in my body."

"Well, no one's gonna force-feed you," Carly laughed, "I can set some plain scallops and mussels aside if you want?"

"What time are you thinking? Because I booked a personal training session at the Nantucket Health Club then a mani-pedi. You know I have to be totally ready for when — well, you never know for what, right?" Remi patted her six-pack abs for emphasis, then stretched out her hands to inspect her nails with dramatic flair.

Carly and Hazel exchanged glances and Carly wondered if Hazel too was doubting Remi's confidence in Burke proposing to her anytime soon. There seemed to be more of a disconnect there than a meeting of the minds.

"Let's say seven-ish? Not too early but before the sun sets," Carly said, as Gus and Burke appeared at the top of the wooden steps that led up from the beach. Burke was undeniably handsome by anyone's measure, but Carly's gaze was fixed on Gus, drawn to him with a magnetic pull she didn't try to resist. Both guys were slick with sweat, the kind that said they'd just crushed a beach run. It was Gus who stood out in sharp focus to Carly. His tanned ropey muscles and sparkling eyes hit her like an avalanche. She had to force herself to unlock her gaze from his and pull herself together.

"Hey, we were just talking about tonight," Carly said, as the guys got closer, "we were thinking seven o'clock for dinner?"

Burke looked from Gus to the rest of the group, "Am I missing something? Did I completely space on some reservation we have or something?"

"Oh, no, Burke, sorry, my fault," Carly chimed in, "Gus and I were planning to make a big pot of seafood chowder for everyone and sit out here at the table with candles and Prosecco or beer — whatever you like. But if you guys have your own plans — that's fine too, whatever! I know sand is trickling through the hourglass of your time here..."

Burke looked to Remi as if for permission, "what do you think, Rem? Sounds good to me."

Remi aimed a pointed look at Burke, holding his gaze a beat longer than was comfortable. Carly couldn't help but wonder if she was silently communicating — *yeah sure dude, as long as you have something bigger planned for later!*

"Sure, whatever," Remi finally said, slurping the last of her green concoction through a stainless-steel straw.

"Thanks guys, for setting this up — what can we do?" Burke said, running his hand through his sweaty, salt-stiff golden hair. "How about like a key lime pie or something for dessert?"

"That sounds really good actually," Carly said, "thank you so much! Not sure where to go for that but..."

"No worries, we'll figure it out," Burke said, good-naturedly, even though he'd just suggested another thing that Remi would not be indulging in.

The guys took turns in the outdoor shower while Hazel and Carly soaked in the soft morning. Hazel recounted more sunset cruise details and showed off her photos while Carly listened and mentally scrolled through her wardrobe to nail down an outfit for her day with Gus.

Chapter Forty-Nine

GUS AND CARLY DECIDED to put a cooler with ice in the back of the Land Cruiser to keep the seafood and produce fresh in case they ended up downtown or driving around. The sun was already hot as they set out, the sky a China blue.

While Gus drove them to Bartlett's Farm, Carly pulled up a recipe she'd bookmarked from Sarah Leah Chase's cookbook back at the house. The crowned queen of the Nantucket food world was famous for her fresh vibrant takes on coastal cuisine. Carly scanned the list of ingredients for the chowder and the accompanying salad they'd planned, double-checking to be sure they'd be able to find everything locally.

Bartlett's Ocean View Farm was out off of Hummock Pond Road past Cisco Brewery. It was set on 200 acres of patchwork fields of corn and flowers as far as she could see — snapdragons, cosmos, gladiolas, lilies and sunflowers. "Too early for corn, isn't it? That would be so great if it was ready now," she said, wondering if mid-west corn harvest was the same time as New England's.

"Too early. Won't be harvesting until July anyway," Gus said, "a bit later in the north. Field corn usually takes about ninety to a hundred days to mature, if I have my facts straight, generally, late April to May is when corn is planted in Iowa and Nebraska."

"Are those the biggest corn-haul states?"

"Iowa is the best place on the planet to grow corn — has a growing season that is long enough and warm enough, deep, rich soils and usually plenty of rain."

"Our weather here is all over the place — probably not a long enough *or* warm enough growing season. And who knows with the rain — like last year we went something like a month and a half without rain! I mean, it was great for summer vacations for sure, but we paid for the drought later. Local Christmas tree growers took a hit — they ended up with all these dehydrated trees — it was so sad."

"Don't even get me started on climate change — ranches out west have really felt the impact these last few years."

"Ooh, that's right, wildfires right?"

"That's only part of it — of course it's all tied together. We rely heavily on snowpack for water, but the warmer winters and earlier snowmelt have cut water availability in a big way, which then impacts irrigation," Gus explained. "And then with the prolonged droughts, all ranchers face the challenges of maintaining the pastures and growing feed. Which ultimately forces us to cut herd sizes or buy expensive supplemental feed. The Colorado River, which is a vital water source, is under huge strain from overuse. It all shortens the growing seasons — disrupting planting and harvesting cycles for hay which really effects forage quality for cattle."

"Oh my God, it's like a vicious chain — you must have to keep finding ways to adapt, that can't be cheap."

"Exactly. We're constantly in the position to have to consider alternatives like sustainable grazing, rotational systems, and drought-resistant forage crops if we have any hopes of staying ahead of the impact of the climate. It's no joke."

"Now there's something you don't see on *Yellowstone*." Carly loved listening to him. The intensity and purpose he projected. He was dedicated, insightful, and discerning. No wonder his father wanted him in charge.

The air inside the market smelled earthy and sweet — of freshly watered tomatoes on the vine and cut grass. There were tall galvanized buckets of cut flowers, wooden crates of produce, and trays of herbs — basil, dill and mint filled the air. They chose parsley, tarragon, and two heads of tender butter lettuce. Then Carly put some arugula, a sweet onion, and four ripe peaches in her basket. She wanted to buy every beautiful thing. Being there made her wish she was a gourmet cook and could create culinary masterpieces, effortlessly, from sunup to sundown. But she could follow a recipe and hope for the best — she had a feeling Gus was in a similar category.

"Doesn't this place make you want to live strictly farm-to-table? Produce fresh from the garden is so inspiring." Gus said with unguarded sincerity, and it was as though he'd plucked the thought right from her mind.

She looked up at him as he spoke, his earnestness snaking through her. August Wilder was a study in contrasts — this thoughtful, generous man packaged in a rugged, strong exterior. It was such a desirable combination yet it left her completely off-balance.

She imagined being on his horse behind him, her arms wrapped tight around his muscled form, her body flush against his as they rocked in unison with the galloping strides. The heady blend of freedom, connection, and the rush of adrenaline was so real she could taste it. What was he thinking, staring back at her?

"Did we get it all?" he asked, "Check your list. Oh, look at that spread of cheeses — we needed some for the salad, right?"

"You seem pretty good at this — do you cook at home?" He couldn't possibly be that guy who did it all *and* looked the way he did. This wasn't the movies.

"I, um, well, once Emelia and I moved in together it became trial by fire or go hungry. She's an extremely busy attorney, and even if she'd had the time, cooking would be the last way she'd spend it."

His serene expression dissolved, replaced by a furrowed brow and concern narrowing his eyes. It was the first mention of this person, this Emelia, this ex-fiancée, and it landed between them like a challenge. Carly wasn't sure she was ready to meet it. This was her chance to uncover his relationship status! He was definitely speaking of her in the past tense, but her words wouldn't come.

"Well, you do seem to know your way around your vegetables and cheeses," was what came out. A missed opportunity for clarity. But she'd decided to let hope hang, untouched and shimmering, like a bubble from a wand.

"And yes, we'll need some goat cheese for the salad," she said, consulting the list on her phone once more. "Oh — and do you think they sell the chorizo here that we need for the chowder? It calls for smoky, sweet chorizo?"

"You know, they must, because their breakfast sandwich menu I saw actually features a sandwich with a farm fried egg and their house chorizo sausage. Let's check over here."

Who knew food shopping could be such a feast for the senses? Every vivid color, fresh aroma, and potential flavor was amplified by the anticipation of the meal they'd planned—and by the simple fact that she'd be spending so much time in Gus's company. Her mouth watered.

From Bartlett's Farm they went to Glidden's for the seafood. They walked into the simple shack that was the fish market and took in the spread before them. There were thick meaty swordfish steaks, ruby-red tuna, the delicate cod fillets, and jumbo shrimp. There was a pile of cherrystone clams, scallops, and the glossy blue-black shells of the mussels. There was also homemade guacamole, marinades, rubs, sauces and compound butters. The smoked bluefish paté seemed very much like something she should try — another time, she decided.

"This is incredible," Gus said, "seafood this fresh is a little harder to come by in Colorado." He tried to distract her with the lobsters crawling around in their tank and pay for the whole thing. She'd barely gotten her card out in time to split the cost at Bartlett's.

"Dude, I told you, we're doing this fifty-fifty." She shoved him playfully out of the way to put her card on the counter with his as their order was packed. "Not that I don't appreciate it..." And she *did* appreciate it, feeling taken care of, but she saw herself as self-sufficient and capable — one who could and would pay her own way.

She'd learned to distrust relying on anyone else, and had long since stopped expecting anyone to show up for her. But there they were, on an island thirty miles out to sea; they'd been plucked from their usual roles and she was feeling a little unmoored. And that changed everything.

They tucked their finds in the cooler and decided to head into town. Gus mentioned feeling like his wardrobe could use some island-inspired flair, and the first place Carly thought of was Murray's Toggery. She was pretty sure there was no way August Wilder was going to want to rock any of that preppy stuff, but she figured — let him see for himself.

Walking into the shop felt like a step back in time to some kind of old-fashioned clothier, it was easy to believe that it was one of the island's oldest businesses. Looking at all the bright pastels and vivid patterns, Carly wondered how the island's style had evolved from its Quaker-simple roots to this.

The men's section was a riot of madras and bold colored prints. There were belts and shorts embroidered with whales, spinning racks of whimsical ties, piles of folded polo shirts in every color, and an entire wall stacked with the iconic faded red pants. *Home of the Nantucket Red* the sign said, describing their legendary status.

Carly put a hand to her mouth to stifle a laugh.

"What," Gus said, "you don't think I could pull off some pink pants? Or some of those pistachio shorts with the little anchors? Paired with one of these pale yellow polo shirts — collar popped?" he said, with a fun accent, pointing to an ensemble like a game show host.

"Yeaaahh, no. And, dear God, why would you want to? I mean, no offense to the uber-preps out there but, no. This is just not you. Let's try Force Five up the street — way cooler vibe — think classy, casual, surfer aesthetic with a little edge."

"So, I'm classy with an aesthetic edge, huh?" That grin again, that started out slow with just a curve of his lips, then spread right up into his eyes lighting up the space between them. Carly was sure her face was on fire. "Then what are we doing here in Trip Chadwell's closet? Let's go," he said, threading is fingers with hers. Which split her focus into foggy tendrils.

They were holding hands. Walking down Main Street of this magical place that looked like a child's toy village. Affection filled her as she registered again how easy he was to be around, how much she genuinely liked him. Her heart was a helium balloon, and his hand was solid and strong wrapped around hers.

Chapter Fifty

O**N THE DRIVE HOME** Carly felt the buzz of an incoming text, Paige. They'd been playing text tag for days. Of course she was already laying the groundwork to be a no-show the following weekend. Carly wasn't surprised, but disappointed nonetheless. In true Paige fashion, she wanted to know all about the cowboy from Colorado — *was he hot? On a scale from one to serial killer...* Carly burst out laughing then took a sneaky side pic of Gus driving, thick hair whipping in the wind.

> Jesus H Christ — tell me you're hitting that!! Goddamn, your vaj has been closed so long a Spirit Halloween's gonna move in

"Holy shit, Oh my God, Paige," Carly said, to herself but out loud, cracking up.

"Private joke?"

"Yup," she said, making a popping noise on the P.

∞

"Taking the cooler along was the call," Gus said, chuckling, hefting it out of the back of the car once they were back at the house, "glad I thought of it."

"Ha, ha, very funny," Carly said, "stick with me, cowboy, you might learn something." She felt completely relaxed and sated; it struck her that it had been too long since she'd felt that way. Spending time with Gus wasn't just easy, it raised her up. She was discovering a version of herself she hadn't known, a version she was beginning to cherish, one that filled her with optimism and hope. She was more used to denying herself these things.

They moved in companionable silence putting the seafood and produce in the fridge and deciding on a time to start the prep. "Oh," Carly said, reaching to squeeze his arm, "and we can't forget to be at Sconset Market right at four o'clock for the baguettes hot out of the oven. Or, one of us anyway."

"Got it. And you said Burke and Remi were in charge of dessert?" Gus said, reaching into the fridge for a cold beer.

"Well, Burke anyway — can't imagine Remi knowing her way around a bakery. Sorry — that was mean," Carly said, reaching for his beer to take a long sip.

"I can't figure those two out," Gus said, "Burke is like this larger-than-life kind of guy — down to take it all in and enjoy everything, and Remi..."

"And Remi lives in a small, lonely world of one. I totally hear you and I don't get it either. She's like the opposite — denying herself so much all the time and for what? I mean is it sustainable? Those bikini contests? Where's all that going? And how do you just stop being one way and then be like, okay, bring on the cupcakes and ice-cream, my bikini era is over?"

"I don't think that's how it works," Gus said, "someone like that, with that kind of discipline and self-control, doesn't just do a 180. It seems more like she's someone afraid of losing control. And if she's so good at denying herself something as fundamental as the joy of eating, then she probably tends to suppress other desires and emotions too — trading external goals for her own personal joy."

"This is pretty intuitive, Gus, I mean it makes sense — do you know someone like that or something?"

"Yeah, actually my sister's best friend growing up suffered from what's called Body Dysmorphic Disorder. All she could see in the mirror were her flaws — nothing that anyone else would notice — but she was extreme with her diet and exercise. To anyone else she came across as super disciplined and motivated. But really she was overly anxious and obsessive about what she thought she should look like — which made it almost impossible to maintain any kind of relationship, personal or professional."

"*Body Dysmorphia* — I have heard of that," Carly said, "it must be kind of like when someone with Anorexia looks in the mirror and sees a fat version of themselves — even though their dangerously thin."

"Exactly. And Remi strikes me as someone who funnels her self-worth into what others think of her, and she equates 'good' with the perfect body. It's actually a sign of vulnerability more than strength."

"And no amount of external validation would be enough, would it? Like no matter how many contests she might win or how many people say they'd kill to have a body like hers — it will never be enough."

"Helloo, anybody home?" It was Antonia at the screen door. Gus excused himself to make some calls while Carly and Antonia grabbed some lemon iced tea and sat out on the porch in the shade to catch up.

"Well, darlin, your day sounds just divine — I'm so happy for you!" Antonia said, putting her arm around Carly's shoulders, "And I'm proud of you for opening up your heart — I know how tough that is. Gus seems like just the most delightful man; strong and kind and sooo handsome — this could be the beginning of something then, maybe?"

"Slow your roll, woman, I'm just trying to be in the moment, you know?"

"I sure do and good for you. And I can't wait to taste this chowder y'all been working so hard on, what a beautiful evening it's going to be. Now what can I do to help?"

Carly was again tempted to say she didn't need any help. But she was starting to feel butterflies in her belly about everything turning out the way she envisioned, *and* about prepping and cooking side-by-side with Gus. She decided to ask if Antonia would help her set the table and plate the salads when the time came, her enthusiasm was contagious. Teamwork was such a comfort.

At three-forty-five Carly stepped back into the house, hoping to find Gus up and about, but the place was quiet and empty. She considered texting him but figured he might be tied up with work concerns. Deciding not to interrupt, she hopped on a bike, and pedaled to Sconset Market for the fresh bread. The rhythmic sound of her tires against the road helped settle her thoughts and check things off in her mind. What kind of a wine stash did they have? She wished she'd thought to check — or better yet, that she'd assigned someone else to beverage duty. Maybe she would text Gus after all from the store — and if need be, she'd pick up some wine next door. A quiet thrill rushed through her thinking of the evening ahead.

Cell service was spotty and Carly's texts to Gus wouldn't go through. She bought the two warm baguettes tucked snugly into paper sleeves and stepped into the wine shop next door. She chose three bottles of sauvignon blanc which she decided would complement the seafood perfectly. The wind played with her hair on the ride home, and the sight of bread and wine nestled in her bike basket made her smile and feel like she'd pedaled straight out of a Parisian postcard.

Once back at the house, Carly decided she wanted to luxuriate in a hot shower before she started chopping the vegetables, cleaning the seafood, and measuring the ingredients for the chowder. There was something about being naked outside with the ocean air and the open sky above and hot rivers of water flowing down her body. She was tempted to stay in there until the hot water ran out.

Naturally, at just the moment she was heading back in the house wearing nothing but a towel, Gus was descending the stairs on his way to the kitchen.

"Ah," he said, sheepishly, noting her state of undress, "your favorite outfit. You wear it well," he added, noting the blush starting in her cheeks. "So, I was just coming to see when we should start food prep — but I'll give you a minute." He averted his attention and upon seeing the wine and bread on the counter, commented on how he would have gone with her if she'd asked.

"Um, no worries, I took a bike, it was fine, beautiful actually," she said, from the door of her room, "be right out and we can start."

She threw on cutoffs and a black tank top and piled her wet hair on top of her head thinking she would change before dinner. Back in the kitchen, Gus was lining up the ingredients that needed to be chopped, cleaned and measured. Carly felt a flicker of self-consciousness about the closeness that had bloomed between them — starting at Great Point and lingering through their day in town. Did he feel it too, or had she completely misread the signals? Maybe he was just an easygoing, friendly guy, seeing her in a completely platonic light.

When he bent over to retrieve the deepest soup pot in the cabinet, her breath caught at the view of his perfect ass and that tan slice of muscled back that showed when his t-shirt rode up.

"Oh, good," she said, keeping her voice cool, "I was hoping there was a huge pot under there. If you peel and mince the garlic and onion, I'll deal with the fingerling potatoes and mince the tarragon — is that okay? Onions kill me."

"Sure," he said, standing close enough to her she could smell his Tea Tree shampoo that she'd seen in the shower, "why don't you pull up the recipe so we know what we're doing." A hum of energy rippled through her body at his nearness — a forcefield sucking her in.

She put her phone on the counter, open to the recipe, as they moved fluidly around each other gathering knives and cutting boards, measuring cups and spoons with an intimate synchronicity. She halved the sea scallops and rinsed the littleneck clams while he scrubbed and debearded the mussels.

"I'm starving," she said, "I'm gonna pop a piece of Portuguese bread in the toaster before we start the actual cooking and sautéing — do you mind? Do you want a slice? It's amazing with just butter, I'm telling you." His eyes softened when they met hers — a look of what she could only describe as tenderness. She felt a surprising zing of awareness between her thighs.

She polished off the last buttery bite of toast and chose a saucepan for the fingerlings. Gus stepped closer and gently wiped a crumb from her lips — it felt like a kiss. Wordlessly they stepped apart and she put the potatoes in a saucepan to boil, simmer, and cook to just shy of being tender. Meanwhile, he heated the butter and the olive oil together before adding the onion and garlic, sautéing until translucent. The space was filled with a deep and savory essence.

They stirred in the diced chorizo and watched for its paprika-colored fat to release and crisp. As Carly added the wine, she poured a glass for herself — wanting a warm buzz in her head to match the singing in her body. That one sip made the inside of her mouth feel sunlit.

Their housemates started appearing all around them commenting on the incredible aroma and bustling to do their parts. Carly was liquid and felt like she may as well have been holding up a sign that said *I am dying to kiss this man*. But no one noticed a thing.

The teak table outside was set and the candles were lit — there was a golden glow to the evening with the last of the day's sun stretching across the Atlantic. "Paradise" by Stick Figure played in the background. Reggae was the perfect jam as people drifted in and out of the kitchen, drinks in hand, slivers of conversation and laughter slipping through the screen door as they came and went.

Carly added the cream and watched it thicken, feeling the same warmth unfurling inside her, a deep, slow build that mirrored the richness of the chowder. The halved scallops were scattered evenly over the ingredients in the skillet and the mussels and clams were artfully arranged over the top of the chowder base. She had five minutes to change.

It was a risky choice but she slipped her white halter dress over her head and shook her sun-kissed hair loose. Her eyes had a brightness that was new, bluer against her tan skin. She barely recognized the look in them. From the view of her bedroom window she saw Hazel tweaking the arrangement of blossoms in the mason jars along the table, pinks and purples popped in the gilded light. Antonia lifted a glass of something bubbly to her lips and shared a conspiratorial wink with Murphy who set the eight teak chairs around the table.

 Carly came up behind Gus as he was sprinkling parsley over the top of the massive pot of chowder then lined up the bowls and prepared to serve. Antonia carved fat chunks of bread while Hazel brought two small terrines of butter out to the table with the carafes of wine. Carly watched Gus as he ladled the chowder, spooning in the creamy broth rich with the smoky-sweet chorizo, translucent onions and fragrant herbs.

He took great care to add the same number of clams and mussels and scallops to each bowl. Her heart bloomed.

Once everyone was seated and served, Antonia raised her glass of Prosecco, "To Carly and Gus for creating this lovely evening. May our hearts always be full, our glasses never empty, and may love, new friendships, and memories linger long after summer fades."

The Nantucket air smelled of pine and salt and was as rich as heavy cream.

Candlelight swam in the wine as the moon took over for the sun. Buttery hunks of bread sopped up the last pools of chowder, and laughter floated like confetti in the lavender light. Hazel and Murphy were like honeymooners while Burke and Remi traded passive-aggressive one-liners. And Carly was grateful for Antonia's sense of timing and humor as she seamlessly steered the conversation in the direction of dessert and the much-anticipated key lime pie.

"I'll drink to that," Murphy said, raising his glass, "the perfect combination of sweet, tart, and creamy."

"Interesting," said a gorgeous woman rounding the corner, pulling a Louis Vuitton wheelie suitcase behind her on the flagstone walk, "Gus has used those exact words to describe me."

Chapter Fifty-One

"**E**MELIA?" GUS SAID, WITH his jaw dropping, "what in the world are you doing here?"

Conversation halted and the only sound was the distant wash of waves. Carly could only stare open-mouthed at the fair-haired goddess before them in a poppy colored dress that caressed her curves, accentuating her small waist and putting her perfect breasts on display. In that dress and heels there was something thunderous about her.

Whatever Carly had expected of Emelia, it wasn't this.

But had she really pictured her as some downhome girl in a ballcap and braids with a wholesome pearly white smile who was utterly without guile?

"Well, I'm here to see you, silly," she said, moving closer to the candlelit table, "and doesn't this all look so coastal-cozy — someone pour me a drink, I've had a day."

Antonia was the first to recover from the shock of Emelia's entrance and reached for Remy's untouched wine glass to pour her a drink. What was going on here? Carly felt the rug being pulled out from under her as she tried out scenarios in her brain—had she misunderstood Keith's email after all?

She tried to replay the conversation she'd had with Gus about Emelia in Bartlett's — *had he ever said EX?*

"What is this?" Emelia asked, with a pinched face, after one sip of wine. "There must be something stronger around here — this is some fancy place you got here."

Who was she even talking to — did the world wait on her? Carly realized she knew almost nothing about this woman Gus had asked to marry him. Carly's blood thickened, molasses in her veins, time stretched, slowed.

"It's a sauvignon blanc, Emelia, zesty and clean, don't you think?" Antonia said, with her southern charm on full power, "but we can scare up something harder if you'd like, whiskey? Vodka? We were just about to do dessert, do you like key lime pie?"

Carly was grateful for Antonia's diplomatic grace because all she could see was her perfect evening unraveling right in front of her. Had Carly missed something? Where did this woman think she was staying — with her bougie suitcase and her expectations? While Gus stood and introduced Emelia to the group, Carly rose in a trance to clear dishes. Conversation resumed and Antonia busied herself with finding Emelia some booze.

"You can't stay here," Gus whisper-shouted, "you know, a little head's up would have been nice — why are you here? What's going on?"

Carly wished she was either clearer headed or buzzed to the point of blissful optimism. She poured herself more wine shooting for the latter.

Wow — my check-liver light just went on, she thought. Maybe Gus would just get rid of her somehow, send her into town to get a room somewhere. *What the fuck was she doing there?* Was she trying to reconcile her relationship with Gus? Did she want him back? Did *he* want *her* back? Were they even over?! She felt instantly foolish and crushed.

Wine and prosecco flowed while Antonia and Burke sliced and served the pie. Claiming her seat back at the table, Carly saw Emelia remove her ridiculous Jimmy Choo heels as she and Gus headed for the stairs to the beach. Her stomach bottomed out.

"Hey sweetheart," Antonia said, topping off Carly's glass, "what do we know?"

"Yeah, I'm totally lost, girl, who exactly is she?" Hazel asked.

"Whoever she is, she's a smokeshow," Burke added, earning a punch in the arm from Remi.

Carly reached for her wine, sloshing some on her white dress. She looked down at it, rubbing the spot with her napkin, feeling stupid for thinking she looked so good, for feeling so excited about Gus. "That, my friends, is his ex-fiancée," she said, unable to meet anyone's eyes, "although the *ex* part is apparently up for debate."

"Aw, honey, let's not jump to conclusions," Antonia said, patting her friend's hand, "for all we know he's telling her to pound sand at this very moment."

"Please," Carly said, "I know you mean well, but honestly look at her and then look at me. She's this glamazon, some high-powered attorney, that Gus was going to spend forever with! Not some midwestern bumpkin!"

"Is that how you decided to picture her in your mind?" Antonia asked, "If you pictured her at all? As some unsophisticated rodeo groupie? A buckle bunny with a prairie skirt, boots, and hay in her teeth?"

Carly heard how ridiculous it was. Seeing Emelia in the flesh made Carly feel like a line-drawing of a woman in comparison, barely colored in.

She took her glass of wine and walked down to the chairs on the lawn. The sky had slipped into darkness unnoticed, and the grass under her bare feet was cool and slick with dew. Antonia followed with her own drink in hand, leaving the others to enjoy their dessert and conversation by the swaying light of the dripping candles.

"You two had gotten pretty close, huh?"

"*Had*? You're using past tense now, Antonia?" Carly groaned and bent forward over her legs resting her glass on the wide arm of the chair.

"No, no I didn't meant it like that, sweetie, you *have* gotten closer, anyone can see that! The way he looks at you... it's about time you finally look at him like that too."

"What exactly do you mean by that?"

"That cowboy has been smitten with you since day one, it just took you a while to get there."

"Really?" Carly said.

"Yes, really. Now what shall we do about this Emelia? We need a game plan."

"For all we know they're rekindling the magic right now," Carly said, "he'll look at her and then at me and say *what was I thinking*? Any man would choose her, Antonia, I'm fooling myself. I could kick myself for getting my hopes up, for actually thinking—"

"Stop all that right now. You're a smart, talented, beautiful young woman. That girl may be gorgeous and some hotshot lawyer but they broke up for a reason. And she's got to be in her mid-thirties at least. My guess is her biological clock is stomping its feet and she's fishing in familiar waters."

Carly wanted to feel sorry for Emelia, wanted to feel steady and unshakable about Gus. But Emelia's air of superiority and entitlement left little room for that. "Do you think she's trying to spend the night here with him? Like in his room, his *bed*? Ugh, I need to get a hold of myself here — it's literally my job to be accommodating. But there is no empty room here, Antonia, maybe I could make some calls? I know places are booked forever in advance around here in the summer, but—"

"I've got it! She can stay with me — I've got two empty rooms," Antonia said.

"Really? That would be awesome. Maybe we could get her drunk enough to pass out and tuck her in over there ourselves so she can't reject the idea. I mean, unless he sends her packing tonight, which I suppose is too much to hope for. Oh, that sounds mean — I don't even know what I'm saying. What if they belong together and I'm the one in the way? What do we do? Wait here for them to come back? That seems weird..."

Carly sat back in the deep chair looking up at the sky and took another sip of wine. Her hopes felt distant and coy, afraid to show themselves. The moon was in her favorite phase, a waning crescent, a lucent shaving so fragile it looked like if she breathed on it, it would melt.

Before Carly could register who was approaching from the steps leading up from the beach, her gaze settled on Gus and Emelia — a striking couple, Emelia wearing his new Force Five hoodie over her dress. Their bodies brushed together as they crossed the lawn, an unspoken ease and intimacy evident in every movement. It radiated something deeper than just familiarity.

The thought sent a chill through Carly, a cold knot forming in her chest, she couldn't look away. Her uncertainty rooted her in place. They looked so perfect together, as though they belonged.

They got closer, even Antonia was speechless.

"Hey, you're the nice lady who made me that drink," Emelia said to Antonia, "what I wouldn't do for another."

"Emelia," Gus interrupted, "this is Antonia and she doesn't work for you."

"Does she work for you?" Emelia blurted with a hiccup.

"Antonia does not work here," Carly said, as kindly as she could manage, "Antonia is staying in the house next door. But please feel free to help yourself to a drink inside." *And take off that sweatshirt I helped Gus pick out while you're at it.*

Carly had looked so forward to this night — and it had unfolded like a dream. Until Emelia blew in. Like sideways rain from a clear sky.

"Sorry about this," Gus said, when Emelia was out of earshot, "I honestly had no idea she'd fly to Nantucket."

"What does this mean?" Carly asked, keeping her voice level and free of judgement. She sat straighter in the chair as Antonia excused herself to go help with the cleanup.

He didn't answer right away as he settled in the vacated chair beside her. And the longer he took to answer, the more nauseous Carly felt.

"She wants...she thought...," Gus stumbled over his words, as if knowing how damning each one would be, "she thinks we should get back together."

Chapter Fifty-Two

IT WAS TOO DARK to read the message in Gus's eyes. And before he had the chance to explain, Emelia came sauntering back out to join them with a drink in hand. She plopped herself in the chair next to Gus as if Carly weren't there at all, as though Carly didn't exist in Gus's life. *Did she even?* Had it all been just some wave of a wand? The spell of Nantucket? Carly finally giving herself over to the romance of it all?

"Aw babe, check out the stars — it's like we're back home, it's so clear," Emelia said dreamily, settling deep in her seat, her hair a golden waterfall over the white back of the Adirondak chair.

Had Carly only been a convenient distraction for Gus? A way to pass the time? She'd started to see herself visiting him in Colorado — maybe even staying there if she loved it, if she even just liked it. The potential was a visceral thing.

She was a free agent with remote work. She could see herself retracing some of her grandmother's cattle-drive trips in Wyoming — sleeping on the ground in big canvas tents, eating meals from the chuckwagon at the end of long days on a horse. The photos and moments she'd capture, the stories she'd tell. It had all seemed so wildly possible, she'd let herself gallop away with the idea of it all, had let her heart take flight for a change.

Turning in Carly's direction, Gus said, "I've reached out to every place in the book — no rooms available anywhere. What if, just for tonight, she stays—"

"With me!" Antonia chimed in, appearing out of the darkness to wrap a cashmere throw around Carly's bare shoulders, "She can stay with me. I have empty rooms — we can put Emelia in one until she can find a flight back."

Carly couldn't have loved another human being more than she loved Antonia in that moment. Did she know something Carly didn't? Was Gus putting Emelia on a flight back to Colorado?

"Hey," Emelia started to say, "I thought I was staying here with Gus?"

"Antonia, that is exceedingly generous, are you sure?" Gus interrupted.

"Wouldn't have it any other way," Antonia said, "Emelia, why don't you come with me. Let's get you settled in next door."

Emelia had drunk just enough booze to be pliable and not put up a fight. She did, however, lean drunkenly down to Gus to give him a kiss goodnight and fall in his lap. Making a strip tease out of removing the hoodie she'd been wearing to return to Gus. Cold jealously twisted in Carly seeing the woman's supple breasts almost spilling into Gus's mouth.

With Antonia finally steering Emelia and her luggage next door, Gus and Carly had the chance to talk. Her thoughts swerved and her pulse jackhammered in her head. Was this the part where he let her down easy? Explaining how Nantucket had enchanted him, but his real life—and Emelia—were waiting for him in Colorado where he belonged.

He sat up on the edge of the chair to face Carly and reached for her hand.

"Don't," she said, unable to listen to anything that might start with *I'm so sorry, but...* She couldn't bring herself to look him in the eye and busied her hands pulling the blanket tighter around her.

"No, listen to me Carly, it's not what you think," he said.

"It never is." Everything around them had gone quiet — the table cleared, dishes done, candles extinguished — poof — everyone somewhere else. Carly wondered what time it was — how long had it been since Hurricane Emelia stormed in, sending Carly's helium-hopes scattering, untethered into oblivion.

"You don't understand," Gus said, suddenly standing before her, pulling her weightlessly from the deep chair, until she had no choice but to look into his eyes. "Emelia thinks we belong together—"

Carly tried to wrench herself free from his gaze and his grasp but he held tight, his grip firm, his tone unwavering.

"—but I don't," he finished, his tone resolute. "And seeing her now, after even the brief time you and I have shared, has only made that clearer to me." His hands rose to her face, his thumbs gently sweeping away the tears that fell. Her gaze remained fixed on the steady depth of his, illuminated by the amber of the porch light behind them.

He hesitated, his hands still cradling her face, as if giving her the chance to pull away. But Carly didn't move. His eyes searched hers, flickering back and forth in question. Her breath hitched and her eyes softened, searching his for something she couldn't name. She let him lean in closer, their breaths mingling in the quiet space between them. Time tipped. There was only the faint hum of the night and the distant rhythm of the waves.

His kiss was tender at first, as if afraid she might vanish. But then, as she leaned into him, her fingers curling lightly into his shirt, he deepened the kiss. She was afraid he would feel her heart beating against his as his hands slipped from her face to rest lightly on her waist, drawing her in to his body. The kiss was everything and nothing like she'd imagined.

She'd never felt this way before — a small declaration she could only make to herself. A universe was expanding in her ribcage, stars and planets and all kinds of sparking debris that could destroy her.

When they finally broke apart, their breathing was ragged. But their eyes steady, locked in a connection that felt unshakable. Neither of them spoke — there were no words that would measure up to the moment.

Carly's body buzzed with electricity, her thoughts a hazy tangle of indecision. She'd had a lot to drink. She couldn't afford to make impulsive choices that would make her feel worse instead of better. And as much as she ached to stay, give in to this pull of longing, she knew what she needed to do. She told him goodnight and went to her room alone. If something real was meant to happen with him, it would keep another day.

She draped her white dress over the chair in the corner, making a mental note to wash it, even though the wine stain was barely noticeable anymore. Then she filled her water bottle and set in on the nightstand beside the bed. Her heart felt lighter as she slipped between the cool sheets in a camisole and her favorite boyshorts. She closed her eyes, marveling at how fast life could shift—how you could be so sure of something, only to understand that it wasn't what you thought at all.

She slept the sleep of the dead and woke up as dawn turned the sky to lemonade. She was parched — a thirst water wouldn't quench — she was craving the sweet juice of a peach. She could picture them nestled in the wooden bowl on the counter. Slowly she pushed back her covers and slipped out of bed, opening her door without a sound, tiptoeing into the kitchen. The whole space was bathed in the silken light of daybreak, and sea-drenched air slid in the open windows on the morning breeze.

Carly didn't see him there on the bottom stair in a t-shirt and boxers, watching her sink her teeth into the ripe fruit, its juice trickling down her chin. Until he silently appeared beside her offering a napkin.

He caught her gasp with a kiss, his lips warm and insistent. She couldn't have said which was sweeter, the lush honeyed taste of the peach or the way his mouth claimed hers, stealing her breath. She felt the hard length of him against her flat belly as his hands gently cupped her bottom. Her nipples straining at the thin cotton of her camisole as she rose up and pressed herself against him.

He lifted her, setting her on the counter, pushing her legs apart so he could step between them, his mouth on her neck, his fingers curling around the thin strap of her top and dragging it off her shoulder. The heat and scrape of his teeth on her skin — only later would she be able to process the feeling of what it's like to be completely consumed with wanting someone.

Footsteps on the stairs startled them apart. Then a delicate voice, whispering, "Gus? Where'd you go? I woke up and you were—"

"*Emelia?*" Carly didn't recognize the strangled cry of her own voice.

Her heart launched itself out of an eight-story window.

Carly flew to her room and slammed the door. Before she could hear Gus asking Emelia what the hell she was doing and when the hell was her flight back to Denver.

Chapter Fifty-Three

THE WALLS SHE'D SO carefully erected, the crumbled boundaries, were a pile of rubble in the rearview. She'd cried herself back to sleep and couldn't tell how much time had passed when she woke. The sun was higher in the sky now, streaming through her window blinding her.

A perusal of her Google history from the other night would reveal the following:

- Photography jobs near Denver
- Falling for someone in a different time zone
- Are exes ever really past tense?
- The effects of Yellowstone on women
- Why loving a cowboy could break your heart
- Signs you're fooling yourself
- Time machines

Unsurprisingly, none of these were much help.

All she wanted was to slip into running clothes and leave the house unnoticed. She needed to run long enough and hard enough for her body to ache more than her heart.

Having left her phone behind, Carly felt loose and free as she ran along the tideline that hugged Sconset and the entire eastern curl of the island. The sand underfoot was mush, unforgiving, no firm stretches of packed sand like the wide beaches in Maine. She felt every step, her legs burning with the sinking exertion of every footfall. The wind off the water dried the tears that streaked her face and left a salty crust where it met the sweat on her skin.

If she'd never truly had August Wilder, then what had she lost?

The answer hit her like another wave against the shore. Hope. The daring, new, brave version of herself she'd only just begun to let in.

She stood still, staring out at the surf while the echo of events spiraled around her. If only the waves could stretch far enough to wash the bad stuff away.

She braced herself for whatever — or whomever — she might encounter as she climbed the stairs from the beach and crossed the lawn toward the house. Resolving to let anything that came at her slide away, she steadied her breath.

It was a small mercy to find the house empty. She indulged in a long hot shower outside before even looking at her phone, wishing she could stay under the pulsing warm rain for the rest of her natural life.

It wasn't until she was dressed in her ragged cutoffs and a faded tank top, her hair drying in the sun on the back porch, that she finally checked her messages. There were so few, she didn't know whether to feel relieved or disappointed.

There was a missed call from Antonia and a text from Hazel thanking her for dinner. Then a message from her dad, asking her to check in when she had a minute, and two emails from Keith.

What *wasn't* there weighed more than any single thing that was. She felt numb. Like she'd officially hit her capacity to process crappy things.

"Hey Chicken Little, what's the good word?" Antonia said, coming across the lawn looking like summer incarnate in a strappy, pale yellow sundress and a pair of gold Jack Rogers flats.

"Chicken Little?" Carly asked.

"You remember — that little chick who thought the sky was falling when a little old acorn fell on his head?"

"Okaayyy," Carly said, "talk to me like I'm five — I'm not sure I get your reference."

Antonia sighed as she took a seat beside Carly, putting her hand on Carly's knee. "Darlin, the world is not ending. There is no catastrophe here."

"What are you—"

Before Carly could finish, Antonia continued. "I'm talking about you and Gus—"

"There is no me and Gus! Godammit, I'm usually better at protecting myself from this. I can usually get out of the way before it hits me head on."

"Shh, I believe I have the floor. He told me about this morning — I am so sorry you saw what you saw, but you can't believe everything you see."

Carly puffed out a weak laugh.

"Shh! Let me finish. Emelia slept in a guest room of my house last night — THEN, come to find out, she snuck out before dawn and found her way over to Gus's room — uninvited!"

Her blood vibrated with what Antonia was saying, her heart a mallet against her sternum. She still didn't know what to think. Emelia hadn't been exactly dressed. "But—"

"Did you even give the man a chance to explain? Rhetorical question — obviously you did not. And if I'm being honest, in your shoes I might not have either... but, well, I think this is a conversation for you and him to have, my darling girl."

Was Carly supposed to forgive a man who's ex forced herself on him? Did they fool around? One last hurrah in the sheets? She couldn't get passed that — even though she and Gus had nothing formal between them, even if it wasn't his idea... she just, no, she couldn't.

Was she that damaged?

"Antonia — I'm not sure any of it matters. It's my own fault. I should not need a man, or anyone, to make me feel like a whole person. Right? Aren't we supposed to be modern women? Complete as we are?"

"And who told you that because you might love someone that you're looking for the other half of yourself? *Who started that? We are* complete and wonderful and capable, yes we are all of those things and more. Love isn't about finding someone to complete you, but finding someone who inspires you to grow even more into yourself, amplifying who you already are. Love doesn't fill in your gaps, honey; it celebrates your beautiful wholeness," Antonia said softly.

The words settled over Carly like an embrace and she felt a fullness land inside her. What Antonia had said made perfect sense — it was exactly what she needed to hear. That was how she felt around Gus, as though she became the best version of herself with him. And she couldn't help but poke around in her heart trying out the idea of what might lie ahead.

"It's just that I've never had that — that insatiable thing, you know?" Carly said, pushing her voice past the cork of emotion in her throat. "I want to be near him all the time. If I eat something delicious I want him there to have a bite. If I see something so beautiful, I want to turn to him and point it out. If I hear something funny, I want to call him and tell him everything."

Antonia's eyes filled and she rubbed Carly's leg. "You are worthy of love, sweetheart, let it in."

She knew she had to have a conversation with him. She also knew that she didn't want to be afraid of things anymore — of things that had all the power to hurt her. She'd gotten good at pushing her physical limits — climbing big mountains, swimming in open water, sleeping in the wilderness alone — she could do hard things. It was time to trust her heart with the same unwavering faith she had in her body. Even if she got it wrong.

∞

Antonia had things to do and Carly needed to catch up on her correspondences with her dad and Keith. She got her laptop and returned to the shady porch. It was after noon before she finished and her rumbling stomach let her know it was well past time to eat something. She got up and stretched before sitting down onto the warm stone steps to consider what she wanted. She leaned back on her elbows and tilted her face up to the sunshine while her knees knocked slowly together. Footsteps behind her pulled her from her musings.

Gus took a seat beside her on the step, leaning back without a word tilting his face up to the sun too. His nearness and earthy clean smell sent a sharp bolt of desire through her body.

She had questions she wasn't sure she wanted answers to. A full minute passed before they both started to speak at the same time.

"So, did you—" Carly started to say.

"Nothing happ—" Gus began.

"Nothing happened between you and Emelia?" Carly said, struggling to hide the hope in her voice.

"Nothing. She wanted it to. And I apologize for that. But rather than make a scene when she slipped into my bed this morning — and wake up the whole house — I left the room." His lips twitched into a teasing smile. "Which is when I saw you in the kitchen, ahem, really enjoying that peach."

"Into your *bed*? Wow. Bold."

"Yes. One of the things that makes her a great attorney."

"Seducing people?"

"No," he laughed, "sorry — her unwillingness to take no for an answer."

"Ahh. And where is she now?" Carly asked.

Gus looked down at his watch and said, "On a Denver-bound plane."

They were quiet again. The breeze whisked the heat from their skin, summer birds swooped and sang, the ocean blue-green and expansive beyond them. Gus spoke of the things he still wanted to see and do with her before he left. It was its own small injury — how easily he spoke of leaving. She swallowed the emptiness of it, but it pushed in and stung the back of her eyes.

"It's not enough time," he said, "with you. Carly, I want you to know I never expected this, I—"

"You don't have to say anything, Gus, I get it. Totally unexpected on my end too." She leaned into his shoulder with hers, trying to keep her voice from breaking, "I know you have to get back. Your kingdom awaits!" Her eyes filled and she leaned forward on the step hugging her knees.

He reached for her hand and brought it against him. "I've been thinking. I'll need to finalize the transfer of power back at the ranch in Gunnison, but then you'll come out — see the Rockies, Wilder Ranch, what life is really like there. Does that sound like something you might be interested in?"

The look in his eyes was so earnest, so clear. "Umm, YES," she said, thoughts and hopes galloping. "Are you sure?"

Carly studied him. He was like no one she'd met before — sure of himself in a way that many people weren't. It was clear in how he spoke. His voice was gentle and kind but with a cool authority underneath — like he was only going to speak if he was certain that what he was saying was true. He looked at her with such a purity of intentions that rendered words superfluous.

"How soon were you thinking?" she asked, attempting a casual tone, that didn't quite match the pounding in her chest.

"Are you committed here through August?"

The question hit with a double meaning she couldn't ignore. And it wasn't lost on her that there was only one August she wanted to commit to. But she'd signed on to *Driftwood Dream* for the season.

And the practical side of her instinctively resisted this sudden shift with this man who meant so much to her already.

"Yes, through August," she replied carefully. "But it's not out of the question for Keith to possibly find someone to take my place here. I mean, if that's what you're asking — if you were thinking about me coming out sooner..." Her voice faltered as she suddenly felt exposed.

Sensing her retreat, Gus pulled her closer on the step, grounding her. "I want you to do what feels right for you, Carly. On your own terms, in your own time. I know this might feel like a lot all at once — but I was just thinking, if you're looking for a place to land when your commitment here has been fulfilled, why not Colorado? Gunnison is more stunning than you can imagine, nestled in the heart of the Rockies. I promise you'll fall in love."

"It's getting impossible to know what's real anymore. But, I mean, I *am* a Yellowstone junkie, so I kind of owe it to myself," she said with a laugh, trying to diffuse the intensity.

Excitement sparked at her edges. Suddenly there was a plan, a story to be written instead of a blank page. And at the center of it all was this incredible man she would have the chance to know even better. Even if it didn't last — she had to remind herself to be ready for that — she'd still be in the Rockies! Immersing herself in a whole new world.

Chapter Fifty-Four

T HE LAST DAYS OF the first *Driftwood Dream* crew blended into each other like the green waves rolling in then back out to sea, beyond reach. Each person chasing their own bucket list trying to get it all in.

Hazel and Murphy were radiant, their ease and contentment a stark contrast to the tentative energy of those first days. They shared unhurried kisses, held hands without a second thought as they decided on souvenirs for the kids. It was clear they had rediscovered each other — as individuals instead of just as parents.

Burke and Remi seemed to have arrived at a truth that was obvious to anyone who spent time around them — that they might not be meant for each other after all. Their focus appeared to lean more inward than toward one another. Perhaps they weren't ready to be together — maybe they never would be. They seemed at peace with telling each other, "Yeah, you do you."

Remi was a woman who spent so much time on her own needs that she'd pushed a good man away. It made Carly think about compromise in long-term relationships — and how one can't exist without the other. She realized it wasn't just that Jake wasn't the one, but how little effort she'd put into compromising — and how she'd need to learn that if she ever wanted something lasting.

∞

Once Antonia adjusted to the idea of her ex-husband and daughter visiting Nantucket from Boulder, she beamed with anticipation. Careening into plans and making reservations, some of which would include David. They'd all have to be okay with that. Their visit would overlap with Gus still being on-island, and they'd share a dinner all together — giving Carly a triple-pronged view of Colorado in one shining evening.

Gus and Carly were inseparable in those final days — as if to dare the universe to break apart what they'd found. Every touch became a way for her to memorize his body. She tried to see it as the start of a bigger, better thing instead of an ending. But watching him board that plane headed 2,000 miles west was a visceral rip. Her heart folded in on itself as he disappeared from view.

∞

In the weeks that followed, Carly made a promise to herself not to allow her time to become so inextricably braided with each of the guest's experiences. It would challenge her, she knew, she was a sucker for blurred boundaries. Instead, she would lean into her own Nantucket experience and how it had influenced the direction she wanted to take her craft of photography, wherever that might lead.

With the photographs and essays she'd been inspired to create, she'd been plunged into the stories behind what makes a place unique. She'd have time to immerse herself in the past of *Driftwood Dream* and the loving force that swung out from it, that all started with someone imagining what a house, a space could be. Isn't that how it always started?

She had more questions than answers — and she was okay with that. And she knew she was ready to swim in the essence of a thing, unravel its charm, dive into the enchantment of what made a place special, what made it singular.

As she stretched out on the warm sand, savoring the sun-drenched morning before the next round of guests arrived, her body hummed with a deep current of possibility. A quiet certainty resonated inside her, showing her that she was on the right path, a tingling of the undeniable promise of what was to come.

Epilogue

The next summer

WHEN SHE OPENED HER eyes, it took her a minute to reconcile the view from her triangle tent window. It was breathtaking...prairie land so flat it almost seemed impossible. Craggy mountains rising like a tidal wave heading right for her, tipped in gold from the sunrise that hit the rock from every angle, illuminating the landscape in startling shades of tangerine, crimson and wine. The pine forests and lush summer meadows came alive in the growing light, Gunnison's famous wildflowers a riot of color. Her new home on the western slope of Colorado.

Carly knew what people said: never date a cowboy — you'll never come first. It'll be the job, the life, the horse. She was glad she didn't buy into that. She smiled looking over at Gus, snoring softly from his side of the sleeping bag they'd zipped together and shared. A muscle in his jaw flexed, and his toned body went taut. Tension lined every limb and she wondered what he dreamed about. They'd met almost one year ago — it had been the best year of her life.

She heard their horses nickering softly outside the tent as a new day began — she could think of few sounds that brought her more joy, and no one else in the world she'd rather be sharing it with. Gus stirred sleepily, rolling toward her and tucking her snugly into the curve of his body. She nestled closer, inhaling his warm, earthy scent — a mix of leather, pine, and something distinctly him. She felt the warm insistent press of him against her backside and wondered how asleep he really was.

She needed to touch him, press against him, relieve her heaviness, her swollen ache for him. She shifted her hips ever so slightly against him, rewarded by the low throaty groan that escaped his lips and his hot breath on her neck. Their bodies moved together instinctively, a silent rhythm matching each other's arousal and desire. Sliding off the barriers of clothing, their tangled bodies moved together, pulsing in unison. Each rise and fall, each shudder and sigh, weaving them deeper into each other.

Everything else vanished in her desire for him. In that moment, she felt a profound ache of gratitude — and a desperation for anyone who had never known a connection like this.

After a hearty campfire breakfast of bacon and eggs, they packed up and rode back to the ranch. That evening, they'd join Gus's family for a send-off dinner at the main house before their flight to Cape Cod the next morning. They would take the steamship to Nantucket from Hyannis for the full experience. They'd decided there was no better way to celebrate the anniversary of their meeting than by spending five days on the island where it all began.

It was a stellar day for the thirty mile crossing — a powder-blue sky and light winds. They sat outside in the bow of the ship under the brilliant sun. A summer cowboy hat really was the perfect cover. As the big boat rode the swells and they got closer to the island, Carly thought about all the things that had changed in her life, all the ways she'd grown since her steamship crossing just one year ago. She'd been ambivalent about turning thirty with so little to show for it. But now...

She shared a home in the Rocky Mountains with her best friend, had a horse to ride whenever she wanted, and a career that showcased the best of her talents that taught her new things about people, the world, and herself every single day. She had a man who's company and affection she craved who returned her love beyond measure. Her parents were thriving in their new home and planning a visit to hers. It was everything and more than she'd ever dared dream.

An unexpected tear slid down below her sunglasses. Gus noticed it before she could wipe it away. He carefully took off her Maui Jims so he could look into her eyes.

"What's wrong?"

"Not one single thing," she said, looking deeply into his whiskey eyes, gold-flecked in the sun.

"Well, I'm glad to hear it," he said, taking her hands in his, "because there's something I really need to know. I thought it could wait, but the truth is it just cannot wait another minute, not another ocean mile."

He released her hands and got down on a knee there in front of a boat full of happy people and dogs bound for Nantucket. "Carly, I've spent my life chasing sunrises and riding through open country, but nothing has ever felt as boundless as loving you. So before this boat ride ends, let's start something that never will. Let's make this Wilder ride last forever. Carly Ava Hill, with you, every place feels like home — will you marry me?"

He had to lower her hands from her streaming eyes to slip the ring he'd designed himself on her finger. She got down on her knees to hug him so hard before looking him in the eyes and saying, "Mr. August James Wilder, it would be my greatest honor."

Phones were out capturing the moment, there was clapping and crying and then the rounding of Brant Point. People waved and shouted from the beach beyond, like they knew. That's how it felt to be this happy, this in love — like the whole world was in on it, singing the same song, knowing all the words.

And finally, she knew how it felt to be made of sunlight instead of shadow.

The End

Acknowledgments

This is the page where I express my gratitude to all who contributed to this book coming to life. But since losing my husband, suddenly and unexpectedly, as I finished this story, my life has been turned upside down. And I can't possibly name the hundreds of people who have reached out with kind words, loving thoughts, visits, flowers, meals, hugs, and just to sit with me, cry with me. I am humbled by the love you've all shown my children and me, the heartfelt words you've offered — knowing there are no words.

My greatest thanks would always go to Billy — for his unwavering devotion and support, for picking up the slack at home, with the kids, the animals — and for his beaming love and pride that raised us all up. I know you live on in your children, Billy, and I know I will keep putting one foot in front of the other as I navigate this unfamiliar way of being in the world without you. I'm so grateful for all the years I got with you, no amount would have been enough.

I want to thank my colleagues and friends for their steadfast, daily presence and love: Celia Cole, Cheryl Snowdon, Keri Layne, Susan Dagley, Alyssa Rennie, Lisa Ollenborger, Susie Detrik, Brenda Fife, Susan Jackson, Lisa Heinke, Allison Soucy, and Laura Whiton.

Thank you to my brothers for supporting me in all ways, picking me up and carrying me when I'm down: Michael De Nitto, Mark De Nitto, and Jamie De Nitto.

I stand in awe of my children — Cody, Madison, and Ryder — for their strength, spirit, and humor. They are my pillars.

I'd like to acknowledge Sarah Lahay for another gorgeous cover and interior design, and editor, Sara Oestreich, for her insight and vision, helping me make *Blame It On Nantucket* a more evocative story with relatable and more nuanced characters.

Finally, I'd like to extend my gratitude to Barbara Tibbetts for inviting me to be a part of the 2025 Nantucket Book Festival, and to Tim Ehrenberg (and everyone at Nantucket Book Partners) for including me on the schedule of summer book signings at Mitchell's Book Corner.

About the Author

PHOTO BY: MADISON
ALLENA PHOTOGRAPHY

Doreen Burliss, author of *We'll Always Have Nantucket*, *That Nantucket Summer*, and *Fogged In*, lives in a small town north of Boston. She has three grown children with her late husband, Billy Burliss. Their Nantucket summer vacation will remain etched in gold on the calendar, no matter where they are in the world, or what they're doing. It will be a different place without Billy. *Blame It on Nantucket* is her fourth novel.

www.ingramcontent.com/pod-product-compliance
Lightning Source LLC
Chambersburg PA
CBHW030125010826
48973CB00002B/424